PRAISE FOR *AM*

"*Amber Wolf* is enjoyable as a narrative, edifying as history, and inspirational as a story of struggle, survival, and ethnic pride—the David of Lithuania is caught between the twin Goliaths of Russia and Germany. What can a young girl do? You'd be surprised."

—Steve O'Connor, author of *The Witch at Rivermouth* and *The Spy in the City of Books*

"Captivating. *Amber Wolf* is a compelling story of bold resistance in the face of insurmountable odds. Wong skillfully paints a portrait of the hidden and mostly forgotten people who struggled to survive behind the front lines of the cataclysm of World War II."

—Guntis Goncarovs, author of *Telmenu Saimnieks – The Lord of Telmeni* and *Convergence of Valor*

"*Amber Wolf* is a compelling story that captures the brutal truth along with fictitious elements of Lithuania in World War II. Before my parents passed, I listened to countless hours of stories just like this and the reasons why they fled their beloved homeland. Bravo to Ludmelia for never giving up!"

—Daina Irwin, daughter of Lithuanian survivors

"In *Amber Wolf*, Ursula Wong turns an unflinching yet sympathetic eye on a brutal slice of history. Compelling and engrossing, and almost impossible to put down."

—Leigh Perry, author of the *Family Skeleton Series*

"Ursula Wong takes on a heavy subject: the grass roots of World War II—not of large-scale mass destruction, but of hand-to-hand combat, villager against soldier, deep in the forests of Lithuania. Ludmelia Kudirka is a girl who must quickly grow up if she wants to survive and ultimately fight for her people, her land, and her freedom. In *Amber Wolf*, Wong gives us a story complexly woven, yet easy to follow, and impossible to forget."

—Stacey Longo, Pushcart Prize-nominated author of *Ordinary Boy*

"*Amber Wolf* is a trek into territory that, seventy years after the dramatic events enacted there, still remains largely unexplored. Ursula Wong, using new source material and careful research, has crafted a harrowing, heroic, and at times poetic, tale of people caught up in the cataclysms of war."

—David Daniel, author of *The Skelly Man* and *The Marble Kite*

Amber War

Ursula Wong

Genretarium Publishing ~ Chelmsford, MA

Cover Design by Ana Lucia Cortez

Map courtesy pixabay.com

ISBN: 198359458X
ISBN-13: 978-1983594588

For more information about the author and her works, go to:

http://ursulawong.wordpress.com

First printing, January, 2018
13579108642

Other works by Ursula Wong

Amber Wolf

Purple Trees

The Baby Who Fell From the Sky

With other Authors

Insanity Tales

Insanity Tales II: The Sense of Fear

Insanity Tales III: Seasons of Shadow: A Collection of Dark Fiction

Ursula is available for speaking events and lectures on writing and publishing. For more information, contact her at urslwng@gmail.com or through her popular Reaching Readers website at http://ursulawong.wordpress.com.

Looking for something great to read? Get Ursula's award-winning mini-tales, guaranteed to shiver, shake, and make you laugh. All you have to do is tell her where to send them. You'll get one to start, and a new one every month. Sign up at http://ursulawong.wordpress.com.

DEDICATION

To Steve, with love.

All tyranny needs to gain a foothold is for people of good conscience to remain silent.

—*Thomas Jefferson*

ACKNOWLEDGMENTS

I'd like to thank my friends and writing soul-mates at The Storyside for their support, guidance, help, food, and occasional drink. When the work wasn't fun, you helped me turn things around.

Dale T. Phillips, a man I've looked up to for years, provided excellent comments and constant support. I'm grateful to have such a friend and mentor.

I'm indebted to Genretarium Publishing for the freedom to explore this vast world of writing and publishing.

I'd like to thank my Lithuanian advisors: Daina Irwin, Maria Egle Calabrese, and Frank Ulcickas. You caught errors I didn't see, and supported me more than you know.

Members of my Reaching Readers email list continue to inspire me. I am honored to know you all. Your messages touch and uplift me. Thank you.

My family tolerated almost endless discussions about characters and plot without complaint. My husband, Steve, is my rock. My daughter, Steph, keeps me on track. I love you both.

My last thought is of you, my readers. Out of the thousands of books published every month, and all the books in libraries, bookstores, and online retailers, you've chosen to read mine. Thank you for giving me a chance.

Ursula Sinkewicz Wong
November 2017
Chelmsford, Massachusetts

PREFACE

Amber War is the second in a series of three novels about Lithuanian resistance fighters opposing the Soviet occupation of Eastern Europe. The first is *Amber Wolf*, which tells of the early and powerful days of the resistance movement during WWII, when farmers and office workers take up arms against the Soviet army.

Amber War tells of the situation in Lithuania a few years after the war ends. The US is at peace and her soldiers are home. Europe is beginning to rebuild, but partisans in Lithuania continue their war against the Soviet occupiers while living in dire conditions. Hundreds of thousands of people are sent to labor camps in Siberia. Food is in short supply. Farmers are forced into collective farms. The churches are closed. The population begins to accept that the West isn't going to rescue them from Soviet dominance, and the tide turns. People begin leaving the resistance.

Although chiefly about Lithuania, *Amber War* includes some observations about the post-war situation in Poland. It is by no means good, but it is different from Lithuania. After WWII and the end of the brutal German occupation, Poland undergoes a civil war. At that point it's still in the Soviet sphere, but Poland has its own communist leader and head of state. Poland has far fewer deportations, fewer raids, and in general, less violence.

The basic history in *Amber War* is accurate. The characters are fictional. Some episodes in the story are inspired by events in Juozas Daumantas's memoir, *Fighters for Freedom*. The implications surrounding the Ignalina power plant at the end of *Amber War* are purely fictitious.

The cities and towns referenced in the novel are real, however there are some simplifications. I've removed the special characters that come with the Lithuanian language as they're meaningless to non-Lithuanian speakers. Aukštaitija, an area of many forests, is modified to Auksia. I've done the same with the town of Anykščiai, changing it to Ankia. The Šešupė River becomes the Sesupe River.

While I've tried to be true to native names, I avoid the ligatures and diacritics of the language there, too. I believe the result, for the most part, gives the reader a sense of the of the language in words that can be sounded out phonetically.

The few Lithuanian, Polish, German, and Russian words in the text are italicized and context should be sufficient for the reader to surmise the meanings.

As I continue to strive to understand the partisan perspective, I imagine the deep levels of uncertainty, distrust, and sheer terror the people of Eastern Europe must have endured throughout the war and afterward. I challenge you to imagine a Lithuanian partisan who survives a life of utter turmoil, and in 1991 watches their leader, Vytautas Landsbergis, address the citizens of a free Lithuania. Is that not a moment of pure joy?

For those who wish to read more about Eastern Europe and the Soviet Union before and after WWII, you may find the list of books in the back useful, along with a list of *Amber War* characters. The map gives some sense of the general Baltic region where the *Amber War* story takes place.

MAP OF THE BALTIC AREA

CHAPTER 1

1948 – The Beginning of the End

Dark clouds rolled overhead as a man and woman walked along a deserted road in northeastern Lithuania, looking nervous as if unsure whether they would survive the day. They passed the occasional hedge and grouping of evergreens marking fields still covered in patches of snow. The Auksia forest beckoned in the distance with a mass of ancient trees that were an enchanting shade of green.

The woman's head was wrapped in a brown kerchief, and the man wore a gray cap that covered most of his prematurely white hair, still tinged with strands of blond. An empty arm sling hung from his neck. Both he and the woman wore dark coats, but hers was shorter than her apron. Her skirt hung almost to her ankles, ending just above a battered pair of men's boots.

At the far-off rumble of a truck engine, the woman glanced over her shoulder.

"Get ready, in case they stop," she said.

She put her hand into her pocket, and gripped the Soviet TT semiautomatic pistol she had stolen from a drunken soldier who had wanted more than she was willing to give. With her other hand, she pulled the kerchief down, nearly covering her eyes. A lock of amber hair escaped from behind her ear; she ignored it. She hunched her shoulders, and dragged her left foot in a limp. The man put his left arm into the sling, and added a Kriegar stiletto. The two shuffled along as if they had been walking for miles, and had miles yet to go.

A Russian military truck stopped alongside them, and two Red soldiers got out. One wore the dung-colored uniform of a private. He pointed his semiautomatic Kalashnikov at the couple. The insignias on the other man's jacket indicated he was a lieutenant. He wore a black leather cap with a single red star over the brim. "Papers."

The man with the sling winced as he moved his sore arm to the side and pulled out a document with worn folds from an inside coat pocket. He handed it over.

"Where are you going?" asked the officer as he examined the papers.

The peasant's face became a mass of lines as he looked up. His shoulders quaked, and tears fell to his cheeks.

The lieutenant stepped closer to the man, sniffed, crinkled his nose, and stepped back. "Five minutes with me and you won't be crying anymore. You'll be screaming."

"Uncle?" asked the woman. She put one hand on her companion's shoulder, as her other hand gripped the hidden gun.

The man straightened and seemed to compose himself. He raised his good arm, wiping his nose onto his sleeve. He took a deep breath, coughed up phlegm, and spat it out on the ground.

The lieutenant looked at him in disgust.

"He's tired," said the woman. "We've been walking all day. We're going to the village over there." She pointed at the huts in the distance. "My grandmother died. We're going to her funeral."

The lieutenant gazed at her face. The woman bowed her head, tucking the curl of hair back behind her ear.

"What's wrong with your leg?" he asked.

"I broke it during the war, and it didn't heal right." Her grip on the gun tightened.

The officer squeezed the man's injured arm until he moaned in pain. The officer thrust the papers into his chest. "Filthy animal." He cocked his head toward the truck. He and the private drove off.

The couple watched for a moment, and continued walking down the road.

"I didn't know you could cry like that," said the woman, a smile in her voice.

The man grinned as he put the stiletto back in the belt sheath under his coat. "One of my talents."

The couple went the short distance to a narrow path that headed through the fields. The brown stubble of last year's crop protruded through the snow. They stopped at the first hillock.

A man came down the embankment. He was of medium build, and thin. His most remarkable feature was his magnificent dark eyes.

"Would you like a cigarette?" he asked.

"I don't smoke cigarettes. But it's a lovely day for a cigar." The woman smiled as she took off the kerchief. Her hair tumbled to her shoulders. She pulled a cap from her pocket and put it on, tucking her hair inside. She tied the kerchief around her neck.

"It's good to see you again, Ludmelia." He kissed her on her cheek before looking to the man. "Dana. It's been a long time."

Dana clasped the man's hand. "Julius."

Julius waved, and two more men came down the little hill. Both were dressed in dark, tattered clothing. With caps pulled down over their eyes, Kazi and Stasys were indistinguishable from each other, except by height. They shook hands all around.

Dana and Ludmelia followed them through some brambles to a spot overlooking a broad open field. At the far end stood a farmhouse. Next to it was a shed where a horse and cart waited.

Julius nodded to one of his men. "Check the place out and look in the cellar. The hatch is under the table. We'll wait here."

Ludmelia stopped him. "Let me. I've done this before, and they'll never suspect a woman."

She tucked her hands into the pockets of her coat and headed across the field, her gaze focused on the house. She didn't dare look anywhere else, as an untoward glance might give her away. After all, she needed to appear as a visitor dropping by for a cup of tea and some conversation. Nothing more.

"Hello," Ludmelia called, knocking on the door. It opened and she stepped into a room that smelled of burning wood, fried onions, and potatoes. A plump man with yesterday's beard and a rope belt holding up his pants closed the door behind her. A woman in a white shirt and black skirt stood at the stove, stirring the contents of a pot. One chair at the table in the center of the room had armrests and a tall back with carvings of birds. Beyond a partially open curtain stood a bed.

"I'm in the village visiting. My grandmother just died," said Ludmelia as she crossed the floor and entered the bedroom. "What a nice room."

The woman watched her.

"Do you know my grandmother?" asked Ludmelia as she returned to the kitchen and pulled the table away from its spot on the floor.

"Of course. Would you like a cigarette? It's a good day to stay inside and smoke," said the man.

"I prefer cigars." Ludmelia struck a match, held it to the wick of a kerosene lamp, then replaced the chimney. Holding the lamp in one hand, she bent down and pulled a latch, opening a hatchway to the cellar. The narrow steps led down into an ominously dark space. Ludmelia shivered. The farmer would have warned her to any dangers, but perhaps he trusted her as little as she trusted him. It paid to be careful these days, as alliances changed quickly. She took a deep breath. "I'll get a jar of pears to have with our tea."

As she descended the steps, Ludmelia remembered the terror the night she had found Mama's body on the bed in the kitchen. She had hidden Mama in a cellar, dark like this one. The light flickered as her hands shook. Ludmelia took a deep breath and stepped onto a dirt floor. She passed a bin with potatoes and a wall filled with shelves, some containing jars of fruits and vegetables. She crossed the floor back to the stairs, suppressing the desire to run up the steps and into the light.

Ludmelia commanded her hands to be steady as she closed the hatch and moved the table back to its spot. She opened the outside door and waved. Her heartrate gradually slowed when Julius and Dana came inside. They all shook hands with the man.

"Mr. Zenonas," said Julius. He kissed Mrs. Zenonas on the cheek.

"No one's in the shed," said Dana.

Ludmelia took off the apron and skirt to reveal a pair of trousers. She handed the garments to Mrs. Zenonas, who hung them up in the bedroom.

Mrs. Zenonas filled bowls with soup and put them on the table. She cut thin slices from a loaf of crusty brown bread and placed one beside each bowl. Ludmelia's piece was noticeably larger than the others, and she smiled. Julius and Ludmelia ate at the table, while Dana stood looking out the window, wolfing down his food.

Mr. Zenonas sat. "They bring four or five of us together at once to convince us to cooperate. You know what that means. We'd hide in the woods, but they'd only come back when we don't expect them, and they'd make it even worse when they caught us. After beating us, they'd be sure to give us a little rest. In prison."

"We know," said Julius.

"Besides, they're letting food rot in the warehouse in Rimkai. We barely have enough, people in the cities are starving, and they're letting the food they force us to provide go to waste so that even a pig wouldn't eat it. Lately, the Russians have been coming more often. They expect us to feed them and won't leave until we do. If we don't meet our quotas, we must give up our land and livestock, and join the *kolkhoz*. Whoever had the idea of creating collective farms should be shot. Between feeding the soldiers and meeting the quotas, we're barely surviving. That's what life is about these days; surviving. They haven't come for me or my brother yet, thank God, but it's just a matter of time."

Julius put his spoon down and pushed the bowl away.

"What, you're not hungry?" said Mr. Zenonas. He gripped the side of his chair and leaned forward. "Where are you going tonight?"

Julius looked him in the eyes. "Your brother's house."

"The Russians are going there tonight? How do you know?"

Julius gave him an icy stare.

"We have to warn him," said Mr. Zenonas.

"We can't. We're going after the agent who keeps track of the quota receipts. It will help all of you in the long run."

"But not my brother. They'll suspect he's collaborating with you. What if they suspect me, too? This is too much."

Julius put a hand on Mr. Zenonas' shoulder. "They won't suspect a thing. Besides, we'll protect you and your brother, and you'll be able to keep your farms. Don't worry. We should be going. I want to get there before the Russians."

"Your men are waving from the shed," said Dana.

"Damn," said Julius. "They're coming."

"My God," said Mrs. Zenonas. She snatched up the bread and hid it under some wood in the bin while her husband pushed the table aside and lifted the hatch to the cellar. Ludmelia and Dana stuffed bread into their mouths as they scrambled down the steps. The woman poured the soup from all but one of the bowls back into the pot before stacking the dirty dishes on the shelf behind a row of clean ones.

As he followed the others, Julius glanced up at Mr. Zenonas. "We'll be listening." Mr. Zenonas closed the cellar door. Furniture moved directly above the partisans waiting in the darkness.

"Sit down and eat your soup, Papa," said Mrs. Zenonas. Her voice was muffled.

A few moments later, two sets of footsteps marched into the room. The door slammed.

"You're coming with us," said a gruff voice, the sound muted.

As a chair scraped against the floor overhead, Ludmelia, Julius, and Dana waited in silence near the stairs. Ludmelia thought back to the attic where she had hidden as the soldiers tortured Mama. She was glad it was dark so the others couldn't see her tremble.

"Get me some soup," said the gruff voice. Footsteps, lighter this time, crossed the floor. "What, no bread?"

"Not today. We're out," said Mrs. Zenonas.

"Bring me something to drink." More light footsteps.

"What's the shortest way to your brother-in-law's house?"

"It's far. You go down the road. Please. This way, and then that way. No, the other way." Mrs. Zenonas sobbed.

"Shut up, you stupid cow," said the gruff voice. A spoon clinked against a bowl amid slurping sounds.

In the cellar, Ludmelia almost smiled at Mrs. Zenonas's feigned stupidity.

A heavy set of footsteps crossed the floor.

"Let's go," said the gruff voice.

The partisans below waited through more steps and a door slamming. Furniture scraped against the floor again, and the cellar door opened.

Mrs. Zenonas's face was free of tears, but her demeanor was sad. "They took my husband. I'll bring you as close as I can in the wagon, and we'll cut across the field."

"They'll have guards posted. We'll have to get in position without being seen," said Julius.

"That won't be a problem. I've done this before," said Ludmelia. "We'll have to create a diversion to get everyone out of the house."

"We could wait until they're done and come outside on their own," said Dana.

"The Russians will kill one or more of them as examples to the others. We have to get them out."

"My men will do it," said Julius, smiling. "That's something *we've* done before."

"I'll get your things." Mrs. Zenonas tied a white kerchief under her chin and left the house.

Ludmelia crossed to the window and watched Mrs. Zenonas enter the shed. She came out a moment later, dragging a large sack that she managed to lift onto the back of the wagon with some difficulty. She drove to the front of the house, parked near the door, and pulled the bag inside.

Julius opened the sack, pulling out four Thompson submachine guns. He handed them to the men. He gave Ludmelia a Mosin-Nagant sniper rifle. Her expression softened as she moved her hand over the barrel in a caress that most women would save for a lover.

The men quickly left the house, climbed into the wagon, and covered themselves with piles of straw. Mrs. Zenonas climbed onto the bench where Ludmelia waited, her rifle hidden in the back with the men.

Mrs. Zenonas shook the reins and the horse broke into a canter.

"You're going too fast. Someone might see us and think something's wrong," said Ludmelia. Mrs. Zenonas pulled back on the reins, and the horse slowed.

Later, as the sky turned a bluish red with dusk, Mrs. Zenonas stopped the horse. Ludmelia jumped down and reached in the back for her rifle. The men got down, brushing off the straw, and they all followed Mrs. Zenonas into a field. They moved quickly and kept to the cover provided by the trees and scrubby brush. With the triangle of her kerchief swaying from the back of her head, Mrs. Zenonas looked as agile as a doe. She pointed at a farm, kissed Julius on his cheek, and shook the hands of the men.

As she hugged Ludmelia, she spoke. "My husband didn't tell me, but I know who you are. God bless you, Amber Wolf."

Ludmelia was about to speak, but the woman disappeared into the trees lining the field that led back to the wagon.

The partisans moved to a spot where they could better observe the dwelling. One battered US-made jeep and a military truck were parked outside a small house with a large sloping roof that extended to within two meters of a barrel. Light from an oil lamp flickered in the windows. Inside the barn, a calf called to its mother. A Red soldier leaned against one of the jeeps, smoking. Another stood by, rubbing his arms against the cold.

The quiet felt deadly.

Ludmelia silently made her way to the left, where she had an unobstructed view of the front door. She crawled under a bush as Julius and the other three men disappeared into the barn. Several minutes passed before they appeared again.

Ludmelia waited. She was good at waiting. She lay on her belly, watching the door through the crosshairs of the rifle. She couldn't help but remember all the times she had watched time pass through crosshairs. Each time, using all the fortitude and strength in her, she had taken a life. She had stopped counting her victims long ago.

At an almost imperceptible sneezing sound, the two soldiers waiting at the jeep slumped to the ground. Julius and Dana dashed up and helped Kazi and Stasys drag them into the barn. A few minutes later, Dana and Julius appeared again and moved to the far side of the house. Ludmelia shifted her hips to keep her muscles from stiffening.

Figures passed in front of the windows. Someone fell. Ludmelia grimaced at a muffled crack. A Russian lifted a chair over his head and crashed it down. A man yelled. A figure ran past the window.

Stasys climbed onto the barrel next to the house and hoisted himself onto the roof, his dim shape ghostly against the dark sky. He carefully walked to the chimney, took his coat off, and stuffed it inside.

Ludmelia clenched her jaw, for nothing else mattered right now except the shot.

Finally, the sounds quieted. Soldiers appeared at the windows, trying to open them. One thrust the butt of his gun through the glass, shattering it. The door to the house burst open and a torrent of smoke tumbled out. Three soldiers and a man with an attaché case ran outside, all of them coughing.

The man holding the attaché case paused just outside the doorway. He wore a greatcoat, boots, and wire-rimmed glasses. He looked like an accountant. Ludmelia recognized the scar from his cleft lip and the insignias on his coat identifying him as a member of the NKVD, Stalin's secret police who controlled people by fear and intimidation. She held her breath and positioned her finger just over the trigger. He looked up, as if sensing danger.

Ludmelia dropped him with one shot. He looked surprised, falling to the ground. As the echo of the blast resounded in the cold air, she fired again. Another soldier fell to the frozen dirt amid the staccato of machine gun fire. One by one, the Russian soldiers collapsed, some from wounds, others to scramble away and snatch a second or two more of life before they, too, were shot.

It was over quickly. Julius and the men ran inside and appeared a moment later, helping a coughing, bloody farmer into the fresh air. Even in the scant light from the open door, his face looked swollen. Two more men who looked like farmers came out, holding up a third who could barely stand. His eyes were puffy. It was Mr. Zenonas. His head bobbed as they walked. On the roof, Stasys retrieved his coat from the chimney.

Ludmelia yanked the attaché case out from under the body of the dead NKVD agent. She opened it and pulled out papers, turning them to the light so she could read. They were quota reports tracking the amount of grain each farmer had given to the Soviet state. Many farmers were behind, and faced losing everything. Once the reports were destroyed, there would be no record, and the farmers would have a chance keep their farms and avoid the *kolkhoz*. She handed the papers to Julius.

Julius went inside the smoke-filled house and tossed them all into the stove. He returned to Ludmelia's side, coughing. "Now the Russians won't know anything, and they'll have to take the word of the farmers. This nonsense about fulfilling their quotas will be over, at least until the new crops come in next fall."

"Let's hope the Russians will take them at their word and not make it even worse."

Julius's men came out of the barn carrying a body that they threw into the back of the truck. Dana piled together a fresh collection of guns and boots from the dead Russians.

Ludmelia pointed to the corpses "What are you going to do with them?"

"We'll get rid of them. Even if the Russians find the bodies, they won't be able to recognize who they are. I wish we could use the vehicles, but even if we could cover up the markings, everyone knows what trucks the Russians drive. We'll hide them somewhere and permanently disable them."

Ludmelia and Dana handed their guns to Julius.

"Excellent job," said Julius as he pumped Dana's arm in a handshake. "When people hear about this, they'll be sure to help us. I expect a lot of fresh recruits. Who knows? If we keep it up, we may have those Russians running back to Moscow after all."

He kissed Ludmelia's cheek before returning to his men. Ludmelia and Dana made their way into the darkness past the farm, to the road, and away from the village.

~~

Late the next day, neighbors found Mr. and Mrs. Zenonas naked, hanging by wire from a tree in their yard, skinned like animals, their eyes gouged out. The woman's arms had been hacked off, and they lay like sticks on the ground. The wagon stood in front of the burned-out hulk of the house, next to a dead horse.

CHAPTER 2

From inside a bunker deep in the Auksia forest, Kazi peered through the narrow opening and fired a burst into the bushes near a stand of red oaks. The tiny branches scattered into a fog of snow and sticks the size of needles. His body reverberated from the blast. Even in the cold, the gun radiated heat. He was worried it might seize up, but it was a good German MG-36. Built to work. Built to last. But it didn't matter. He was surrounded by Soviet soldiers.

An explosion rattled the ground. Dirt fell from the ceiling onto Kazi's head, dusting him with bits of earth. The stale air in the claustrophobic space made it hard to breathe, and the dirt walls made it feel like a coffin.

"That was the other bunker," said Stasys.

"Oh no! You all right?" said Kazi.

"All right."

"Algis?"

Stasys glanced down at the body lying on the floor. Algis's knees were bent to the side, his face turned away, an arm stretched out as if beckoning Stasys to join him in his journey to the great beyond. A tint of red colored the black liquid seeping into the ground around Algis's head.

"He's gone," said Stasys.

Kazi stood with his back against the wall and stared into the dim space as machine gun shots clattered outside. A bullet pinged through the tiny window, the sound oddly muted as the projectile impaled itself in the dirt wall across the room. Grains of black soil trickled down to the floor. Kazi stepped up to the small opening and fired another burst. "Damn them! They just keep coming!"

"This is what we get for our men killing that NKVD agent and those soldiers the other night," said Stasys.

A moment later, Stasys spoke again. "I'm out, Kazi." He threw the gun down.

"Use Algis's gun, dammit!"

"I already have."

"Thank God the others from camp were able to get away, but that explosion means we're the only ones left." Kazi grimaced as he fired again. "I'm almost out, too. You know what I have to do."

Stasys leaned against the wall. "Well, we're already in our grave, aren't we?" He managed a dry laugh.

"We're in this together."

"We do this for our families. To keep them safe."

"If the Reds don't recognize us, they won't recognize our families."

"Our sacrifice keeps them alive."

"No time for even a last smoke?" Stasys smiled.

Kazi shook his head. "I'm sorry."

"Don't be sorry. Do you believe in life after death?"

"I don't know anymore."

"It's all right. I believe enough for the both of us."

Kazi extended his hand to his brother. Stasys pushed it aside, embraced him, and kissed him on the cheek. Kazi quelled a sob. Stasys patted him on the back.

The gunfire came closer.

"Wait until I'm dead to mourn me," said Stasys. He wiped his eyes and straightened, his cap touching the ceiling. He saluted. "For freedom and family. I'll see you soon, Kazi."

Kazi stepped back, and fired a short burst into Stasys's chest. The body pummeled back against the dirt as if he were trying to push the wall away. Stasys fell to a sitting position, and leaned to his side in slow motion, his head resting against his left shoulder, his cap falling off, the hair on his head stretching down to the ground, his mouth shaped in an O, as if death's visit had come as a surprise.

Kazi wiped the tears from his eyes. He glanced up at the rough-hewn boards of the ceiling and the dirt visible through the spaces between them. He sat down next to Stasys and put an arm around the dead man.

"God help me."

He brought the grenade that had been dangling from his waist up to their faces. In seconds, they both would be unrecognizable. He pulled the pin. As he closed his eyes, Kazi pictured his young son. His words came as naturally as breathing. "Our Father, who art . . ."

~~

Colonel Karmachov pushed the chair away from his desk and leaned back, putting his feet on his desk. He stretched his arms over his considerable girth as he carefully spread soft butter over the slice of brown bread, covering every bit of it. He gently put the knife down on a plate decorated in a pattern of roses next to a charming demitasse cup filled with strong tea. He raised his pinkie as he brought the savory bread to his nose and sniffed: slightly sweet and slightly pungent. Perfect. At least Mrs. Pagelis knew how to bake good bread, one of the few palatable things to come out of this country. A knock sounded at the door.

Karmachov sighed and put his feet down, placing the bread back on the plate. "Come."

Lieutenant Yuri Svechin, Karmachov's aide, opened the door and marched in. His eyes were in the shadow cast by the visor of his black leather cap emblazoned with a red star. Dirt covered his cheeks. Bits of brush and pine needles clung to his uniform. His compact physique seemed to sag.

"We routed them out," said Svechin after saluting.

"Good. How many did we get?"

"Ten."

Karmachov raised his eyebrows. "That's good. Very good. How many alive to interrogate?"

Svechin shifted his weight. "They're all dead, sir. They blew themselves up."

"Crazy bastards." Karmachov frowned. "How many did we lose?"

"Forty-two."

Karmachov banged his hands on the desk. The butter knife rattled against the plate. "We lost four men for each of those farmers?"

Svechin stared straight ahead, saying nothing.

"We should have deported everyone back in '44. I'm sick of constantly fighting them. I want this to stop." Karmachov felt a sting in his belly as he thought of the raid in the old forest near Vilkija four years ago. His protégé, Roman Zabrev, hadn't returned from the mission, no doubt succumbing to those bloodthirsty bastards. Now, they were causing *him* damage, too, but even worse, they were making him look like a fool. He had to try something different, something they wouldn't expect.

"Did that farmer Zenonas say anything?" said Karmachov.

"No, but just before his wife died, she said 'Avenge us, Amber Wolf.' She was delirious."

"The peasants revere this man they call Amber Wolf, but he's just a criminal." Karmachov shifted his weight in the chair, hoping to offset a feeling of malaise. His career would be in jeopardy for as long as the man lived.

"What does he look like, sir?"

"Young. Light hair."

Karmachov watched Svechin's Adam's apple move up and down as he swallowed. "That couple you stopped on the road near the Zenonas farm. What did the man look like?"

"Like anyone you'd see here. Nothing but a peasant dressed in rags. He had fair skin, a dirty face, and white hair. He was disgusting."

"It might have been him, you idiot! Why didn't you arrest him?"

Svechin steeled his expression, but a sheen of sweat on his brow testified to how uncomfortable he was.

"He was probably involved in the assassination. Why else would the Zenonas woman mention him? Get out there, find this Amber fucking Wolf, and bring him to me. Alive. And do it quickly, or I'll have you freezing your ass off in Norilsk before Easter."

"Yes, sir."

"Go into every village and interrogate every man and woman. Question the damn chickens if you have to, but find him."

"Sir, are we sure Amber Wolf is a man? One of the villagers we interrogated last year said it was a woman."

"Has anyone confirmed it?"

"No. We get very little information from those people, no matter what we do to them."

"Then ignore it. It was probably a lie to take us off the scent. Besides, it's a ridiculous notion. If the stories are true, this bandit has nerves of ice and never misses a shot. It couldn't be a woman. Impossible."

"Yes, sir."

"While you're tracking this Amber Wolf down, get someone in on the inside."

"Colonel?" Svechin tilted his head.

"You heard me. Cut the head off the snake. Find someone to infiltrate the camp. They think they're smarter than we are. But once we know what they're up to and how they're organized, we'll be able to get to the leaders and stop this nonsense once and for all."

Karmachov opened the pearl-encased box on his desk, the only adornment in his living quarters aside from the portrait of Stalin on the wall behind his desk and the framed Soviet flag in the small dining room. He took out a cigarette and lit it. "Who do we have for the job?"

"The last time we tried this, the bandits mutilated our agent before murdering him and hanging him up just outside the barracks. No one wants this."

"Then you can do it. You'll make a fine spy. I hope you learn quickly."

Although still at attention, Svechin's shoulders hunched, and his entire body seemed to sag. "There are a few men in the infantry who might be qualified, but many have already relocated."

"Find me someone!"

"There might be one man. Anton Dubus just started NKVD training in Chernovsty. He was raised here, speaks the language, and knows the people. He even looks like one of them."

"Raised here," Karmachov mumbled. "But can we trust him?"

"He's been in the military for years. I've known him most of that time. He's done nothing to indicate anything but allegiance to Mother Russia." Svechin looked down at the floor.

"Are there any relatives, anyone he's close to?"

"He has a sister." Svechin gazed out the window. For a second, it looked as though his thoughts were elsewhere.

"Good. Bring her in. That way we won't have to worry about his loyalty."

"I don't think it's necessary to involve his sister, sir."

"Do as I say."

Svechin nodded.

"And send patrols out tonight. Check everyone's papers. If anything is out of order, arrest them. If anyone resists, shoot them. These people need to learn that when those damn partisans kill us, we kill *them*."

After Svechin saluted and left, Karmachov's thoughts strayed to the gruesome fate his protégé must have met in the woods at the hands of the partisans. He jammed the cigarette into the buttered bread, releasing a stench of burning fat. "Damn it!"

~~

It was late afternoon in Utena as people hurried past Dana. The largest city in this part of the Auksia forest, the area was known for its beer and sawmills that had once supplied wood for the local farmers carving out an existence there. A few were still operating, but many had been abandoned by owners who had either refused to supply lumber to the communist occupiers or who couldn't get parts to repair their equipment. The city itself was settled over 700 years before. Utena was a great lady who wore her scars with dignity. She had survived fire, the German occupation during WWI, the Bolshevik occupation, and far more. Dana hoped that the great lady would survive the Soviets, too.

With his cap pulled down over his eyes and his deliberate stride, Dana looked as though he had somewhere to go, just like everyone else. But by nightfall, the streets would be deserted, as people avoided the random patrols clouding most of their evenings, by retreating to the relative safety of their homes.

Dana expected the intensity of this night to be different. From the recent battle at the bunkers, where they had lost Kazi, Stasys, and eight others, he expected many patrols to be out raiding homes and terrorizing families. Tonight, he had two jobs. The first was to stay alive. The other was to observe what the Russians were doing and report back. Neither involved helping anyone who might be in danger, and it bothered him, but he would do what he had been told.

His first stop was Pagelis's bakeshop. The bell on the door sounded when he entered.

"All the bread's gone. We're closed," shouted a female voice from the back. In a moment, a small, wiry woman with dark curly hair appeared. She went to the door and closed the shade.

"What are you doing here? It's almost dark," she said.

"Don't burn the bread."

"Not again."

Dana shrugged and went outside. The lock clicked behind him, and Mrs. Pagelis lifted the shade a hand's width. The position of the shade would resonate like a siren, warning the people of Utena that something had happened and they should take care to protect their families and their lives. A man strolling past Dana glanced at the shade, then hurried back in the direction from which he came.

Near the Christ Assumption Church on Vytautas Square, Dana was too far away to feel the cold moisture from the lake, but he shivered anyway. Some people were out along the main streets, while others turned down dirt paths and alleyways. Gradually, the streets emptied and people went into their houses, but Dana stayed outside in the shadows.

He witnessed Soviet soldiers breaking down the door to a house and dragging the screaming occupants away; two women in dresses with buttons down the front. Perhaps they were teachers, or office workers. It made him sick, but he couldn't help them.

That evening, Dana could do nothing but watch helplessly at the terror of the people who were taken away. Usually, the partisans controlled the night, and the Russians controlled the day, but these raids were different. Dana knew they would last for several nights, or even longer. As his mother used to say, *misfortune comes in on horseback and leaves by foot.*

In the few hours of relative calm just after midnight, Dana found an abandoned home still free of squatters, its owners gone to an unknown fate. It felt strange to be away from camp and alone. The solitude gave way to loneliness as he lay on the floor, wrapped up in a blanket he had found in the back bedroom. He stared up at a ceiling instead of the stars. He thought of the strange set of circumstances that had brought him to this place. He bore the scars of his first encounter with Roman Zabrev on his back. He also bore the scars of his parents' death, for he hadn't moved them away before the war started. He had been too busy wallowing in anger for having to leave university for a life on the farm. He had thought the Russians wouldn't stay. After all, what could they possibly want with such a tiny country? When he finally witnessed the deadly hand of the Soviets, it was too late to save his family. He was alive because people he had treated badly had rescued him. He was lucky to have such friends.

The only threads that linked him to his past were people. Ludmelia, Jurgis, and Vadi were with him every day. It had been years since he'd seen Simas, the one-eyed farmhand who had treated him like a son. Other partisans were like family, too, but many were dead. If the Soviets ever left and Dana lived, he would need years to mourn for all the people who had lost their lives to Russian bullets and bayonets.

Later, Dana awoke to a pounding, and thought his days of freedom were over. He reached for his rifle and groaned, remembering he had hidden it in a stack of wood outside town. If he had been captured with it, it would have meant certain death.

At the sound of muffled voices, he crept to the window. Four soldiers entered the house next door. Dana went out the back, anxious to avoid yet another sight that tore at his heart. He ran down an alleyway to a hedge bordering a dirt road leading away from town. He had seen and heard enough.

As he walked, he paid attention to everything hitting his senses. He froze at the sound of a child crying for his mother; he dove into a ditch at the howl of a feral cat. He didn't feel safe until he was back in the arms of the Auksia woods.

~~

While Chernovsty was a charming city of narrow streets and elegant buildings where even the train station looked regal, the NKVD school was as forbidding as the gloomy winter's day. Everything in the room was gray, including the walls and especially the view. A filing cabinet stood next to the window. Apart from the volumes of manuals in the bookcase, the room was bare. Svechin sat behind a desk, watching Anton Dubus nervously settle into a chair, and thinking that his pale skin and light, curly hair belonged more on a woman than a man.

Svechin spoke first. "I need you to go into Lithuania."

"Holy Christ. Anything but that."

"You have to. If you're successful, it may make your career. I want you to infiltrate the partisan organization in the Auksia forests near Utena. We need someone on the inside to get us information about their plans. I'll help you as much as I can."

"It's a death sentence."

"You can do it. You were born there. You speak the language, and you're clever. All you need is time and a little luck to pull this off. There's a partisan called Amber Wolf. The peasants revere him. Find out where he is. We need to capture him alive for interrogation."

"If I find him, how do I get word to you?"

"Get yourself arrested. The partisans will like that. It'll give you credibility."

"And when they kill me, I'll be even more believable. What about Katya? Are you planning a mission for her, too?" Anger ran through Anton's voice.

"I'm bringing her to Utena. Karmachov's orders."

"What for? Has she been arrested?"

"Calm down. She'll be fine. I'll take care of her, but you better not warn her."

"I don't have any choice in this, do I? When Katya and I were living in Lithuania, no one helped us. They saw how our grandmother treated us. And no one even asked if we were getting enough to eat. That place is not my home. I care as little about those people as they cared about us. Katya is all I have in this world."

"Then this is your chance for revenge."

"Fine. I have no allegiance to them. Just keep Katya safe and away from Karmachov. I've heard about his reputation with women. Promise me."

"I'll do everything I can."

CHAPTER 3

In the Minsk boarding house where she lived, Katya Dubus had an understanding with the owner, a hairy, middle-aged fellow who understood the value of a ruble. Katya paid him to smooth over any complaints from the neighbors, and to screen her nighttime visitors, as drunken soldiers and ex-soldiers often felt entitled to free favors after having saved the motherland from the Nazi fascists. Occasionally, the owner wanted more than rubles. Katya hated the pig, but had to put up with him in order to survive. Every time he prepared to screw her, he insisted she wear an old set of his dead wife's underwear. The garments hung on Katya's thin frame, and she found wearing them disgusting, but she did it because she had to. He was like all the others who got into her bed: nothing special, nothing different. As her grandmother used to say, *all cats looked gray in the dark.*

The night had been long, but the money good. After Katya had bathed, scrubbing the stink of too many men from her skin, she put on her woolen nightdress, and thought about taking a walk tomorrow, if it was sunny. It had been a cold winter, and she could never seem to warm up. The prospect of feeling the sun on her face brightened her spirits as she walked through the large bedroom where she ran her business, to a door that most people would think was a closet. She used the key hidden under the carpet to unlock it. She picked up the oil lamp from the table and went into a meticulously clean room just big enough for a bed and a nightstand with a photograph of her with her younger brother, Anton. The picture was in an ornate silver frame, and had been taken in 1941 in Minsk just after she had moved here. It was the most precious thing she owned. Behind their smiling faces, the light glimmered through the leaves of a black almond tree. It was the last thing she saw every night before drifting off to sleep, and the first thing she saw every morning. She put the lamp on the nightstand, doused the light, and got into bed.

She dreamed of her mother calling out to her from the other side of a long wall. Katya ran along the bricks looking for the end, but it kept growing longer. Her mother knocked and called her name. Katya awoke with a start before realizing someone was at her door. She assumed it was another customer, and took the time to put on a robe and slippers before answering.

"Hello, Katya," said Svechin.

She smiled, tilting her head in confusion. The twist in her stomach came next.

"I need you to come with me," said Svechin as he walked in through the doorway. He went to the table and poured himself a drink, tossing it down in one gulp.

"I can't just leave. I have appointments to keep." She searched Svechin's face for a hint of assurance that things were all right. "Something has happened to Anton."

"He needs you."

"My God. Has he been hurt?"

"Get your things. I'll take you to him. Hurry."

Katya grabbed the lapels of his jacket. "Tell me!"

Svechin bent his head as if he couldn't bear to say the words.

She squelched a sob. It only took her a few minutes to dress and pack a small bag. In the second before leaving the room, she remembered to take the photograph in the silver frame. She lay it on top of her clothing and rushed out to where Svechin waited.

They went outside to a military truck. The driver started the engine as Katya climbed in beside him. Every time he shifted gears, he brushed her leg with his hand. It was annoying, but she was too worried about Anton to do anything. As they drove, she settled into the uncomfortable space between him and Svechin.

Gradually, she inched closer to Svechin. With another person present, intimate conversation was impossible, but any bit of information in a glance or touch would help soothe her nerves. He reached into the pocket of his uniform, pulled out a packet of cigarettes, and offered her one. She took it, and light from the match gave her a glimpse of his eyes. She could usually tell what he was thinking from his eyes, but this time they said nothing. She pressed her leg against Svechin's, hoping for some gentle pressure in response. He trembled; nothing more.

After Anton had joined the Red Army, he brought Svechin to the boarding house. Even though Svechin was handsome, she resented that he was there interfering with the little time she had with her brother. But Svechin had politely stood for her when she came in from the kitchen with a tureen of soup. He had helped her with her chair when she sat down at the table. He had let her talk with Anton without interjecting some personal story that directed attention away from her brother. Most of all, he had brought her a tin of chocolates with soft caramel centers; her favorite sweet. Svechin had smiled as he watched her eat one after dinner.

The evening had flown by. Anton's head nodded sleepily as he sat in an overstuffed chair. Katya sent him to bed in her little private room in the back of the apartment.

She poured Svechin another glass of vodka and they sat on the worn velvet couch. Svechin talked about his father, a military man who had died in the mud of Warsaw in 1920, and his mother, a pianist. Svechin didn't have the patience to learn a complex instrument like the piano, but she had tried to teach him anyway. He was never very good at it. She had enrolled him in the best schools she could afford. She caught typhoid fever in 1929, and was gone. He was fourteen years old. After being handed from relative to relative, Svechin joined the army, although he was barely old enough. There he met Anton, and from the start, they'd shared a camaraderie based on two things: having a mother who left them when they were young, and having to fend for themselves early in life.

After finishing the story, Svechin had leaned back into the cushions, his gaze directed to the dark recesses of the room that still held faded glory in the worn rug on the floor and tapestry hanging on the wall. He did something no other man had ever done. He had asked Katya about herself. The men who gave her money either boasted about their accomplishments or said nothing. This nicely built man with the sculpted cheeks had shared something of himself, and had shown genuine interest in her. Katya was touched. She'd moved closer to him, and they kissed. They made love on the couch. He didn't grunt like the other men. He was gentle, and when they were through, he had held her in his arms.

Before he left, Katya had asked him to take care of Anton. He had looked at her quizzically, as if her request were odd. She had told him how hard it was to survive. Besides, what did she know of the army and its ways? She wouldn't be there for Anton, and he needed a friend. Smiling, Svechin had promised to look after her brother, and she had blushed.

~~

Katya gave in to the growl of the engine as the constant motion of the truck lulled her into an uneasy quiet. After sunup, they stopped on the roadside near a forest. The soldier poured fuel into the tank from containers in the back, and Katya squatted behind some bushes to urinate. When she got back, Svechin gave her a jar of lukewarm tea and biscuits. As they stood beside the truck, she sipped the tea. "Tell me something. I can't stand not knowing."

Svechin touched his mouth before speaking. "We're going to Utena."

"Anton's there? He hates Lithuania," said Katya. She stepped up to him and looked him directly in the eyes. "Is my brother all right?"

"If you don't come willingly, he'll be in danger."

Katya's eyes grew wide. "What's going on?"

The driver started the engine. Svechin shook his head. "We have to go."

He held the door open, and Katya reluctantly climbed in.

Svechin stayed with the driver the next time they stopped to fill the tank. Katya seethed at Svechin for not telling her more, but she had to go with him. She had no choice. She had to know if Anton was all right. The last time they stopped, it was dark. Katya's body was sore from the constant rattle of the ride, and she almost fell as she stepped down from the truck, but Svechin caught her. He held her in his arms for a moment.

"I'm sorry, Katya. I had no choice," he whispered. His expression was unreadable and his demeanor unchanged, even after the exhausting ride.

"Is this a hospital?" said Katya.

Svechin didn't answer. She took hold of his arm. Her fingernails dug into his jacket.

"I've made sure you'll be as comfortable as possible under the circumstances. Do what you're told, and no one will hurt you. Just go along with what Karmachov wants. Stay alive."

"I'm being arrested?" Panic seized Katya's voice.

"I'll get you out as soon as I can."

He turned away without further explanation and took her satchel from the back of the truck. She followed him into a large brick building, and down a flight of steps. A soldier walked behind them. They passed a line of dark cells to an open door. Svechin put Katya's satchel inside the door, and stepped back into the hallway. He nodded to the soldier, who gave her a shove. Katya tripped into the room. The soldier slammed the door shut and locked it.

"Yuri!" Katya's heartbeat echoed in her throat as she pounded on the wood, feeling the stab of Svechin's deceit. When she realized no one was going to answer, she sat on the bed and took account of her surroundings. Her satchel leaned against the wall where Svechin must have left it. Judging from the carpet on the floor and sheets on the bed, it may have been a room for guards in the cell block. A small window provided an eye-level view of the ground. A difference of color on the dull wall near the door showed where a bureau had once stood. The ceiling was gray from cigarette smoke. A bucket lay in the corner; the only sanitation. The room smelled of sweat and urine.

Katya rubbed her scalp with the tips of her fingers, feeling her silky curls, a feature she shared with Anton. She remembered the picture and opened the satchel. She took it out, kissed it, and held it over her heart. She closed her eyes and escaped to a day long ago when she and Anton were very young. She had been pulling the feathers out of a pillow and scattering them over the bedroom floor while Anton slept next to her. Katya had frozen when Mama came in.

"Look at the mess you've made." Mama had smiled, taking Katya's hands, and they danced in the feathers.

"It looks like snow!" Mama said.

Katya laughed as she chased the little puffs drifting back to the floor.

Grandmother barged in. "What are you doing, teaching your children to be pigs? I already have enough pigs out in the pen."

Anton awoke and began to whimper.

Mama picked Katya up as if to shield her from the old woman's words. "Don't worry. I'm going!"

"Where are you going, Mama?" Katya asked as she patted her mother's hair.

"To Russia to find your father. When I do, we'll marry, and I'll send for you and your brother. We'll eat *vatrushka* every day. Do you remember *vatrushka*, Katya?"

"Yes, Mama."

"We'll have it with sweet tea."

"Can I have mine with milk instead, Mama?"

"Yes, my love. You can have all the milk you want."

"Make sure you stick to your plans. I want you out of here," said Grandmother. "You're a disgrace. I can barely stand how the neighbors mock me because of you and your bastard children."

"You won't have to worry about me."

"You spit in water that I have to drink."

"And I'll send for my children."

"Good."

The old woman left, slamming the door shut with a loud bang. Anton sat up in the bed and wailed. Mama put Katya on the bed next to him and kissed Anton's cheeks until he stopped crying. Then she lay down with her children.

In the morning, Mama was gone.

~~

A key turned in the lock, startling Katya back to the present and the reality of being held in a jail. A guard entered and jerked his head, indicating she should follow him.

A voice screamed inside her head. *What do they want with me? Is Anton all right?* The soldier stared as Katya slowly ironed out the wrinkles in her skirt with her hands. They lingered on her hips.

"Help me get out of here, and I'll give you a night you won't forget," she said.

He looked at her as if considering her suggestion, but shook his head.

"Think about it." Her shoulder brushed his chest as she passed him and entered the dimly lit hallway. They went into the stairwell. Katya's feet felt like lead as she climbed the steps. She paused at the first landing next to the door that led outside. The guard shook his head again, and she continued her climb into hell.

Three flights up, they entered a foyer that held a door and a window. Katya's reflection stared at her from the glass. The guard knocked, waited for a voice, and opened the door. Katya took a deep breath and stepped over the threshold.

The room was lit by a desk lamp. It wasn't bright enough to see everything clearly at first, and the effect was unsettling. A man who reminded her of a walrus sat behind a large desk. She had seen a walrus before in the Baltic off Poland. Both creatures had the same posture and layers of fat, although the man behind the desk wore a military uniform. He didn't stand, offer his hand, or speak. She assumed he was Karmachov. He had a large white food stain on his jacket, which looked like sour cream.

Two chairs stood in front of the desk whose only adornment was an empty dessert plate and a cigarette box laced in mother-of-pearl. Against a wall was a file cabinet. Perched on top was a typewriter, a bottle of vodka, and several glasses. A door to one side was open; it led to a dining room. The door on the other side was closed. Katya guessed it was the bedroom. She sat, even though a chair hadn't been offered. She crossed her legs. "Good evening, Colonel."

A corner of his mouth twitched. His face was covered in pimples. He sat back and crossed his fingers over his sizeable belly, watching her. She settled back in her chair, willing her hands to remain steady as she waited for Karmachov to speak.

"Svechin didn't tell me how beautiful you are."

Katya bristled at the compliment. "Where's my brother?"

"He's safe for now."

"What do you want with me?"

"You'll stay here as my guest and hope your brother does his job. He's doing some work for me. Let's say that your presence will help him focus. If he fails, you'll both know what it's like to die for the motherland."

She clenched her jaw. "What job is that?"

"A secret mission." Karmachov smiled.

The full impact of Svechin's betrayal seeped in. They needed her for leverage against Anton. His assignment had to be dangerous; Svechin had broken his promise to protect Anton. Svechin had deceived them both. "There's no reason to talk of death, Colonel. I'm sure we can be friends."

She stood and went to the file cabinet. She held up the bottle of vodka. "Would you like a drink?"

He grunted, which she took for a yes. She poured out the liquid into two of the glasses. She handed him one. She held her glass out, and he clicked his to it. She sipped while he quickly swallowed his drink and made a face.

"Good." He belched.

Katya smiled through her disgust. She filled his glass again.

Karmachov took his pistol from the shoulder holster, and locked it in the center drawer of his desk. It would give her great pleasure to use the gun on this pig, but then Anton would suffer, too. She went over to the door to what she guessed was the bedroom and glanced over her shoulder. "Aren't you coming?"

CHAPTER 4

In a barracks at the Tomsk Oblast labor camp in Siberia, Victor Kudirka started awake. His body was so cold that it hurt to move. As he forced himself up and off his thin straw mattress, he wished that he would die now and end the suffering. He had made that wish every morning for the last seven years. But he pictured his wife Aldona's soft face, and his children, Ludmelia and Matas, wondering what they looked like now. The thought of them convinced him to survive for another day, so that he might see them once again in this life. If not for the memory of them, he would have given up long ago. And yet he didn't know if his family was alive. He didn't know if his beautiful wife had followed his instructions to escape the Soviets and flee to the forest with their children. He didn't know if his years teaching them to survive in the woods had mattered. All he could do was hope. Today, like every day, it was enough to get him out of bed.

He rolled off the low shelf onto the floor, landing on his hands and knees. From there, he painfully stood as his bones cracked. He moved his shoulders and stretched his back. He rubbed his hands together and blew warm breath onto his fingers.

Victor made his way past other shelves and places on the floor where bodies breathed heavily in sleep. He went to the stove, where he coaxed a fire to life. The flame, small as it was, warmed him a little. Sometimes, after working outside all day and walking on the slippery road back to the drafty shack, the mere thought of flame warmed him, but it was never enough to truly make a difference.

As the fire grew, bodies stirred, except for the one closest to the door on the far side of the frigid room. Even under the thin blanket covering his head and shoulders, *that* body had the look of the stillness Victor knew all too well.

He sighed and turned his back. Either the man would rise or he wouldn't. Victor was too tired and too sad to run to him and rub in the warmth that might ward off death. He had done it before, and all it had done was steal Victor's energy and spirit when the poor soul had died anyway. Death always came, no matter what he did or didn't do.

Victor sprinkled a few broken tea leaves into a pot of water and moved it toward the flame, next to another pot containing the same thin soup they had eaten the day before, and the day before that.

"Victor, bring me my tea," said a voice.

"Get your own tea, Hektoras," said Victor.

"Shut up fools, let us sleep," mumbled a voice.

"Why do you get up so early?" asked Hektoras, his voice lower and softer.

"I need some peace and quiet before you start talking."

"I talk because I feel obligated to entertain the brilliant Victor Kudirka. If you'll excuse me, I need to piss."

Hektoras wrapped his blanket around his shoulders and pulled on his boots. At the door, he murmured, "Pardon me." The body lying there didn't move. Hektoras tapped the leg with his foot. Nothing.

"He's dead," said a man with crooked teeth and feverishly bright eyes who was watching from his shelf. He rubbed his hands together with an insane vigor, almost as if he was happy about it.

Hektoras glanced up at Victor and sighed, then put his hands under the arms and pulled the body outside for the detail of prisoners to collect, along with all the others who had died during the night. They would be dumped into a mass grave just outside camp. Hektoras came back inside carrying the dead man's blanket and shoes. He spread the blanket out over his mattress, and hid the shoes under his bed.

Victor helped himself to his allotment of food: one cup of tea, one bowl of soup, and one crust of bread. It wasn't enough. Ten times this wouldn't have been enough. Other hungry people watched from their beds. Snatching an extra crust of bread or mouthful of soup meant a beating and relegation to the spot on the floor next to the door, where the cold night air crept in. Some prisoners said it was where death slept. One thing the guards never had to do was police the allotment of food, for the prisoners took care of that themselves.

Men rose, moving to the food or the door depending on whether the need to eat or empty their bladders was greater. Voices spoke in different languages: Russian, Latvian, Polish. It was not a problem, for Victor spoke all those languages, as well as English and German. Only Hektoras spoke Lithuanian in this shack. That alone made him feel like a brother. Hearing the guttural singsong of his native tongue made Victor think of home, Aldona, and his children. He prayed to God every morning and every night that they were still alive and well.

Besides Hektoras, a few other Lithuanians lived in the camp, having been snatched from their lives by Stalin's deportations in a deliberate intent to annihilate the best of Victor's generation and ultimately rid the earth of their nationality. *And why? Because Stalin is afraid of us?* Victor scowled as he carried his cup and bowl to his bed and sat.

When Hektoras returned, he stood in line for his tea and soup. He took his food to Victor's bed and sat down. Hektoras rambled on while Victor tried to block the upcoming drudgery of the day from his mind. All too soon, a Red soldier came into the room and commanded them to line up for the long walk into the forest, where they harvested trees with dull hand tools.

Victor and Hektoras managed to fall to the back of the line, as usual. It was the best location, for they could shuffle along a little more slowly, saving energy. If they got close enough to the truck behind them where the soldiers inside laughed and smoked, they could imagine the warmth from the engine. Occasionally, they could feel it.

Something was in the air today: a brighter sun, a warming of the usually frigid air. Victor could feel the glimmer of hope that always came with the first hint of spring.

About half a kilometer from the work site, a man broke from the line and ran toward the woods. The line came to a halt as the escapee, whom Victor recognized as the man with crooked teeth from his shack, raced around stumps, bits of pine, sawdust, and chips of wood. He ran with abandon over the scarred remains of the forest, his arms flailing like a child's, tatters from the hem of his coat fluttering about his legs. He laughed hysterically as he ran, gasping occasionally for breath.

Hektoras shook his head. "It's the end for him."

Two soldiers climbed out of the truck, smirking as though they were glad for the break in their routine, and pausing for a moment, as if enjoying the show. First, they tapped their cigarettes on their boot soles to extinguish the embers, and put the remains in their pockets for later. They raised their guns slowly, deliberately, as if they had nothing else to do. The man was pumping his arms and legs, darting from side to side, still screaming with laughter as he ran around the stumps and branches.

The soldiers took aim and fired. The blast from the guns hurt Victor's ears and he covered them with his hands. The escapee's arms flew out to the side as if he was giving himself up. He hovered for a moment midair, and then fell onto his face.

A soldier called out, "On your way." The line trudged on, leaving the body where it lay.

At the job site, Victor and Hektoras worked with axes, carefully trimming branches from trees they had felled yesterday. Any mistake meant a cut or an injury, and here, in the coldest conditions, with barely enough calories to sustain an inactive body, let alone one working at hard labor, injuries rarely healed, hastening the inevitable spiral toward death.

An hour into the workday, a prisoner was selected to start a fire for the guards. It was a coveted job, because it was easy and meant warmth for a while. Victor glanced at the lucky man with envy. The soldiers sat on logs and stretched their hands out toward the growing flames. They laughed and talked and offered each other cigarettes. Victor gazed at the fire whenever he could, imagining how it felt. It helped a little.

Lunch was a warm drink and a crust of bread. Victor and Hektoras sat together on a log while they ate, their legs and shoulders touching. They took tiny bites to make the food last.

"When do you think we can escape?" whispered Hektoras, holding the cup close to his lips so the guards couldn't see that he was talking.

"Escaping is not the problem. Surviving is the problem."

"If we saved a little food every day, we would have enough."

"They barely give us enough to live, let alone saving any."

"Victor, we have to try. I must see my wife and my baby. I can't bear being away from them any longer."

"The only way we can get food is to steal it. Then we could wait for a storm and disappear. We'd have to avoid the nearest town, for that's where they'd look for us."

"Do you know where that is?"

"Not exactly. But I know there's another town, further away to the west. I heard the guards talking."

"Is there hope, Victor?" Their whispers cut off as a guard came near.

The afternoon's work was like the morning's work, and like the work they had done the day before that, and the day before. Finally, the men assembled for the long walk home. Victor and Hektoras weren't near the truck this time, as Victor's numb hands couldn't release the axe handle quickly enough for them to get to the coveted spot first, so they walked in the front of the line, where the wind was the coldest. Victor's body was so frigid he could barely bend his knees.

At the clearing where one of them had decided that morning he would suffer no more, the line stopped. The body was still there, but someone had stolen the hat, boots, and jacket. The dead man lay on his back with his pale arms and legs extended as if he were enjoying the warmth of a summer's day. One of the trucks drove up and prisoners lifted the man's arms and legs, unceremoniously tossing the body into the open back. The truck stopped at the pit where other frozen bodies waited for the earth to thaw so they could finally be buried.

"It's too bad we have to die to get a ride in the truck," murmured Hektoras.

The line plodded on until they reached the barbed wire gate of the compound. They stood in the yard for evening count that always seemed to take longer in the colder weather. Afterward, they went to their shacks. Men climbed up on their shelves, making themselves comfortable however they could. Some went to the stove where they set fire to the little bit of wood available. Others moved the pot to the heat.

As usual, Victor ate slowly, sitting on his bed and cupping the bowl with his hands to warm them. The meal was never enough. The prayers for his family were never enough. The sleep that followed was never restful, for it took Victor hours to warm himself. Every time he shifted on the bed, his arms and shoulders ached. When he finally slept, he entered the same airless and lightless abyss he entered every night, often waking up gasping for breath.

CHAPTER 5

The jeep cut its lights as it rolled to a stop in a remote section of northeastern Lithuania, about sixty kilometers from Utena and the Auksia forest. Anton Dubus sat in the passenger seat as the engine idled, enjoying the warmth for a second longer. He exhaled, nodded to the driver, and got out. He quietly closed the door and the jeep drove off. Anton quickly walked toward the trees, the sound of his feet on the gravel crisp against the fading sound of the engine. He stopped at the frozen dirt near a line of receding snow. The vehicle's lights snapped on just before a curve in the road. He waited until darkness took over again. When he was satisfied that the distant sounds he heard were animals and not men, he put the knapsack on his back, dug his fists into his pockets, and walked with a step as light as a wolf's.

The night was bitter, the air raw. In an hour, even his eyes felt cold. Gradually, the trees became more distinct against the horizon, and little by little, light brought the promise of warmth. At daybreak came the creak of wooden wheels, along with the clomp of a horse. Anton opened his coat and reached for the Luger tucked in his belt, but stopped before drawing it. After all, he should look like just another man searching for work and a place to call home; nothing special or unusual in this part of the world. An old farmer came into view, driving a cart. Without stopping, the farmer cocked his head toward the back. Anton nodded and hopped on, grateful for the offer of a ride.

They passed trees and bushes, and a long expanse of fields rimmed in a thick border of wild rue, dry and brittle from the cold. Anton rested his elbow on the side of the cart, letting his head nod and his body sway as he constantly scanned the roadside, observing that nothing had changed since the last time he was there.

He and Katya had lived with their grandmother in a nearby village, where the paths between dwellings became so muddy in the spring as to be almost impassable. He remembered the neighbors talking with his grandmother and stopping to stare at him whenever he came into view. He remembered his mother's scent that resembled sweet tea, but he couldn't recall her face, even though he had spent most of his childhood trying to. Eventually, the foolish expectation that she would walk in through the door at any moment had changed to anger for leaving him and his sister alone with that witch of a grandmother.

Grandmother hadn't starved them, but she certainly hadn't loved them. She had told them that work would be their salvation from having been born innocent bastards—but bastards nonetheless. Work was the only way to show God they deserved a place in heaven. So, they worked. Katya and pigs had been the companions of his youth, and he constantly smelled of the rotten stink of the sty. One night after Grandmother had gone to bed, Katya had held out the soft underside of her shapely forearm. At fourteen, she was already beginning to look like a young woman. "It's from the oven, Anton. It still hurts. This time I'll have a scar."

Anton examined the wound, and rubbed his own forearm as if he shared her pain. "I'm sorry."

"It's not your fault. I hate her." Katya started to cry.

"She might come in and see you. Don't give her the satisfaction."

"She hates us as much as she hates Mama. She wants me to do everything in the kitchen now, but I won't. I'm going to leave."

"Where will you go?"

"I don't know. Someone will take care of me. I know men like me. I see them watching me."

"What men?"

Katya had shrugged. "Will you come with me, Anton?"

Anton left the memory behind as he jumped down from the cart when the farmer turned the horse onto a narrow path leading through a field. Anton waved his thanks, and the farmer and horse clomped on as if their paths had never crossed.

When the farmer was out of sight, Anton urinated against a tree, then sat down on a stump for a breakfast of bread and sausage from his knapsack. He ate snow to quench his thirst, but craved a glass of hot tea. Somewhat revived, he walked for three more hours before cutting through the trees to a village he knew. His grandmother's friend had lived there. If she was still alive, he hoped she would give him a meal and a place to stay for the night in exchange for a few rubles. He approached the cottage through two small fields. Chickens clucked along the wide path leading to the hut. The thatched roof still looked sturdy. The wood underneath was dark and weathered.

An old woman answered his knock. He recognized her scowl right away. It took a few minutes for her expression to show surprise and recognition. It only took a second longer for it to change back into a scowl. She pointed an arthritic finger at him. "I remember you. Your grandmother, God rest her soul, treated you like a son, and you ran away, leaving her to take care of those pigs all by herself. You're the son of a whore. You have no father. Get out of here, you scum!"

That they had known each other long ago didn't appear to matter. Anton felt his neck get hot at once more being called a bastard. He had thought those days were over, but he should have expected more bad treatment from these people.

Angry and bitter with memories, Anton returned to the road. Perhaps Svechin was right. This mission was his chance at revenge. If he did is job well, the partisan resistance would end, at least in the area. Russian families would eagerly move into the deserted homesteads, knowing it was finally safe. Those natives who had survived the war and its aftermath would be absorbed into the motherland. They'd speak Russian, sing Russian songs, and become good communists. Gradually, their culture would fade away, and Lithuania would be gone. The thought bolstered his spirits, but he was still hungry and cold, and needed a place to spend the night.

Anton was weary by the time he noticed a trace of wood smoke in the air. There came a slow banging that sounded like a drum. When he discerned a cracking sound, he realized that someone was outside splitting wood. He crossed a carpet of pine needles to a clearing and a cottage, where a dark figure was working on a woodpile. The building had a large door, and a low fence that marked a kitchen garden covered in snow. A shed stood in the back. Even through the cold air, he recognized the stink of a pig sty. The only person who seemed to be around was the man chopping wood.

Wood brought the prospect of warmth and hot food. Hopefully, it would be offered willingly. A man wielding an axe wasn't an obstacle Anton wanted to overcome, unless he had no other choice. He patted the Luger's handle still tucked under his belt, and stepped into the clearing.

"*Labas*," called Anton.

The axe cracked through the wood, snapping it into two perfect halves. The man pulled up on the handle, releasing the blade from the stump. With the axe still in his hand, he straightened and turned to Anton. "What do you want?"

Stunned at hearing a woman's voice, Anton responded. "That's hard work for a woman. Can I help you?"

The woman had dark hair. Her gaze bound him like a rope.

"Please," said Anton. "I'm hungry. If I help you, will you give me something to eat and a place to sleep?"

The woman watched him for a moment, as if deciding whether to trust him or to kill him.

"What are you doing here?" she asked.

"Looking for work."

"You won't find any."

Anton looked down at the ground, and then glanced back at the path that brought him here. "It's just for one night. It's very cold."

"Where are you from?" she asked.

"Dysna."

"That's not too far. Why don't you go home to your wife?"

Anton shrugged and hung his head, seizing the opportunity to play the grieving widower. The woman nodded and to Anton's surprise, wiped her eyes. "I know what it's like to be alone." She handed him the handle of the axe, and went into the cottage. As he chopped, Anton noticed the woman watching him from a window. She came out after a while, carrying a pail. She handed it to him.

"Feed the pig," she said. "When you're done, clean out the chicken coop in the shed. Dump the droppings on the pile in the back."

She called over her shoulder as she returned to the cottage. "After you finish with the chickens, get back to the wood."

"What's your name?" asked Anton.

She didn't answer.

Gritting his teeth, he fed the pig, hoping she didn't have more chores in mind for him. He was already tired. It was almost dark by the time Anton finished with the chopping. He was so hungry it felt like his stomach had collapsed into his spine. He loaded his arms with cut wood and knocked on the cottage door. It opened and he went inside. Flames roared in the fireplace behind a table and chairs. The room smelled of onions and cabbage cooking in a savory stew. A bed in the back of the room had rosary beads draped over the headboard.

Anton dropped the wood into the bin by the fireplace. He took off his cap and tucked it into his pocket.

"Sit," said the woman, pointing to a large chair with a cushion on the seat at the head of the table. She dished out two plates of stew and set one in front of Anton.

He put a large spoonful of food into his mouth and huffed. "Hot."

"Of course, it's hot. It just came from the pot." The woman chuckled as she put a chunk of bread on the table in front of him.

Anton blew on each bite before putting it in his mouth. He was so hungry he barely chewed, and didn't look up until he finished. He glanced longingly at the pot still on the stove. The woman stood, and brought him a little more. This time, he ate slowly enough to taste it, and it was wonderful.

"How did your wife die?" asked the woman.

Anton licked his spoon and put it down. The woman was neither young nor old, and exuded a wholesome energy. She had an hourglass figure. He would enjoy seducing her, if he could summon the strength. Most soldiers went to whores, but he never could, because he knew what Katya did. It had been a long time since he'd been with a woman. "I never thought it was possible to miss another person so much." He closed his eyes for a moment as much for dramatic effect as to make up a good story. "The Germans shot her. I wasn't home. A neighbor told me. I should have been there. Maybe I could have saved her."

"The Russians killed my husband. Bastards!"

Anton put his hand over hers and gently squeezed. "You poor woman."

"Any children?"

"None."

She shook her head. "That's too bad. If you had a child, you wouldn't be alone. All I have is my pig, a few chickens, and this place."

"I know pigs. They smell like home to me."

The woman smiled as she reached for a bottle and two glasses on the shelf. "I save this for when people come to visit, but no one does any more." She poured some out. "*I sveikata!*"

"You're here all alone in the woods. Are you safe?" Anton yawned, trying to think of a way to get her to talk openly, for perhaps she knew something that might be useful to his mission.

"When the soldiers come into the area, I hide. That keeps me safe enough."

"Tell me about your husband."

They drank and talked some more. In the warm room, with food and vodka in his belly after a long day's walk and hours of chores, Anton only half-listened. His head dropped to his chest.

He awoke to a murmuring. The woman was kneeling by the bed, and the rosary beads were in her hands. It brought back visions of his mother kneeling next to him as she prayed. He was too little to know the words, so he had mumbled nonsense in harmony with her voice. When they were through, Mother kissed him on the head. He ached to remember her clearly in the waves of images that were nothing more than vague recollections from his childhood. Her face always faded when he focused on it. He let his eyes drift shut again, hoping to see his mother in his dreams.

Anton awoke to the crackle of burning wood. He was still in the chair. A blanket covered him. His back was stiff.

"I thought you were going to sleep all day," said the woman, smiling.

Anton glanced out the window. The dark sky was becoming lighter with the dawn. He pulled on his coat and went outside. He stood next to a tree, unzipped his trousers, and pissed on the snow clinging to the bark. As he finished, the door to the cottage opened and the woman set a pail outside on the front step. "Go feed the pig." Almost as an afterthought, she added, "And clean out the pen where she sleeps."

Anton set his mouth in a grim line as he remembered how Grandmother had ordered him about all the time. But he hadn't had breakfast yet, so he did as he was told.

After finishing his chores, he entered the cottage to the smell of good Lithuanian bacon frying. The woman, whose name he still didn't know, was setting the table, pouring hot tea into cups, and cooking eggs. He sat in the same chair he had slept in, thinking that he would remember this breakfast for a long time. It was nothing fancy, but the bacon was delicious, and he had four eggs on his plate.

When they were done eating, the woman handed him a sweater. "It belonged to my husband, and it will keep you warm under that jacket."

Anton was dumbfounded by the kindness. "Are you Russian, or Polish perhaps?"

"Of course not. Why would you think so?"

"No reason." He smiled. She must be from Ukraine. She was far too civil to be from here.

The woman donned boots and a coat as Anton put on the sweater. It smelled of apples. She ushered him out the door, said goodbye, and headed toward the shed.

Anton adjusted the straps of his knapsack, and made his way back to the road, wondering if he should have left some money for her. But even with the gift of a sweater, he had earned everything he had gotten.

He walked through the day and into the afternoon light, often thinking of Katya. Together, he and his sister had survived their grandmother and the war. If he survived this mission, he'd take her away from that boarding house and the way she made her living. She had never told him what she did, but it wasn't hard to piece together the old satin bedcover, the endless supply of vodka, and the fact that Katya had money to live even though she admitted to staying home all the time. They'd find a place in the Russian countryside where they could live in peace for the rest of their lives. It pained him that he couldn't send her enough money to leave that existence right away, as she had done so much for him. She had taken him away from a hateful grandmother. She had even ventured into marriage for his sake. She had found him a mentor in the army. To avoid being a burden to him financially, she let Russian men take her to bed.

As the scent of the forest grew strong and the shadows cast by the trees grew long, Anton heard the creak of old timbers and the rush of water. The moisture in the air became so cold that it stung his lungs. A waterwheel came into view, moaning as it slowly turned. The saw was gone, as well as the engine that powered it. During the war, there was no fuel, so wide belts were brought back to run the saw with water power, but even those were gone now. The shed where planks had been stacked had collapsed. All that remained was a rotted floor covered with leaves and pine needles, and a nearby shack with a crooked chimney. Long before the war, the shack had been an office and a place for the owner to sleep when he chose to spend the night.

Anton went up to the shack's door, the wood gray with age. Its bullet holes were a reminder that the war had touched even this obscure corner of an unknown woods, in a country most people didn't even know existed. He knocked, not expecting an answer, but one couldn't be too careful. People lived anywhere these days, and a surprised squatter could easily say hello with a weapon. He pressed an ear against the wood, lifted the latch, and pushed the door open.

A window shrouded in spiderwebs let in just enough light to see the basics of a room that smelled of dust and stale smoke. A dilapidated fireplace was along one wall, and a narrow bed along another. A small table and a broken chair were in the corner. Everything was covered in a thick layer of dust. He pulled out a candle from his knapsack and lit it with a match. He let a few drops of melted wax fall to the table, and set the candle in it. In an instant, the soft light made the filthy room look almost homey.

Anton put his Luger down on the bed. He reached for the flask filled with vodka in his side pocket, hoping it would help loosen the tongues of people he met. He also took out a small photograph of him with Katya, taken seven years ago after he had helped her settle in Minsk. He wiped away the lint clinging to it. They were both smiling. He had carried it with him since he joined the army. He had it with him during every battle. So far, it had protected him.

A partisan would never carry a picture of a loved one, for they feared the Russian reprisals. From this moment on, he had to act like a partisan. He kissed the picture, lit a match, and picked up the photograph. His hands shook as stared at his sister's lovely face. The fire burned his finger and he blew it out. He put the photograph back in his pocket. He'd destroy it later if he had to, but for now, the picture would remain his good luck charm.

He went to the fireplace, placing half-burned sticks of wood over nesting material a mouse had left behind, and paused. Someone might see the smoke. He didn't want visitors, but decided that was unlikely. He tucked the gun under his belt, went out into the twilight to gather wood. He came back inside, and made the fire. After holding his hands out to the warmth, he ate from the dwindling store of food in his knapsack.

He dragged the cot to within a few feet of the fire, and lay down fully clothed, using the knapsack as a pillow. He placed the Luger at his side. He stared at the ceiling covered with dust and cobwebs, thinking of the turn of fate that had brought him here. Even though

Svechin had been promoted sooner and more often than Anton, he was like a brother. He had kept an eye on Anton, even getting him accepted to NKVD training. Svechin had helped Anton get the choicest and least dangerous assignments until now.

His last meeting with Svechin had given him a cold feeling of foreboding. If he could infiltrate a partisan cell, which would be no easy task, he had to be ready to take advantage of any situation where he could do damage, possibly even killing someone. Svechin couldn't help him. No one could. Once Anton was with the partisans, he was sure they wouldn't let him out of their sight. Even more worrisome was the prospect that Russian soldiers might come after him, for they wouldn't know he was a spy. They'd think he was a partisan. In addition to all this, Svechin was holding Katya captive to ensure Anton's loyalty. Anton closed his eyes, but sleep didn't come.

He was thinking that the man who was like a brother to him might be his enemy.

CHAPTER 6

Life in Utena returned to a strange new normal over the next few weeks as the fury of the Soviet patrols gradually died down. Despite this, people continued to reel from the senseless violence. During the day, men lucky enough to have jobs shifted along with dour expressions on their faces. Even those working on the forced labor crews building an airstrip outside the city looked more terrified than usual. No one lingered on the streets, except for lines at Pagelis's bakery, the butcher shop, and the grocery store, where women comforted each other with hugs and handkerchiefs as they waited hours for food. Often, a glance over the shoulder showed a face tortured with doubt that the relative quiet was really a Soviet trick. It was impossible to tell the difference between the expressions of people who had lost a loved one, and those who still waited for that horror to happen. After dark, the streets remained empty, for anyone caught out at night would be stopped. Such encounters were nothing compared to being beaten or shot, but they could lead to an arrest and deportation, so nighttime activity was mostly limited to Soviet soldiers and their communist friends traveling to Lukas's grog house, then back to their beds.

But this night was different. Ludmelia, Dana, Raminta, Jurgis, and Vadi were in the city, doing all they could to stay out of sight. In the vicinity of Lukas's establishment, a pair of drunken Red soldiers burst through the door and tripped down the worn wooden steps. The partisans ran into an alleyway to avoid them. The swell of voices sounded until the door slammed shut. With their arms draped around each other, loudly singing a Russian bar song, the two drunkards walked one way, then turned around and walked back in the other direction.

When the soldiers were out of sight, the partisans continued through the maze of streets and back alleys. At the base of a small hill, they stole past a broken column and the statue of a knight lying in the dirt, next to the iron fence that had been crushed in its fall. They followed the snow-lined path to the top where an old church stood against the haunting glow of a full moon, like a grand dame looking down on the town.

Ludmelia motioned for the others to wait in the graveyard next to the church. She stepped to the back door and forced the lock with her knife, freezing at the sharp clack as it unlatched. A moment passed in which she listened without breathing. Then she went in, gun drawn and ready, mindful of every creak, interpreting shades of gray to a table, chairs, glasses, crosses, and doorways. She looked inside the rooms along a hallway, and opened a closet that held robes and vestments. She passed an alcove. A figure was there, barely bright enough to see. She raised her gun before realizing it was a statue of the Virgin Mother next to a basin where babies were blessed. Ludmelia leaned against the stone and exhaled before going into the nave. She made the sign of the cross and briefly knelt at an altar decorated with a large bouquet of flowers. Ludmelia touched a bud. It felt dry and brittle, but in the dark looked alive and vibrant. She breathed softly, waiting to hear others who might be breathing as they hid in the cavernous room. No one was there, except for God. She owed Him many prayers for all she had done and all the lives she had taken, even though killing for her country didn't feel like a sin. In God's eyes, it was. She believed that one day she could atone for her past by doing good, and God would forgive her. She crossed herself a second time, and spun around to the sound of footsteps. Dana came into view.

"Get the others," she whispered.

He went out the door as silently as he had come.

Ludmelia ran her fingers through her amber hair. Her dirty jacket and trousers weren't the dress she should be wearing to a wedding. Few people were getting married these days, for the Soviets had closed the churches, and had sent most of the priests to labor camps. The ones who remained free had fled into the woods, some to fight.

She said a prayer for Papa, hoping he was still alive. She prayed for Matas, her brother, who had already given his life in the fighting. She prayed for Mama, who had died while saving Ludmelia from the soldiers. Thinking about a person should bring them back, especially in a church where such miracles were possible. Jesus's dim outline shone in the stained glass above the massive wooden door, his hands pressed together, his expression serene. Though the space was empty, it felt like others were with her. "Mama?" she whispered.

Silence.

"Matas?"

If the dead could come back, this place would be full of poor souls whose lives had been cut short by a war that just wouldn't end, at least not for them.

"Papa, are you there?" She pictured Victor Kudirka's face. She hadn't seen it in seven years, and wondered if he had changed. She wondered if his cheeks, that had once been rosy as apples, had become thin and gaunt. Ludmelia fingered the cloth on the altar, missing her father as keenly as on the day the soldiers had taken him away. She spoke to him often, and he often answered. She wanted him back, and for her life to begin. That couldn't happen until the fighting was over. For now, fighting *was* her life. The dead flowers quivered in agreement.

At the sound of a lonely creak, Dana entered. Behind him came Raminta, and then Vadi and Jurgis, the farmhands who had worked on Dana's homestead before the barn was destroyed by the Soviets. Ludmelia relaxed until she noticed the last man; a stranger. Dana held up his hand. "This is Father Burkas."

The priest nodded, stepping forward. A gun hung from the holster on the strap over his shoulder. "After what I've done, I don't know if God still thinks of me as a man of the cloth."

"You can perform a wedding ceremony, can't you?" said Ludmelia.

"I can say the words. I just hope God is listening."

"He is."

"Where's the bride?"

Raminta stepped forward. "Here I am, Father." She took Jurgis's hand.

"Be quick," said Ludmelia. She adjusted the semiautomatic hanging from her shoulder. She considered taking it off for the few minutes they would be there, but a partisan is never without her gun.

"Words are important at a wedding," said Father Burkas.

"If it's not brief, it may be the last ceremony you perform."

Ludmelia opened her knapsack and pulled out a hand-woven shawl that was a delicate white, and had belonged to Mama. She also pulled out a stubby bouquet of pussy willows tied together with a strip of cloth. She draped the shawl over Raminta's shoulders, covering part of her jacket. She wrapped Raminta's fingers around the stems and kissed her on the cheek as Dana went outside to watch for soldiers.

In a church abandoned except for a few lonely partisans, a couple bound in love stood before a priest who carried a gun. He spoke. "We are gathered together in this house of God, to witness the marriage of this man and this woman. In a different time, the church would be full of flowers and people we love. Still, the bouquet in the bride's hands is as beautiful as a thousand blooming buds. While the church is not full of family, the few people standing with you risk their lives to protect your joy and your future. How can a marriage starting with such love not be blessed?"

A sob escaped from Raminta's throat.

"In this time of turmoil, it's more important than ever to cling to the ones we cherish, and remember the importance of love and children to carry us through to better times. Now join hands," said Father Burkas.

After the words linking the young partisans in holy union had been said, and the blessing had been given, Jurgis leaned in to kiss his bride.

Dana rushed in. "Trucks!"

They all dove to the floor at the rumble of engines.

The hard wood against her cheek reminded Ludmelia of the night she had spent hiding in the attic. The old fear came back. She felt the urge to vomit, but didn't. Despite everything, she had wanted to kill those soldiers as much as she wanted her heart to continue beating. She felt the same way now.

Light from the headlights cast Jesus's presence in colors that grew brighter with every passing second. Ludmelia grasped the gun. The engines grew louder. Jesus glowed. She aimed her weapon at the door. The light waned and the sound of the engines faded.

Ludmelia hung her head in relief as the others got to their feet.

"Thank you, Father," said Ludmelia. "We'd better get out of here."

Jurgis gave his new bride a quick kiss, and took her hand. They filed out as silently as they had come. Ludmelia was the last to leave, glancing back at the altar and offering another silent prayer to Papa, hoping he was still alive.

CHAPTER 7

Several kilometers outside of Utena, the Russians were building an airstrip, and they needed more men. They had found Anton on market day several weeks ago, and had pressed him into service, like any other man, able-bodied or barely so. Anton was healthy and stronger than most, so he was a prime candidate. Most men forced to join a labor crew would consider it bad luck, but it was just the opposite for Anton. Every day he was with a group of twelve men. None were paid, except for a meal, and their choice was either to work or be shot. So every day, that's what they did. The work of clearing trees, shoveling, digging, and wielding a pickaxe was backbreaking, but it gave Anton a chance to talk, listen, and learn. Every bit of information was useful, for he knew little. So far, his reward for this effort was a sore spine, calloused hands, and a sense that his mission was going to take forever.

Anton was the last to climb down from the military truck that dropped off the crew on the outskirts of town. They were picked up from and delivered to the same spot every day, did the same work every day, and grumbled the same swear words under their breath every day. The only thing that changed was the part of their bodies that hurt the most. He wanted to go to the shack at the sawmill and rest, but this was the only time he had to do his real job, and that was finding partisans.

He practically dragged himself through the streets of the little city toward Lukas's bar. Russians and communists drank there, but it was worth visiting, in the hope that partisans masquerading as communists were there too. This would be his first time inside, as he was concerned that partisans would think he was a Russian sympathizer. But he had to do something.

Anton passed the market that was open only on Thursdays, but avoided the street housing the military barracks and the commander's quarters in the old brick building that had been taken over by the Soviets. It had once held offices for the provisional government during the brief period of freedom after the Great War, but now it housed soldiers who didn't know that Anton really was one of them. A cluster of cells in the basement was used to detain criminals and dissidents until they were shipped to the barren east and a future of cold, desolation, and death. He wondered how many men and women were inside awaiting their fate. A pain touched his heart as he wondered if Katya was there, too. It was an old nothing street in an old nothing place. And he had nothing to do but wait and watch for his chance, hoping one would come quickly, before Katya came to any harm.

~~

In a snug house, two streets away from Utena's gymnasium, young Tilda Partenkas looked up from the sheet of mathematics problems as the clock on the mantle ticked a comforting rhythm. Many of the answers her friend, Ona, had provided were wrong. She glanced at Ona sitting on the other side of the dining room table, chewing her fingernails. Tilda realized that her friend might never understand the concepts of geometry. Mathematics came easily to Tilda. Her teacher had begun to secretly tutor her in advanced concepts and already she was surpassing him in knowledge. Ona was barely passing her exams and needed more tutoring, but it was past the hour Tilda should have left for home. It was already getting dark outside. She considered spending the night at Ona's house, but Mama and Papa would be frantic with worry, not certain where she was.

Tilda put on her coat, grabbed her books, said a hurried goodbye, and rushed out the door. She ran until she was out of breath and wondering why she had to go so fast. So what if it was almost dark? It wasn't even late. Besides, it wasn't ladylike to run.

She stopped to catch her breath outside the bakery where Mr. Pagelis sold bread, catching a glimpse of herself in the window. She touched her shiny brown hair and thought she looked quite grown-up for a fourteen-year-old girl. She glanced down the street. At least she wasn't far from home.

Mama was going to be angry with her though; Papa, too. They would punish her for being so late, but what could they do? Already she couldn't go out; no one could. She couldn't visit her friends, except Ona, and that was just once a week. There were no freedoms to take away. The Soviet occupation was already punishing her more than her parents ever could.

It wasn't fair having to live like this. The streets were almost empty. No one was going to harm her. Mama had told her never to be out after dark because of the Russians, but she was just a schoolgirl. What could they possibly want with her? Tilda turned back to her reflection in the window. She smiled and twisted a lock of hair around her ear. She turned and almost bumped into two Russian soldiers. She screamed.

One soldier grabbed her by the hand. She pulled against it. *Are they going to shoot me? Interrogate me?* In a rush, she remembered the stories about the horrible things the Russians did. It hurt to breathe. Her legs grew weak.

"What have we here?" asked the other soldier. He wore a hat and had a beard.

"An angel has fallen from heaven, right into our hands," said his companion. He was tall and clean-shaven. His uniform was very neat.

Tilda leaned away from the soldiers, as if mere inches could make a difference. Oh, how she wished she had listened to her parents!

At that moment, Anton came down the street. He saw the three of them, and his arms extended out toward an invisible partner as he gracefully twirled and danced while humming Tchaikovsky's "Waltz of the Flowers." He stopped next to the gaping soldiers and grinned. "Comrades, let me buy you a drink. I'm feeling happy today." Anton moved his hand to his coat pocket.

One of the soldiers pulled his weapon forward and pointed it at Anton.

"Comrades, don't worry," laughed Anton. He clumsily pressed his thumb and index finger together, reached slowly into his pocket, and pulled out a flask. He passed it to one of the soldiers. "I've been building the new airstrip, but it's been lonely living at the old sawmill, and I crave company. Come. Let's celebrate the motherland and the Lithuanian women who warm our hearts as much as vodka warms our souls."

The soldier took the flask from Anton's outstretched hand and drank before handing it to his companion. "Get out of here," he said.

"Drink up, I have more," laughed Anton.

The second soldier took a drink and put the flask in his pocket. "You heard him. Get out of here!"

"Let's go to Lukas's bar. It's just down the street," said Anton.

The soldiers exchanged a glance.

"Come, comrades. It's where we can have some real fun. Throw this little fish back into the lake to grow."

"What's your name?" asked the bearded soldier.

Anton spoke his name with a hand flourish and a bow.

"Go home before we get angry and arrest you."

"No, no, no." Anton shook a finger. "I want to go to Lukas's."

"You don't want to fool with us."

"Come closer. I want to tell you a secret." Anton put his arm around the soldier who last spoke. The soldier stepped back and punched Anton in the stomach. Anton gasped for breath as the soldiers laughed. As he straightened, Anton stepped closer to the soldier who had hit him. He stepped back with his right foot and raised his fist. Before he could crash it into the man's jaw, the other soldier let go of Tilda's hand and cracked Anton on the head with the butt of his rifle.

Tilda raced to the corner before glancing back to Anton as he was dragged away by the soldiers.

~~

Hours later, Tilda awoke in her bedroom to a knocking on the front door downstairs just below. The sound was barely loud enough to be heard, yet as persistent as a hungry mosquito. Her first reaction was to hide under her blankets, for Papa had told her the Soviets came in the middle of the night, when people were asleep and at their weakest. Then she realized they would come smashing in, not knock softly so the neighbors wouldn't hear.

She hadn't told Papa about the soldiers stopping her on the street and how Anton Dubus had saved her. She thought Papa would get mad at her if he knew how close she had come to real danger.

She crept out of bed and went into the room where Mama and Papa were sleeping.

"What is it, Tilda?" he asked. Mama opened her eyes.

"Someone's at the door."

"My God, *Dieve*," whispered Mama as got up. She ran to the closet and began throwing clothes into a satchel.

"Wait, Mama, let's see who it is first," said Papa as he got out of bed. He rose slowly, as the work in the labor crew had made him perpetually tired. The Soviets didn't care if a worker had a bad back, if his muscles were sore, or if he was old. They just made him work, no matter what. And doing extra jobs for the partisans from time to time made him even more tired, although mostly he just listened to conversations and reported what he had heard. The Russians killed for less. It was much easier when he had been caretaker at the University of Kaunas. There, at least, he could sit and rest for a few minutes when his back hurt.

While Mama waited on the landing and Tilda looked out through the balusters, Papa put on his pants and plodded down the stairs. He took a deep breath. "Who is it?"

A voice answered, and Papa and opened the door.

Mr. Pagelis stepped inside. "Is she all right?" He was clutching his hat in his hands, and smelled like fresh dough.

"What are you talking about?" asked Papa.

"Go to your room, Tilda," said Mama.

Tilda didn't move.

"Your daughter," said Mr. Pagelis. "There was nothing I could do. They would have killed me, you understand." He wiped his forehead with the back of his sleeve. "I have a business to protect, and a wife."

"Come inside," said Papa as he took Mr. Pagelis by the elbow and led him to the sitting room.

Mama ran down the stairs. Tilda followed her but stopped in the hallway, watching the adults as they hovered around Mr. Pagelis. Mama lit a candle, as the electricity had been turned off hours ago. Papa poured a drink for the little man.

"I'm so sorry," whimpered Mr. Pagelis as he gulped it down.

"Enough with being sorry. Just tell me what happened," said Papa.

"Soldiers came up on your daughter earlier this evening. They were in front of my shop. I saw them with Tilda. Didn't she tell you?"

Mama cried out.

"I couldn't do anything that involved the Russians so openly. I couldn't take any risks."

Papa stiffened. "My little girl was in danger and you did nothing?"

"I wanted to know if she got home, if she's all right. My God, my God."

Mama was crying.

Tilda was too afraid to move.

"Tilda," said Papa. He didn't raise his voice, but she knew the tone.

She slowly walked into the room.

"Did soldiers hurt you?" he asked. His face grew dark.

"No, Papa."

"What did they do to you?"

"Nothing, Papa. I was running home and bumped into the soldiers. I was scared, but Anton got them away from me."

"Anton?" asked Papa.

"Anton Dubus. He gave the soldiers a drink. Then they hit him and dragged him off. I got away."

"She's ruined," wailed Mama. "What are we going to do? What if there's a baby?"

"Nothing happened?" asked Papa.

"No."

"Thanks to God," said Mama.

"Don't lie," said Papa.

"Please Papa, I'm telling you the truth."

"We'll have to get out of here. If they come back for you . . ."

"Nothing happened."

"Mama, pack our things. We'll leave immediately."

"Papa," pleaded Tilda.

Mr. Pagelis blew his nose into a handkerchief. "I'm glad she's all right."

Papa scowled. "Get out of here! Doing nothing is as bad as helping them."

"I had no choice! You know how it would be if the Russians caught us. Besides, she said nothing happened."

Papa took Mr. Pagelis by the arm, dragged him to the door, and pushed him out. He closed it and clicked the lock.

Tilda sank into Mama's chair. "I don't want to leave."

"Listen to me and do as I say. Dear God, when will this end?" Papa sat down, rubbing his forehead.

"Where are we going to go?" asked Mama. "Who is going to help us? The borders are closed. We're trapped."

"We'll go to another town."

"Russians are everywhere."

"We can go into the forest."

"What do you know about living in the forest? You're a handyman; a janitor. What do you know about living in the wild? How could you sleep on the ground with that back of yours?"

"I know people!" Papa's face was red.

Mama knelt at his side. "The people you know will be our deaths. They don't help us anymore. All they do is take. Tilda can stay home from school with me from now on. I will teach her. She doesn't have to go to school."

"What?" asked Tilda.

"She'll be safe at home with you." Papa grabbed Mama's hand.

"She'll never go out alone again."

"Yes, Mama. She'll be safe with you."

Tilda ran up to her room and sprawled out across the bed, crying into her pillow so no one would hear. She wouldn't see Ona anymore, or any of her classmates. Mama could barely add, let alone tutor her in mathematics. Her life was over. Papa was hateful, and Mama, too. No one understood her.

~~

Anton opened his eyes to the glare of a light. His jaw hurt so badly he thought he was going to lose a few teeth. The back of his head throbbed. His hands were tied to a chair. "Where am I?"

"Tell us about your partisan friends." The man who spoke rested his backside against a table and leaned forward. He was close enough for Anton to see a faded scar on the side of his face and smell onions on his breath.

"I need to speak to Lieutenant Svechin."

"It's good to need things. I need you to tell me where the bandits are hiding."

"Colonel Karmachov, then."

"What do you need him for? You expect him to care about a filthy pig like you? No one cares about you. You are alone. Your friends abandoned you for being so stupid as to hit a Soviet soldier."

A guard hit Anton in the nose. Blood flowed down his shirt.

Onions again. "Where is the camp?"

"Tell Lieutenant Svechin that Anton Dubus is here."

"Why should I, fool? First, you tell me something."

"Just tell him."

"You don't understand— I give the orders here."

The guard hit him again. Anton fell into darkness.

He awoke in the same room. His head crackled with pain. He was still in the chair, but his hands were no longer tied. A fat man sat behind the table, sipping a glass of tea; it must be Colonel Karmachov. Lieutenant Svechin stood behind him.

Anton rubbed his wrist from where they'd been bound. The guards were gone.

"Your sister Katya was here a few minutes ago. I've never seen a grown woman carry on so at the sight of a little blood," said Karmachov.

"Katya's here? Let me see her," said Anton. The veins in his neck pulsed as he turned to Svechin. "You said she wouldn't be harmed."

Svechin poured a clear liquid into a glass. He handed it to Anton. "Here, drink this. You'll feel better."

Anton scowled at his friend as he took the glass. Svechin handed Anton a handkerchief. Anton used it to wipe the sweat and blood off his face. He handed the cloth back to Svechin.

"Well, at least you look like you've been interrogated. The bandits will expect that," said Karmachov.

"Let Katya go. There's no need for you to keep her here."

"Katya's a little insurance policy so you don't start spying for *them*. But don't worry. She's treated well enough." Karmachov grinned.

"Do what you want with me, but let her go. She hasn't done anything."

"I'll let her go once you've proven yourself," said Karmachov.

Anton took a drink, the vodka's sting transforming his expression to that of a man under duress trying to think clearly. "I listen when the men from the labor crew talk. Utena is a hotbed of partisans. They roam the woods and disappear into crowds in the city." Anton paused. "The camp is in Auksia."

"Of course, the camp is in Auksia! You've told me nothing." Karmachov's face turned purple around the jowls.

"I need more time. It's a massive place."

"Look, fool. I need you to infiltrate that camp. Now go back out there and get to work."

Anton creased his brow as he glanced at Svechin, who looked away.

CHAPTER 8

The Siberian day was warmer than usual for this time of year, and after walking back to the shack where they lived, Victor and Hektoras sat on the steps outside, sharing a cigarette from the package Hektoras had received from his wife. It was almost empty when it arrived, as the guards had taken the choicest morsels and most of the clothing for themselves, as usual. But they always left something and delivered the packages; the Soviet government, in its benevolence, ensured that gifts from home made their way to the intended recipients. In Hektoras's box, there remained a tin of crackers, a pair of socks, a package of candy, three packets of cigarettes, and the most valued gift of all: a photograph of the baby. Later, the valuables would be stuffed into their hiding place below a loose floorboard under Hektoras's bed to protect them from thievery by the other prisoners. But for now, he and his friend were outside eating crackers, enjoying the first cigarette they had smoked in months, and feeling almost human.

Victor gazed with longing at the photograph of the grinning child, remembering his own family. He didn't dare imagine a happy reunion, for it was just as likely he would receive devastating news. He lived in a state of limbo where every second passed slowly, and he wouldn't let himself think of the future.

He had written a letter to Aldona, and another to the Dagys family who lived next door in Kaunas. He didn't dare write to Aldona in Vilkija or to the Ravas family, as it would be too easy for the Soviets to make a connection. Since he'd received no responses, he wasn't even sure his letters had been sent.

A maid from Estonia who cleaned the building where the guards lived had mailed his letters during her one of her monthly trips into town, or at least said she had. He'd given her the last of his money, knowing she might just drop the letters in the garbage and buy something for herself. She had grown fat and disappeared. Months later, Victor heard that she had been sent away to have a baby. Now, with no one left to mail letters for him, he pined in silence.

Hektoras held up the photograph and wiped his eyes. "My son has gotten big, and he's never seen his father. Will he ever know me, Victor?"

"He will."

"We've got to get out of here, somehow. If I could save some of this food . . ."

Victor put his hand on his friend's shoulder. "This food keeps us from starving. Without it we'd surely be dead."

Hektoras sighed and wiped his face with his sleeve. "Tell me something to keep me from going mad. Tell me how you came to be here."

"The less we know about each other, the better."

"You've known me for almost a year, yet have told me little about yourself."

"We shouldn't be talking like this."

"Will it make any difference? Will it make our time here any worse?"

Victor looked over his shoulders before speaking. "You know I'm a history professor. I've made studying the past my life's work."

Hektoras took a puff of the cigarette and passed it to Victor.

"So much of what happened in the last fifty years was inevitable. One action led to another action, which led to another and so on, like the October Revolution and the Great War. They were both predictable events. It wasn't inevitable, however, that men like Hitler and Stalin would come into power."

Victor took a deep drag and held in the smoke. "Before the war, I knew Russia would occupy Eastern Europe again. It was only a matter of time."

Hektoras raised his eyebrows. "How could you know?"

"It was logical. The Russians have occupied our country many times. It made sense that they would find their way back here eventually.

"I taught my children everything I could about surviving in the woods. My daughter Ludmelia could shoot better than any man I know. She has the heart of a warrior. I told Aldona what to do if I was taken. At first, she refused to believe that prison or deportation was even a possibility.

"When I expressed concerns to my colleagues, they encouraged me to write about it, and I did—but no one paid attention to the obscure journals that accepted my papers. Then a few of us started writing pamphlets warning the people of an invasion and encouraging them to prepare themselves. Our students passed them out to everyone they could. Over time, our message became clearer and eventually, when the Soviets invaded, we encouraged people to resist the occupation.

"And they did. Many left their families to search the woods for escape routes, and places where they could camp and store armaments. Some of us began to plan how to resist the Soviets and drive them out of our country.

"My pamphlets became popular, but as always, the problem was knowing who to trust."

"You expected the Russians all along."

"During the first Soviet invasion in 1940, my wife, Aldona, was terrified and wanted us to run away, but I didn't want to leave my country."

"No one escapes from the Soviets."

Victor put his elbows on his knees. "I wanted to fight, but Aldona wouldn't stand for it. I continued working and writing. When I least expected it, they came for me. It was 1941. The Soviets raided our offices at the university and loaded us all onto a cattle train. Now, here we are, living off the bounty of Siberia. And you, Hektoras—how did you come here?"

"I was a mathematics teacher at the gymnasium. I taught algebra and geometry to teenagers. That made me a real threat, didn't it?"

Victor put his hand on Hektoras's shoulder. "You're my countryman, and I trust you. I want you to know who I am because you're the only friend I have left."

At a shuffle behind them, one of their bunkmates came outside. The two men exchanged glances, and finished smoking the cigarette in silence.

~~

Utena's old buildings looked timeless under the early morning sun as Marius Partenkas bent down on the street in front of Pagelis's bakeshop, tying his shoelace. He stood and glanced upward, willing the rays to warm him. Dana Ravas passed by, carrying a sack over his shoulder. The men took no notice of each other. They were just two strangers in a town full of people who often acted like strangers whether they knew each other or not.

Dana went into Mr. Pagelis's bakeshop. A moment later, Marius followed him inside. The door rattled shut, clanging a little bell. The room was small and almost filled by two tables and chairs. The air was rich from the sweet scent of bread baking. Dana was taking small packages from the sack he had placed next to the glass counter in front of the door to the ovens. Baked goods were usually displayed there, but it was empty today, as it had been every day for years. Before the war, people had swooned over the delicacies Mr. Pagelis had made: sweet cream cakes and butter cookies. At Easter, Mrs. Pagelis, who made all the bread, had treated her customers to wonderful *pyragas* made with golden raisins. When she baked, a warm scent spilled out into the street and lured people in.

"Why were you following me?" hissed Dana.

"We have to talk," whispered Marius.

Mrs. Pagelis came in from the back. Her forearms were spotted with flour. She picked up one of the packages Dana had placed on top of the counter, then bent down to the sack and looked inside. "Raisins, rye flour; oh, what I can do with these," she mumbled.

"When will the bread be ready?" Marius asked.

"It'll be ready when it's ready," said Mrs. Pagelis, taking out another package. "Either wait or come back later, but I'm too busy to chat." She went into the back of the store with the packages in her arms, leaving the men alone.

"What's wrong?" asked Dana.

"When Tilda was on her way home last night, two soldiers almost . . . my God. If they had hurt her, I don't know what I would have done."

"She's all right?"

Marius nodded. "A man called Anton Dubus gave the soldiers something to drink, but they hit him and dragged him off. Tilda got away. Who knows what will happen next time?" Marius wiped his eyes with a handkerchief. "Is this Anton Dubus one of ours?"

"The one who lives out at the sawmill?"

"That's him. He's in my work crew. Tell Julius he must help me find a place where my daughter will be safe. After all I've done, he owes me."

"We're grateful, Marius. But you know if we give up, they win, and that's not good for anyone. Besides, we need every man we can get." Dana clasped the older man's shoulders. "Keep your eyes and ears open. Find out all you can about this Dubus fellow. I'll be in touch."

The bell over the door clanged as Dana left. Mrs. Pagelis returned to the room and went back to the sack, where she removed two more packages. "What are you still doing here?"

Marius shrugged and left.

CHAPTER 9

A casual observer might have concluded that this secluded part of the Auksia woods was the most peaceful place on earth. The trees were hearty and big. The frosty air smelled fresh and clean. But as the observer came closer, he might have wondered why anyone would have piled pine branches and leaves together in this deserted spot. As he drew even nearer, he would have seen tents hidden under the piles, eleven of them, and paths in the snow leading to each one. As he gazed beyond the tents, he would have noticed a lone woman with a blanket over her shoulders, sitting on a rotten log, chewing a crust of bread.

Ludmelia Kudirka was remembering four years before, when the Reds had invaded the old forest and she had tracked down the local Soviet commander, Roman Zabrev. Though long dead, he was one of the ghosts that still reached out to her in dreams that left her breathless and wanting to scream, but unable to utter a sound. She remembered receiving the code name Amber Wolf, and leaving that forest for another, to escape the wrath of the Soviets. She remembered the blessed week of quiet while she had waited for the partisans in her old cell to join her in the new forest, where they would start their work all over again.

During that first evening alone in the woods, late in the summer of 1944, she knew Roman Zabrev was finally dead, but her mind kept drifting to the image of Zabrev's ghost wandering through the woods. She cursed herself. Life here was difficult enough without conjuring up spirits.

She had sat on her blanket, listening to an owl's hooting. Leaves on a nearby silver birch had begun to turn gold. She had opened her knapsack and carefully pulled out the scraps of paper retrieved from the garden on the night she had fled from the cottage in Vilkija. One held Papa's signature. Her fingers lingered over it, trying to feel something of him.

She laid the fragile pieces on her blanket and fitted them together piece by piece, like a picture puzzle. Gradually, she recognized names at the bottom: *V. Kudirka, A. Kudirka*, and *B. Ravas*; Papa, Mama, and old Mr. Ravas, Dana's father. A fragment was missing, and she wondered if it held even more names she'd recognize.

The smudged paper was a letter to the head of the Lithuanian Army, asking for help in creating a Soviet resistance group in Vilkija. It proposed stockpiles of weapons, ammunition, and supplies to be hidden at various locations in the forests. The letter mentioned centralized oversight of resistance missions and an organization known to only a select few. Partisan groups would pool resources for larger missions while retaining a level of independence. The letter suggested military order, and a dozen details that Ludmelia couldn't see because of her tears. The words resonated with a joy and foreboding that left her shaking, for what Papa had outlined years ago was already in effect.

Mama and Papa had always been part of this. Her brother, Matas, may have known as well, but she wasn't sure. Being left out of something so important pained her, and made her feel untrusted. She had known only one side of the people closest to her. Now, their secrets lay in front of her on these filthy scraps of paper.

Leaving Kaunas for Vilkija had been part of Papa's plan. Her learning how to shoot and how to survive in the woods had been part of his plan, too.

Ludmelia picked up the only thing she had left of her family, and brought each piece to her lips, dirt and all. She tried to detect Papa's scent, but all she recognized was the smell of soil and mold. She lit a match and brought the torn bits to the flame, staring at the tiny flash and the ash that drifted down to her blanket. Piece by piece, she destroyed all the papers reminding her of a past that had been secret until now, and would remain secret forever, as her family legacy went up in smoke.

Mama had never searched for Papa. She had never returned to Kaunas. She had never even written to the neighbors asking for news of him. When the cattle train had taken Papa away, it was as though Mama reconciled to never see or hear from him again. Maybe Papa had told her not to search for him. Maybe he had thought it too risky. Maybe Mama was too scared to do anything but hide. But it had done no good, for in the end, there was no hiding from the Soviets.

Ludmelia loved her mother, but her reluctance to search for word of Papa was too much to accept. Ludmelia had the strength to do what Mama couldn't or wouldn't do. She had the time, the means, and the sense that if she didn't at least try to find out about him, she'd regret it for the rest of her life. It was up to her to find news of Papa's whereabouts, and it had to be done before the others joined her. She had identity papers in her knapsack from the raid on the prison. Someone in Kaunas might know something. She had to try. She might never get another chance.

Early the next morning, Ludmelia got a ride on a truck headed for the dairy processing plant in Vilkija. When the driver let her out, she was just down the road from the cottage where she had lived with Mama for most of the war.

Ludmelia hid in the shade cast by a cluster of trees and watched the front door for any indication that someone was inside. The building seemed to be intact. The doors and windows were closed. Nothing moved, and that meant Papa wasn't there. It had been silly to hope that he was at the cottage waiting for her. No one had such good fortune these days.

Saddened, she turned away and went to the cold cellar tucked into a small rise behind the house. She had left Mama's body there, wrapped in a quilt from the bed in the kitchen. Ludmelia's heart steeled itself at the sight of the open door. She approached cautiously, even though it was unlikely that soldiers were hiding inside waiting for her. She didn't want to see the dead body and relive the pain of her mother's passing, but she had to know it was there and safe.

"Mama?" she whispered.

Ludmelia stepped into the darkness of the windowless room. Nothing lay on the floor. The quilt from the kitchen was gone. Mama was gone. Stunned, Ludmelia hoped for a moment that it had all been a horrible dream, and that Mama was still alive in the cottage, stirring the stew for supper.

She ran to the house and went in through the door. The narrow bed in the kitchen was on its side. The bloodstain on the mattress where Mama had been shot told her that she hadn't been dreaming. Mama was dead, and someone had taken her away from the cellar where Ludmelia had left her. She made the sign of the cross and prayed that a kind soul had found Mama and had buried her. It was all she could do.

A startled mouse ran across the table where a pot held the crusted remains of a meal. The bedroom was in tatters as she had left it the night she had escaped, although it looked like someone had recently slept on the bed. Squatters, no doubt. She picked through the wrinkled clothes on the floor and found a skirt and a blouse.

Ludmelia put them on. She found Mama's shoes hidden under the bed, and put them on, too. They fit well enough. Next, Ludmelia went to the dresser. She took out the bottom drawer and reached in for a small cloth package. She opened it to find Mama's good kerchief, made of a delicately woven soft white cloth, big enough to double as a shawl. She put it in her knapsack.

She stopped at some heather near the cottage and hid her rifle, pistol, and her clothes, before heading down the road toward Vilkija and the train.

Ludmelia bought a ticket and sat on a bench looking like a nervous young lady as she fingered the forged papers in her pocket that identified her as a student at the Vytautas Magnus National University in Kaunas. Classes were finally in session again, and that presented an opportunity to find some of Papa's associates who might have heard something and know of his whereabouts. She felt naked without her gun, but couldn't go all over town with a Soviet Maxim slung over her shoulder, or Papa's pistol on her hip. All she had was her hunting knife hidden in her knapsack under a loaf of bread, a piece of cheese, a piece of sausage, and Mama's kerchief.

The train to Kaunas was an hour late when it finally coughed into the station. Ludmelia passed a guard before climbing the steps into the car. Her palms sweated as she scanned the faces of the passengers, careful not to linger too long on anyone. She feared that someone might see through her flimsy disguise and recognize her for the partisan that she was. She went to an empty seat next to a man in a brown suit. He looked up from his newspaper and smiled at her when she sat down. She closed her eyes and pretended sleep to discourage any conversation. Eventually, the sway of the train lulled her into a dream, where she scratched at the dirt walls of a cellar with her bare hands, looking for Mama.

A shrill whistle, puffs of steam, and the smells of hot metal and burning coal greeted Ludmelia as she climbed down the steps at Kaunas station. People wandered about the makeshift platform, the old station having been reduced to rubble years ago by German bombs. The bustle she remembered from before the war was gone. In its place hung a strange tension, as if each person posed a threat, and each step would draw the attention of the Russian guards waiting at the gate to the street.

A bent old woman with gaunt cheeks stepped up to Ludmelia. "Do you have anything to eat? There's no food here." The woman grabbed Ludmelia's arm. "Please, something to eat."

Ludmelia dug into her bag and pulled out the bread she had taken from the camp in the old forest. As she moved to break off a chunk, the woman snatched it out of Ludmelia's hands, tucked it under her coat, and hobbled away.

Ludmelia sighed. These were desperate times and desperate people. She wondered if she and Mama would be begging for food if they still lived here. As she closed her knapsack, the old woman came hobbling back. With the tenderness of a mother giving up her baby, the old woman handed Ludmelia the food she had taken. Tear filled eyes looked up from a face lined with wrinkles. "Here," she said. "I'm not a thief. I'm just hungry."

Ludmelia placed it back inside the woman's coat. "No, Mother. Take it."

"Thank you," said the woman. She straightened a little, turned, and walked away.

The guards checked papers randomly as people passed by. Ludmelia stepped up to a woman wearing a red kerchief, hurrying toward the guards and the street. Ludmelia thought that two women together would draw less attention than a single woman traveling alone. Besides, the woman in the kerchief looked like she made this trip often. The guards would be less likely to bother a person they saw all the time, even if she was accompanied by a stranger.

"It's a lovely day, isn't it?" said Ludmelia.

The woman glanced at her and kept walking. They were twenty steps from the guards.

"I wonder if it's going to rain," said Ludmelia, smiling.

The woman walked faster. Ten steps.

"Well, if it does, we'll get wet, won't we," laughed Ludmelia as they passed right in front of the guards.

As the woman walked away, Ludmelia waved and smiled. "Goodbye. It was nice seeing you." She headed in the opposite direction. Ludmelia didn't blame the woman for being unfriendly and suspicious of a stranger, since any wrong word could get one questioned, arrested, or even shot.

The walk to the university would have been enjoyable if she hadn't been constantly watching for soldiers. Ludmelia followed the path to the old stone building where Papa had worked, opened the heavy wooden door, and climbed the steps to the third floor. She went to the end of the hallway and knocked on Papa's door. She breathlessly waited to hear his voice telling her to come in, but there was no answer. She tried the knob. It was unlocked. She pushed the door open and went inside.

The furniture was in the same place as before: the desk in front of the window, the bookshelves, and the straight back chairs in front of the desk. There was no mess of papers or books crowded into the shelves. Barely ten volumes stood in a single neat row. Everything was orderly and in its place. It didn't look like Papa's office anymore. There was no sign of him.

Still clutching to the wild hope of finding a familiar face, Ludmelia knocked on another door. Again, no answer. She opened it and walked into a dusty room devoid of any signs that a person still occupied it. Paper lay strewn on the floor. The desk had been overturned, the drawers missing. The few books that remained had been opened and tossed on the floor. She noticed the stink of urine.

She opened another door to an office piled high with old furniture. A chill ran up her spine. There was no sign of anyone she knew; there was no sign of anyone at all.

As she closed the door, a woman appeared at the opposite end of the hallway. She wore a wool skirt, a white blouse, and glasses. She glared at Ludmelia.

Ludmelia smiled. Her steps on the wooden floor sounded like a ticking bomb as she walked toward the woman.

"What are you doing here?" asked the woman.

"I'm looking for Victor Kudirka's office," said Ludmelia.

The woman hesitated.

"I'm new here," said Ludmelia.

"Are you a student?"

"Yes."

"How do you know Mr. Kudirka?"

Because I'm his daughter, you fool, thought Ludmelia. "I heard that his history course was wonderful."

"He hasn't been here for years." The woman didn't smile as her eyes traveled over Ludmelia. Her thin lips pursed into a line. The air crackled.

"My mistake," said Ludmelia.

"Wait here and I'll get someone to help you."

"All right."

As the woman walked down the steps, Ludmelia took off her shoes and followed her down, staying out of sight. The woman went into the building next door. Ludmelia turned in the opposite direction and ran barefoot to the tree-lined path. She sat on a bench to put on her shoes, and saw the woman in the wool skirt hurry back inside with a soldier.

Ludmelia pulled out Mama's kerchief and put it over her head, tying a small knot under her chin. The cloth fell to her shoulders, covering part of her blouse. She ran to a student strolling along the path and kept pace with him as she asked for directions to Vytautas Avenue. At a crosswalk, she cut through shrubs and went back to the city streets.

She headed to the lane where she used to live with Mama, Papa, and Matas, passing their old house without giving it more than a sideways glance. The curtains were open. Mama had left them closed.

Ludmelia went next door and climbed the steps to the building where Mrs. Dagys had lived with her husband. She took a deep breath, knocked, and waited. She didn't even know if Mrs. Dagys was still alive.

The latch clicked. The door opened a crack and a worn face appeared. "What do you want?"

"Is that you, Mrs. Dagys?"

The woman's eyes were dark and sunken. "Ludmelia? Can it be?"

Mrs. Dagys pulled Ludmelia inside and down a dark hallway to a kitchen that looked like it hadn't been used in a long time.

"Sit. I'll make us some tea. Let me go to the corner for some bread. Oh, they probably don't have any. Why are you here? Is everything all right?" Mrs. Dagys sat and grabbed Ludmelia's hand. "It's so good to see you, my dear. How is your mother?"

"Dead," sighed Ludmelia.

"Oh no."

Mrs. Dagys cried as Ludmelia told her the story.

"Why are you still here? You said you were leaving for Germany," said Ludmelia.

"I won't leave my husband."

"But he's in the cemetery."

Mrs. Dagys shrugged.

"How bad is it?"

"My friend has a farm in the country and gives me food, but I can't go there often. I have no money, but I have my jewelry, at least for now. There's very little food in the city."

Ludmelia opened her bag and pulled out the few items she had left to sustain herself for the trip back: a small piece of sausage and some cheese.

Mrs. Dagys stopped crying and stared at the food. "I can't take this."

"Please. I'm not staying for long."

Mrs. Dagys put water in the kettle and placed it on the stove. She put Ludmelia's food on plates, as if giving each morsel the presence it deserved. She put down knives, forks, glasses, and a bottle of vodka from the shelf.

"We have nothing to eat, but we can get more than enough to drink." She poured the liquor into glasses.

"I thought you might have heard from Papa."

"You've gotten no word from your father in all these years? My God." Mrs. Dagys shook her head.

To Ludmelia, the pain from fearing him dead became even sharper.

"Don't give up hope, my dear. Just because you haven't heard from him, it doesn't mean anything."

They talked of past times and people who were gone. On her way out, Ludmelia kissed the old woman on the cheek and left. Her sadness seemed to grow during the walk to the train station. She had hoped for success, but now the uselessness of the trip and unnecessary risk she had taken weighed heavy in her heart. She felt empty from gaining nothing; not even a morsel of news. That she had even tried to find out about Papa brought her no comfort, and no consolation.

The guards were still on the train platform. Ludmelia moved behind a group of young men carrying books, probably students. She tried to look like she was with them. The old woman who had taken Ludmelia's bread that morning sat on a bench nearby, just outside the gate. Her coat bulged. Ludmelia assumed it was the bread. The guards approached and stepped up to the students, demanding to see their papers. Ludmelia's hands automatically went to her hip, but there was no gun there.

Thin young hands, some shaking, handed folded documents to the guards.

"So, you're students, eh?" The guard asked the question with a derision that surprised Ludmelia. He had a scar on his left cheek.

The tallest man among the group of students, nodded.

"These draft exemption cards must be forgeries. You're too old to still be in school."

"We're all studying medicine at university," said one, handing him a book. "Look! We're taking a class in chemistry."

The guard shoved the book away. It landed on the ground with a thud.

Ludmelia inched back. The old woman touched her elbow. "Walk with me, dear," she whispered.

"You're coming with us," said the guard.

"We've done nothing wrong!" said the tall man. A guard hit him in the mouth, driving him to his knees.

The old woman took Ludmelia's arm and led her past the guards toward the tracks. She brought Ludmelia to a bench and they sat down. "Stay with me. The guards see me every day and pay no attention to an old woman."

Even though the commotion died down, the people in the crowd spoke in low voices. When the train pulled in, the old woman patted Ludmelia's hand. Ludmelia climbed up the steps into the car without looking back. Once in Vilkija, the walk back to the cottage was uneventful. Ludmelia found her clothing and guns, and went back into the forest that felt like home.

~~

The years since that trip to Kaunas blurred in a rash of missions. The only constants were Ludmelia's friends: Dana, Raminta, Jurgis, and Vadi. They had managed to survive, even though many hadn't. She hadn't seen Simas and his eye patch since he had left camp in 1941.

After 1945 and the end of the war, the fever to expel the Russians gradually waned as supplies dwindled and support failed to arrive from the West. The first offer of amnesty had come from the Soviets in 1947. Any partisan who turned in their guns could go back to a normal life, but what was normal under a communist occupation? Ludmelia thought that the Russians would imprison anyone who surrendered, and that the offer of amnesty was a trick. But a few men took it, hoping to find their families and a better life. For most, amnesty meant that instead of starving in the woods, they starved in their homes. Instead of Soviets going into the forest to find them, they raided their houses at night.

Now, in 1948, Russians were still deporting people, and many were leaving the cause. That anyone would give up their fight for freedom pained Ludmelia, but there was nothing she could do. Between those who left willingly and the partisans who had died in battle, there were very few remaining to fight, so cells of partisans were combined to provide enough men for the missions they still undertook.

CHAPTER 10

Ludmelia left her remembrances of the years that had brought her here, and snapped back to the present when Julius joined her. He said nothing as he paced between two pine trees. She was still sitting on the log; she had eaten the bread. The forest was quiet and cold. The other partisans were inside their tents and a light snow was falling. Raminta was at the cook tent preparing something to eat, as usual. She hadn't stopped smiling since her wedding.

Julius hadn't changed much since they had first met. It amazed Ludmelia that even after leading the district's partisan groups for four years, Julius still looked handsome, even carefree. His code name, Lightning, didn't fit his personality. He was thoughtful and deliberate, although the impact of his missions had been as deadly as a lightning strike. Despite his untroubled appearance, Ludmelia had recently found him sitting alone in the woods, holding his head in his hands, looking like a man too weary to go on. She had wanted to comfort him, but before she could, he sat up and smiled, as if nothing were wrong.

Julius was clever and intellectual like Papa, but of course, they never had time to just sit and talk. A partisan's life had few moments for distractions. Still, before every mission, Julius took her aside and told her how smart and strong she was. It made her believe she was going to succeed, even when the odds were against her. It proved he had feelings for her. What else could it be? He was a wonderful mystery: friendly, although aloof, and gentle, yet strong. He was a tangle of contradictions she wanted to sort out. Once they were done with the fighting, life with Julius might be quiet afternoons reading in front of a fire, and friends discussing politics and history over dinners that lingered into the night.

Then Dana joined them, sitting down next to her on the log, his shoulder touching hers and bringing a sensation of comfort. He was her childhood friend. Their missions had taken them through hell together, and he still sought her out for advice and sometimes just a quiet word. He had evolved more than any of them since coming into the woods. He had learned how to fight, and never flinched when faced with danger. He was kind and considerate to everyone in camp. She trusted him and knew he would do anything for her. But unlike Julius, Dana carried the strain of every encounter with the Reds on his face. The years of combat, constant risk, and sleepless nights had left their mark. At twenty-eight, he was two years older, but could easily pass for a man twenty years older, especially with hair that was predominantly the color of fresh milk. She was certain he was in love with her, too. When she pictured herself living with Dana in a house full of children, bustle and laughter, it made her smile.

She wondered which future she really wanted. She could see herself with either man. As much as Ludmelia yearned to know love in a world free of Soviets, thinking about it was a dangerous distraction. The people in camp needed her to be alert and focused. They depended on her to plan and run missions that brought them back alive. They needed the anger and constant twist in her belly that kept her mind and instincts sharp. If she lived long enough to choose between Julius and Dana, it was sure to be the hardest decision of her life, and recently, she found herself thinking about it more often.

Julius spoke first. "There have been a dozen sweeps through Auksia since you took care of that NKVD agent. After what the Russians did to Mr. and Mrs. Zenonas, the people in the village are too scared to help us, and with the loss of Kazi and his men, our ranks have never been so thin. The reprisals are severe everywhere, not just here. It's all over. People are frightened. They want to get on with their lives and have some sense of normalcy after all the years of fighting. The West hasn't helped us, and we can't hold on much longer."

"Normalcy isn't possible when you're an occupied country," said Ludmelia.

Julius continued to pace, as if he hadn't heard her.

"We'll move," said Ludmelia. "We can always find another forest and more people to help us."

"We need to be where the Russians are. It's where we're the most effective. But it's also where *they're* the most effective," said Julius.

"Effective?" Ludmelia shook her head. "We haven't been effective in months. We're getting weaker by the day. So we killed a NKVD agent and a few soldiers. It's nothing. There are tens of thousands more Russians here now than right after the war. The Soviets are starting to anticipate our moves. They're stronger than ever. *We* need to be stronger. I say we hit them where they live. I say we go after Karmachov. We'll kill him and dangle him from a tree. We'll do to him what he did to Mr. and Mrs. Zenonas. *That* will bring the people back to us. Until we're granted our basic human rights, we'll deny the Russians theirs." Ludmelia jumped to her feet. "We're not Soviet puppets. One more good strike is all we need to send those bastards back to Moscow."

"We've been hitting the Soviets for years. Without help, we have no chance of winning. We've known that since 1944. Besides, we can't kill Karmachov. He's surrounded by soldiers all the time," said Dana.

"The West sold us out at Yalta and Potsdam, and yet we still wait for their money and troops like obedient children." Ludmelia twisted her mouth in disgust. "They have the most powerful bomb ever known to mankind, and they could use it to bring Stalin to his knees. Yet they do nothing!"

"Maybe they don't know," said Julius.

"Don't know what?" said Ludmelia.

"We've going forward with Operation Bolt." He looked at her warily, as if expecting another outburst.

"We can't afford to lose you, too." Ludmelia looked down at the ground, her heart empty from the mere thought of Julius leaving.

"What's Operation Bolt?" asked Dana.

"It's time for one of us to leave for the West and tell them what's happening here. If they know what the Russians are doing, they'll act. Look at what happened to the Nazis at Nuremberg. What the Russians are doing here is just as bad, or worse, and no one knows except us. If one of us could get out, he could tell the West that we're fighting for our lives. He could convince them that here, the war isn't over, and the Russians are beating us down," said Julius.

"We smuggle letters out, and all those who escaped before the war tell the story. Some of us have even culled together radio transmitters from spare parts, but no one is listening," said Ludmelia.

"Maybe the letters don't get to the right people –or maybe they don't believe what they read."

"They don't believe it because they don't want to believe it." Ludmelia sat back down as if already weakened by what she was about to hear. "When are you leaving?"

"Not long. You'll be escorting me through the frontier and getting me safely through the border into Poland. Make sure Dana knows the details, too. Once I'm with our supporters there, you'll go to Birzai for another mission. Karmachov isn't our target right now. It's something else.

"Three high-level NKVD officers from Moscow are coming here for inspections. They present us a chance to do damage politically. They're your target, Ludmelia."

She stared at Julius, her mind already at work.

"It'll be dangerous; that's why I'm giving the job to you. They'll be heavily guarded. After you take care of them, the Russians will come at us like nothing before. Our people will evacuate camp, but I need to be in Poland before anything even starts."

"Tell me more about the agents."

"They're visiting various military encampments in the country. We know they'll be in Birzai next month. Exactly how and when you do it is up to you. Vadi can help—you'll need him. But don't tell anyone about this until I'm gone. The less people know, the better, in case they're captured and interrogated."

Dana put his hands on his knees. "What do you want me to do?"

"Help Ludmelia get me out of the country, and then help her with the mission. Don't underestimate the Russians. Those men will be protected. You'll need some luck to pull this one off," said Julius.

"I never rely on luck, because luck needs to fail only once. Then you're dead," said Ludmelia.

"Well, you'll need it this time, because there's almost no one left to help you with the job."

"I know someone who might want to join us," said Dana.

Julius raised an eyebrow.

"There's a man who's been working on a labor crew for a few weeks. He lives at the sawmill. Anton Dubus."

"How do you know him?"

"Marius Partenkas told me about him, and he's checking him out. Dubus saved his daughter from some Russians. He interrupted them so the girl could escape."

"Tilda?" Ludmelia looked surprised. "She's barely a teenager. I remember her from when we lived in Kaunas before the war. We lived on the same street. Mr. Partenkas worked as a janitor at university when Papa was there."

"Marius is getting nervous. He's terrified for his family," said Dana.

Julius put his hand on the younger man's shoulder. "I'll need a lot more convincing before I can trust this Anton Dubus. In the meanwhile, I'll see what we can do for the Partenkas family. It just may not be much right now."

"If Dubus checks out, we can give him a task or two to test his loyalty," said Ludmelia.

Julius smiled. "You're always one step ahead, Ludie."

~~

Julius gazed after Ludmelia as she walked away with Dana. Her face reminded him of a woman he had known many years before, in the outline of her chin and the way she held her head. But the two women couldn't be more different. Ruta was as gentle as a warm breeze. Ludmelia was a tornado; beautiful and wondrous to look at, but capable of massive destruction.

These days, he was too consumed with Operation Bolt to consciously let memories join him in the rare moments of peace and quiet he had each day. But Ruta entered his thoughts whenever she wanted. Over this, he had no control.

He had no doubt what he still felt for Ruta was love, even after all this time, even though she might be married by now. He didn't think she was, though, for he believed love only came once in this life. And with all his heart, he believed she loved him. He had met Ruta in Vilnius where he was studying political history and indulging his passion for military strategy. He read Sun Tzu, Clausewitz, Creasy, and many others. Ruta was studying to be a nurse. She had lived in the United States when she was a child, but her parents wanted to come back home. They crossed the ocean in a ship, and moved into a house near Vilnius. Some friends from school had introduced her to Julius, and he asked her to help him perfect his English. He was drawn to her tender nature like a bee to a flower. Eventually, they talked of marriage, but Ruta feared war and wanted to go back to the United States. Julius couldn't imagine raising his children anywhere but here.

In 1939, she left for a place called Chicago, and Julius joined soldiers eager to protect their independence under a young government that was barely surviving. In 1940, he sought out Victor Kudirka after receiving one of his pamphlets from a friend in Kaunas. With the older man's encouragement, Julius joined a fledgling partisan movement, where he honed his skills as a planner and a strategist. Julius felt his country should strive for nothing less than a system where open debate and popular vote determined the political climate. He already knew the path to freedom would be lined with bodies.

Julius's passion for freedom had sustained him for a long time. But all the fighting and fear of the Soviet occupiers made him yearn for a warm bed and a peaceful life. Neither were within his grasp until the night he dreamed of Ruta racing to him on a white steed. By the next morning, he had hatched a plan to get someone out of the country who could speak English, had intimate knowledge of what the Russians were doing, and had connections in at least one major city in the United States. That someone would coordinate with intelligence groups and politicians to get supplies, agents, and support into the country. He called it Operation Bolt when he laid out the details to his superiors. To his surprise and delight, they had agreed. Julius was on his way out.

~~

Raminta led her new husband past the sentry and deeper into the woods. She found a spot where they could sit and talk, far enough away from the buzz of camp for a little privacy.

"I have something to tell you," she said.

"You're going to take me away from all this." Jurgis gestured at the woods, grinning.

"Yes. I'm pregnant."

"Really? I didn't think it was possible, not with all the stress and turmoil going on. This is wonderful." Jurgis scooped Raminta up in his arms, and swung her around in a dance. "You're going to make a wonderful mother—and I, a handsome father." He kissed her.

Raminta twisted out of his arms.

"What's wrong?"

"How can you ask that question? I can't bring a baby into camp. I can't work with a baby suckling on my breast. We'll have to leave if I'm to keep the child."

"If you keep the child? What do you mean? You're going to give it to someone else to raise?"

"A doctor can stop the pregnancy, if we can find one."

"Kill it? You can't kill my baby! That's nonsense. How can you even think of such a thing? It's the worst sin of all."

"You know I can't have a baby at camp."

"We'll leave."

"I don't want to leave."

"Our cause is hopeless. How can we possibly win against the Soviets? They've even brought in expert trackers and dogs. They know what forests we're in. They're killing us off." He took Raminta by the shoulders. "We can't win."

"I don't want my little girl raised under a bloody red flag."

"Even though we can't win, a part of me doesn't want to give up the fight. We've sacrificed too much to see it all come to nothing. But I would give up everything for my child." Jurgis took off his beret and ran his fingers through his hair. "How do you know it's a girl?"

"I'm sick all the time. How else would I know?"

"I would love to have a girl."

"Our only hope is to try to get out and find a new home."

"We can't leave the country. The borders are closed."

"I don't want to leave. I was born here and I want to die here."

"But we have no place to go."

"We can find an abandoned homestead. Maybe we can go back to Dana's farm."

"There's no barn anymore. We'd have to build one. If Russians squatters are living there, I'd have to drive them off."

"Don't be ridiculous. If you did that, soldiers would come and take you away. What would the baby and I do with no one to care for us?"

"We'll find a way. There are plenty of other abandoned homes."

"I hope so, because you're going to be a father. And unless he decides to come with us, you're going to have to say goodbye to your brother, Vadi."

"More than that: we're going to have to find a way to tell Ludmelia."

~~

Ludmelia brushed away the diagram she had drawn in the snow, containing early ideas on how to execute the mission involving the three NKVD officers from Moscow. The snow had stopped falling, but it was still cold. Her stomach growled. Life in the forest was harder than ever. Food was an issue, and farmers could no longer support the partisans, as they barely had enough to eat on their own. Out of desperation, some partisans raided homes and took food. Others worked during the day on the collective farms in exchange for food, although it was rarely enough, and helped on missions at night. In addition to hunger and exhaustion came the feeling that they were risking their lives for nothing. Even so, each departure made Ludmelia's heart feel heavier.

Instead of spending most of her time organizing missions, Ludmelia had to constantly find people to fight for the cause, and food to sustain them. As the years moved on, there were fewer animals to hunt in the forests. There were fewer birds. Pets were a rarity. Occasionally, the partisans raided a food warehouse, but the Russians were guarding those now, and the partisans couldn't afford to lose more men. It felt like they were living on a cliff and the rocks under their feet were falling over the edge.

Raminta approached with cups of hot tea.

"Shouldn't you be bringing tea to your husband instead of me?" asked Ludmelia.

"He's resting."

"You're unlike him. I was surprised when I heard you loved him, but I'm glad you're happy."

"In peacetime, I might not have even noticed Jurgis. We have different friends and interests. But the war made us equals. Instead of seeing a farmhand, I see a brave and unselfish man. Maybe he sees me for my essence, too. At least I hope he does."

"And what is your essence?"

"A woman who cherishes life."

"And what's *my* essence?"

"You're a warrior."

Ludmelia scoffed. "Well, I know how to kill Russians."

"One day, I hope you learn about love, and see how generous it can make you. Every time my husband goes out on a mission, he risks everything. He goes, though, because he loves his country as much as he loves me."

"Sometimes I wonder if I do this because I hate the Russians more than I love my country."

"I worry that after this is over, hate will be all you have left."

"I need hate to get through the day. Hate has defined me. It's defined all of us who fight."

"You have a Russian name you're proud of because you loved your namesake, your great-aunt. Her mother married a Russian, and gave her a name that lives on in your family."

"My great-aunt was a wonderful woman and I loved her."

"Our hatred may run deep, but we're all connected, whether we like it or not. Some men fight honorably and some like rabid dogs, but that has nothing to do with whether a person was born here or two hundred kilometers to the east."

A vein throbbed in Ludmelia's neck, and she pursed her lips. "It has *everything* to do with where we're born."

"Since you're already annoyed with me, I may as well tell you." Raminta gazed into her cup. "I'm pregnant."

"How can you bring children into this? They'll have no future with the Soviets here."

"They'll have hope, just like Jurgis and I do."

"Hoping for something accomplishes nothing. We have to act!"

"I'm tired of this. I've been fighting for too long. All I want is a husband and a baby. It's all I need to make me happy."

"So, you're abandoning me."

"No, Ludie. You're like a sister to me. I just can't fight any more. Not all of us are as strong as you. Please don't be angry with me. I couldn't bear it." Raminta brushed away the tears from her cheeks.

Jurgis came over and sat next to his wife. He put his elbows on his knees and stared at the ground.

"When are you leaving?" asked Ludmelia.

"Today. We're going to Dana's old homestead," said Jurgis.

"Just be careful. You don't want the Reds coming after you for driving away squatters, or killing them. What about your brother?"

"Vadi is staying here with you."

Ludmelia breathed a sigh of relief.

Raminta choked back a sob as she nodded at Jurgis. "I'm going to take care of him, and he's going to take care of us." She put her hand on her belly.

"We want to raise our child together," said Jurgis.

"Is there anything I can say to get you to stay?"

Jurgis stood and hugged Ludmelia. Raminta kissed her on the cheek. Ludmelia watched as they went to Vadi's tent. Jurgis was small and wiry; his brother tall and muscular. A stranger wouldn't have suspected they were brothers at all, as they were so different in appearance. But it was clear from the way they hugged that the separation would be hard on both.

An hour later, Raminta and Jurgis disappeared into the forest they knew so well.

Two more gone. Ludmelia wandered around the camp trying to quell a feeling of desperation. Jurgis was one of her best men, and Raminta could wield a bow and arrow better than anyone she knew. Ludmelia had two missions to worry about: getting Julius out of the country, and killing those three NKVD officers from Moscow. She was desperate for more men.

The camp seemed quieter than usual, the sounds dampened by a cloud of sadness, no doubt from Raminta and Jurgis's departure. She remembered old faces and voices, many gone, and how their innocence had faded bit by bit after each mission.

Even the forest was different—less of a sanctuary, less peaceful. Maybe some men who had left might come back, but it was unlikely. It was better to sleep in a bed than on the ground. It was better to find someone to love and have children with than to endure this cruel and bloody existence. But it meant giving up their cause. She wondered if anyone cared anymore, except for a few lonely partisans. She thought of Papa and this time, he was silent.

Ludmelia found her favorite stump and sat down to think. Anton Dubus came to mind as a possible recruit. She had no reason to trust him; she didn't even know him. If he checked out and passed her tests, maybe she could take a chance and add him to their diminishing ranks. She really had little choice. She hoped she'd be lucky with him, even though the idea of relying on luck left her with a feeling of dread.

Ludmelia rubbed her arms. The movement pushed the sadness down a little, and the forest around her spoke through the leaves brushing against each other in quiet greeting. Life would go on, and she needed to see if somehow, she could continue to make a difference.

"I've been looking for you," said Dana.

Ludmelia moved over so he could sit next to her.

"What do you want?" he asked.

"What do you mean?"

"From life. What do you want from life?"

"I want the fighting to be over. I want the Russians to be gone."

"But for you. What do you want for yourself?"

She felt the soft brush of Dana's shoulder. She had never been asked this before: not from Papa, Mama, or even Julius. She wanted to answer, but the words caught in her throat, as if voicing her dream of having a man to love would make it impossible to achieve.

Dana glanced at her. "I want a family of my own. When I was young, I couldn't wait to leave home, and now I can't wait to find one for myself."

Ludmelia felt that all too familiar twist in her belly. "Everyone here is your family, at least those who are left. You belong here. This is where you have to stay."

"I suppose you're right, but I want to be like Raminta and Jurgis. I want children. I want a legacy. I want to live forever."

"No one lives forever."

"Those who change the world do. Sometimes I wonder if history will be kind to us, and whether future generations will see us as heroes or fools."

"Maybe the answer will depend on how successful we are, if we survive long enough."

After Dana left, Ludmelia kept repeating his message: *those who change the world live forever*. The problem was that they couldn't change the world without help. A few tired men and women couldn't hope to defeat the Russian army. Besides, no one knew who they were. They lived in the shadows. It was how they survived. History wouldn't remember them. They wouldn't be written about in books. They wouldn't be heroes unless they *won*. History only remembered the winning side.

Ludmelia glanced up at the sound of voices. Julius was standing next to his tent with a stranger, whose back was to her. He was of average height and build, but very compact. An automatic hung from his shoulder. Julius hugged the man as if he were a brother. The man raised his hand as if beckoning Julius to wait. He turned around and walked toward her.

She knew only one man with an eye patch. Ludmelia stepped up to him and slapped him in the face.

"Good to see you, too," said Simas, massaging his cheek.

"That's for leaving Vilkija when you did."

She stepped in close and put her arms around him in a hug. "This is for coming back. I thought you were dead." She glanced around him. "Isn't Vera with you?"

"We were living in a woods north of here. The Russians found us. Many people didn't get away. Vera was one of them. Me, with a bad leg and half my vision, I survive."

"Not her, too."

"She was a good doctor and a better friend."

Ludmelia nodded. "I didn't think I'd ever see you again. Are you here to stay?"

"No. I'm old before my time, and I can't fight any more. My only value is that I know people, and they'll do things for me if I ask them." Simas looked over his shoulder at the camp tents that looked tattered, even under their covering of snow and pine branches. "Are they all dead or have most left?"

"A bit of both," said Ludmelia. "And you, what happened after you left us in Vilkija?"

He shrugged. "I wandered the woods, going from camp to camp. Sometimes I joined a mission here or there; sometimes I just walked away. I spent a lot of time thinking about Eda."

"I still do," said Ludmelia remembering her friend's tragic end. "So why are you here?"

"I'm the one who lined up the guides to get Julius out. Operation Bolt is alive and well." Simas pulled out a flask and offered her a drink. She took it.

Ludmelia flinched as she swallowed. "It's not a good idea. We need him here, not in some foreign country. They're not going to listen to him. They're probably not even going to agree to see him."

"I'm not so sure about that. There are a lot of our people in the United States. If he can rally them together, they can make the government do something."

"I'll believe it when I see it."

"Many are dying for our cause, but the Russians keep coming," said Simas. "Without the West, the Russians will eventually kill us all, and that will be the end of our noble war, unless Julius is successful in convincing them to help us."

Ludmelia nodded, and the ghosts of the warriors who still wandered the woods had nothing more to add.

CHAPTER 11

The area directly behind the water wheel was large enough for Anton to sit comfortably, even providing a flat rock for that purpose. He was home early, for after finishing his work on the labor crew, he had gotten a ride from a mechanic who was on his way to Salakas to fix a truck. From this vantage point, Anton could avoid the cascade splashing into the stream while watching his shack. It was a perfect place to hide. Ever since his encounter with the young girl outside the bakeshop, he'd expected a visitor, and now waited for one. Waiting had never been a chore for him. He had perfected the art in the years after his mother left, when he had learned patience and to expect nothing.

Utena was small for a city, and word spread fast. He hoped that helping the girl had been enough to get him noticed by the right people and that someone would visit to determine if he was a true patriot. He was certain that at least the girl's father would come to thank him. Either way, he wanted to observe his visitor and see what they did when they thought he wasn't home.

Dusk was approaching when a man appeared along the path leading to the shack. He was old and wore a loose jacket. He carried a sack over his shoulder. Anton recognized him from the work crew, but they had never spoken. The dumpy-looking fellow wasn't what Anton believed a partisan would be.

Anton flattened himself against the wall of stone and dirt, trying not to get wet as he inched along past the falling water and onto the path that led to the shack. He observed the man stepping up to the door and knocking. The man shifted the sack on his shoulder, the weight appearing to bother him. He opened the door and went inside. Silently, Anton followed.

The intruder stood by the wall where Anton had hidden his Luger behind a loose board.

"What are you doing?" said Anton.

"Oh. Excuse me." Marius turned around. "You must be Anton Dubus."

"Who are you?" Anton came closer.

"I knocked, but no one answered," said Marius, visibly shivering. "Tilda is my daughter. You saved her from those Russians the other evening. I wanted to come by and thank you."

Silence.

"Here." Marius held out the sack. "My wife put some food together for you. A few jars of beets and some bread. She still thinks I married her because of her delicious beets." He laughed nervously as he placed the food on the table.

"What's your name?"

"Marius Partenkas. I live in town with my family. I'm grateful to you."

"How do you know where I'm staying?"

"Tilda told me. Besides, people talk."

"*Who* talks?"

"Just people." Marius looked like a child who was about to cry.

Anton moved to within inches of the man's face. "Are you here to steal from me?"

"Oh no. I just wanted to . . ."

"You're Russian, aren't you?"

"What? No." Marius shrank away. "Please, I just wanted to thank you." He pulled out a flask with a shaking hand, and offered it to Anton.

Anton sat on the bed and watched the little man for a long minute. He took a pull from the flask and handed it back. Then Anton reached into his pocket for a packet of cigarettes and offered one to his guest. Marius took it, the cigarette quivering in his mouth as he tried to light it, finally succeeding after several tries.

This man is an idiot. "When you're not in a labor crew, what do you do for a living?" asked Anton.

"Long ago, I was a janitor at Kaunas University. We moved to Utena in 1944. I was a handyman until the Russians forced me to work on the airstrip. How about you?"

"I'm from a village not far from here where my sister and I lived with my grandmother. She had pigs." Anton recalled the threads of truths, lies, and omissions he had formulated weeks ago for this very purpose.

Marius took a drink. It seemed to calm him.

Anton continued. "I left when I was young. My sister and I moved to the countryside west of Vilnius. She married a man from Poland and I lived with them. We made the unfortunate mistake of moving to Krakow in 1939, just before Hitler came to visit."

"Were you involved in the fighting?"

"I had no choice. I was conscripted into the Wehrmacht. The Germans had me doing jobs unfit for any human." Anton paused for effect. "When the Soviets invaded Poland, the Germans sent me to the front. I killed as many Russians as I could before fleeing to my homeland. But when I got to Lithuania, I found it was even worse here. But this is home to me, and now it would be almost impossible to leave, even if I wanted to."

"We never seem to get along with the Russians, do we?"

"Don't talk to me about those bastards. It would be better if they got out and left us alone. If it were up to me, I'd start by getting rid of the guards on the labor crew." Anton frowned, but he had nothing to lose and everything to gain in observing Marius's reaction to his bold words.

"Words are like glasses of weak beer. They do nothing," said Marius.

"One man can't do much by himself."

"So, you want to help?" Marius handed him the flask.

"If the opportunity arose." Anton shrugged before taking another drink. "But there's no opportunity."

"Opportunity is a strange thing. It comes and goes like a garden snake. If you're not watching, you won't even see it cross your path."

Marius thanked Anton again and left.

Anton watched him go down the trail back toward town, wondering if he'd just been interviewed. Maybe Marius Partenkas wasn't as stupid as he had thought.

~~

Tilda stopped at the sound of voices in the kitchen.

"We have to leave," sobbed Mama. "Staying home is unbearable. We sit inside all day long waiting for the Russians. Even if I locked Tilda up in her room, eventually something would happen and the soldiers would get to her. I know it."

"No, Mama. If she stays home, she'll be fine, like you said. The Russians aren't coming for us. I can't leave the labor crew; the Russians won't let me. But soon, I won't be going out at night."

"What if things don't change and you're gone even more? What if they need you in the woods? You think they're going to help us, but they're not."

"Let's wait and see."

"No! I can't stand the thought of Tilda being here, and all the danger. We have no choice."

Tilda opened the door. Mama and Papa sat at the kitchen table, bent over cups of tea, the room lit by only a candle. Mama looked up, her face drawn, her eyes dark and cloudy.

Tilda slumped into a chair.

"We should have left before the war. You know I wanted to." Mama blew her nose into a handkerchief.

"We thought it was best to stay, for Tilda. She has friends here and school. We thought it wouldn't be so bad." Papa wiped his eyes as he turned to his daughter. "When I look at you, I still see the little girl who climbed into my lap every night for a kiss and a story. But you're almost a woman already. You should leave."

"You're coming with us, aren't you?" asked Tilda.

"If I don't report for work in the morning, the Russians will come looking for me. If they see you're gone, you won't have a chance to get very far. Besides, there's something I have to do tomorrow night."

"It's for them, isn't it?" snapped Mama.

"We'll leave tomorrow night after you get home. We'll hide. We'll be fine. You have to come, too." Tilda's cheeks stung from fresh tears.

"We can't wait," said Mama. "There are things you don't know. If the Russians come for us it will be bad, especially for Papa. There's nothing here for us anymore. It's dangerous to even breathe, and the future, who knows? Someplace else, we might have a chance to live a normal life. We'll have to leave everything behind and walk to the border. It will be hard, Tilda, but it's what your Papa wants." Mama covered her face with her hands.

"You'll join us when you can, won't you Papa?"

"Pack your satchels. You have to leave while it's still dark out."

~~

Late the next day, as long shadows stole along the frozen ground, the laborers in the work crew climbed down from the truck. All but one looked old and tired as they went in their respective directions; some toward town and others toward their houses in the forest or one of the nearby villages. Some went in pairs, some by themselves. Several men limped. Others walked hunched over from sore backs. No one talked.

The most able man among them, Anton was the last to climb down, as usual. The guard who had been watching got into the cab and the truck drove away, leaving Anton alone. He cupped his hand around a match flame and lit the cigarette hanging from his lips. He shivered, as the chill that typically came at dusk had already settled in. He lingered for as long as he dared, in the hope that something would happen. But no one had contacted him since he had helped Tilda Partenkas a week ago, except for her dolt of a father. Anton was beginning to wonder if risking his life for her had done him any good at all. It felt like he was back at the beginning. Marius Partenkas had proven to be useless, refusing to talk even when they were working side by side. It was time to meet new people and make new connections. Maybe it would be better to move closer to town and the opportunity Marius had talked about. At least it would save him the walk to the sawmill almost four kilometers away. It was equally possible that Marius was a crazy old man who didn't know anything. Damn, how he hated this place. He seethed at Svechin for forcing him to come here.

He didn't suspect anyone on the work crew was a partisan, but in truth, he didn't know. All he had was the suspicion that if the partisans were interested in him, they would have done something by now.

Anton finished his cigarette, and dropped the miniscule remnant of ash and paper into the snow as he went down the road. The trees became tall and dense, the spaces between them dark, and fewer houses stood among them. When he reached a lonely stretch of road, a voice behind him called out: "Hello, my friend."

Marius Partenkas stepped out from the trees. "I want you to take a walk with me."

"I'm going home."

"Please. Indulge an old man."

"Go to hell."

Marius unbuttoned his worn overcoat to reveal a gun tucked under his belt and another in a holster. He pulled out the Luger and waved it in the direction of a snowy path that led into the forest. "That way."

"Do you recognize the gun?" said Marius. He was pointing it at Anton's back as they walked. "You should. It's from that loose wallboard near your bed. Normally, having a gun would mean that the Russians haven't found it yet, for they would have shot you. You know, most of us like to keep our valuables buried in the garden. But if you were working *for* the Russians, it would mean something entirely different."

"Give it back, thief!"

"In time. It turns out I know someone who knew your grandmother. It seems you two didn't get along very well. My friend said you knew everything there was to know about pigs. Personally, I prefer cows, but we're all different, aren't we? They also said you and your sister ran away, leaving your grandmother in a bad way. The woman said your mother was a whore."

"Bastard!"

"Relax. I'm only telling you what my friend said. When were you married?"

Anton looked away as he thought of his conversation with the woman who had been chopping wood. He had told her he was married; it was part of the lie. That Marius had managed somehow to find her in that remote area made him feel even colder. "We got married in Poland. In 1940. We were young and happy. After all these years, the memories still hurt. I don't like to talk about it."

"Ah. Much of your time in Poland remains a mystery to us, although some of our friends there confirmed you lived west of Vilnius when it was part of Poland."

"I told you what I did there. I don't know what you're up to. Give my gun back and go bother someone else. I want to go home."

"We need to understand your true loyalty. If you want to help us, here's your chance."

Anton scowled to mask his surprise as they approached a clearing where a man was tied to a tree. He wore the greatcoat that most soldiers favored. He was neither old nor young, but his hair was mostly white. His face was red and wet with tears.

"What is this? A Russian soldier? Are you crazy?" said Anton.

"Please let me go. I don't know anything more," sobbed the soldier.

Marius raised his free hand as if to slap him on the face, but stopped. "I'm sick of your sniveling." He put the Luger under his belt, and handed Anton a M1895 revolver from his holster. "It's already loaded. Kill him. One in the chest. Right there." Marius pointed to the soldier's heart.

"Why should I?"

"To prove yourself."

"I have nothing against this man. I don't even know him."

"Please don't kill me," begged the soldier. "I won't say anything. Please. I have a wife and a child."

"He's a Russian, Anton. Make the world a better place." Marius smiled.

Anton took the gun. If Svechin ever found out he had killed a soldier in cold blood, it would be his own death. Svechin cared about his men, while many officers didn't, often ignoring news to avoid any official responsibility. But if things went well over the next few months, there would be no witnesses left alive to contradict the lie he would have to tell to cover his actions. He thought of the men he had killed in battle, and hesitated. The need to fire when being fired upon was very different from executing a crying man who was tied to a tree.

"Please no!" The soldier wept.

Anton couldn't miss, and a wound wouldn't be good enough. If he refused to shoot, Marius would kill him, for he had seen too much already. He had to kill to save himself. He had to kill for his mission. He pictured his grandmother and pointed the gun at the soldier's chest. He squeezed the trigger. In the retort and smoke that followed, the man slumped against the rope. His head fell to his chest. Anton lowered the gun. At least it was over.

"The first execution is the hardest," said Marius beaming, as he took the gun from Anton's hand.

The soldier looked up.

Anton took a step back. He hadn't missed. The man should be dead. "What the hell! Is this a joke?"

"Is that good enough for you?" called the soldier.

A figure who had been hiding in the trees stepped forward. The guns he carried probably weighed more than he did. "Honesty, Dana. You're a grown man, but you cry like a baby."

"What? Who are you? How is he not dead?" said Anton, startled as much from the strange events as from hearing a woman's voice.

"They're blanks," said Ludmelia as she approached the tree and untied the rope.

Marius slapped Anton on the back. "Well done."

Anton's hands shook and he put them in his pockets, his surprise and trepidation overshadowed by anger for what they had put him through. It felt like he was in a den of snakes. "Now what?"

"You come with us," said Dana.

Marius shook hands all around, handed Anton his Luger, and went back down the path toward the road.

With Dana in front and Ludmelia in the back, the trio trudged deeper into the woods. In the fading light, Anton did his best to avoid low branches and ruts in the ground. He glanced at Ludmelia. Her hair was tucked into her cap, and she wore a long dark coat over a pair of trousers. She held a semiautomatic in her hands. A second one hung over her shoulder. Her skin was rosy from exposure to the elements. Her cheeks were round and firm. Her neck gracefully extended out from the rough collar of her jacket. The tilt of her head held a femininity that was hard to mistake, but except for that face, she looked like a tough little man.

"Watch where you're going," she snapped.

Anton tripped on a dead branch and fell headlong into the snow.

Dana helped him to his feet and dusted off his pants and coat as Ludmelia scowled. "So, you think this is going to work out well?"

Dana frowned. They continued to a road and headed away from Utena. Anton was numb from exertion and cold by the time they reached a village that had been completely burned out. All that remained were the black remnants of framing and chimneys, in an area that was as still as a grave.

CHAPTER 12

Every day in the Siberian forest, Victor struggled to do just the bare minimum of work necessary to avoid a beating. Survival was a thinking man's game. Lack of action had to be subtle, unnoticeable. Otherwise the work wore away bodies until they slipped into death. The struggle to save himself filtered into everything he did: walking, lifting, chopping, carrying, sawing, living, and even breathing.

Besides the physical strain, the forest was dangerous. Men weakened by illness, extreme fatigue, or a moment of distraction, could fall and hurt themselves, or injure someone else. It caused everyone to isolate themselves. No one could work alone, but it became normal to rely on others as little as possible. All the men eventually brought this sense to everything they did, talking less, sharing less, and shutting themselves off to interaction. A few men fought the isolation, but many didn't. When a blade went into a leg or arm, no one helped the sufferer except Victor. If the wound was sufficiently severe, the guards would let the victim rest before walking home with the others. The injured were barely fed during their convalescence, and were always told to return to work long before they had healed.

All winter, the weather had seemed interminably bad, until a few sunny days appeared and lifted Victor's spirits. Then came the news that they were moving to a new camp. Victor and Hektoras sat inside, somberly preparing for the separation they expected in the morning.

"You're like a brother to me," said Victor.

Hektoras nodded and swallowed a sob.

"I don't know when . . ." Victor couldn't say anything more. He couldn't let his feelings out for others to see, and for the Russians to see. He couldn't let them out because once he did he might never be able to control them again.

That night, Victor thought of his family, hoping for comfort and sleep, but rest wasn't possible. He would face the unknown again, and he simply didn't know whether he could bear new guards, new people, and new disasters. It was just too much. He was too tired. He felt older than he ever thought he'd live to be.

When the room grew light, he tended the fire in the stove and moved the pots over the heat, as always. Hektoras rose from his bed and trudged out of the shed without even saying good morning. They lined up outside as they did every day, except today they held their tattered possessions tied up in their blankets; everything they possessed in the world.

A guard read names from a sheet of paper, directing men who were little more than walking skeletons, to different trucks. They lined up and climbed into the back as they were told. Victor heard his name called. He didn't look at Hektoras. He couldn't let the guards see that leaving his friend behind was like a father leaving his son. He climbed into the back and rushed for a spot near the cab where the wind wouldn't whip around his head. He glanced up. Hektoras was climbing into the truck. Victor wiped his eyes as his friend made his way forward. It couldn't be. Good things didn't happen here. But was it possible this once?

"Today's our lucky day," said Hektoras as he squeezed into the seat next to Victor.

They drove for hours deeper into the forest, over roads so rough that Victor's stomach felt like it had taken residence in his throat. About midday, the truck passed through a barbed wire gate and stopped. Victor climbed down to his new home that was even shabbier than his previous one. He was happy though, for the first time in a long time. His friend was with him. He still had someone he could trust, and who would help him if he needed it.

Victor Kudirka's first day at the new camp was brutal. A tree fell, crushing two men. One coughed up blood and died within the hour, while the other died just before the walk home. They drove the bodies to the mass grave outside camp and tossed them in like sacks of garbage just like at the old camp. There were no words, no blessings, nothing. Just garbage.

By the time the prisoners arrived at the camp, it was almost dark. Everyone was hungry and miserable, but that was nothing new. When the pitiful meal was ready, the men carried their portion of soup and bread to a place where they could eat it in relative peace. Some went to the shelves where they slept. Others sat on the floor. The men acted the same as they did every evening, except for a deeper quiet from realizing that the fate of the two dead men could easily have been theirs.

The peace changed when the man from Riga spoke up. "Fill up my bowl, as you fill up the others," he demanded of the man from an obscure village in the German countryside who was dishing out supper.

The man from Germany shrugged. "It's all the same. I put the same in all the bowls. One ladle. That's all you get. That's all anyone gets."

"I see what you're doing. You fill the ladle for them. For me, it's less."

"It's all the same."

One man pushed the other. Victor didn't know who pushed first. Those who had their soup scurried away so they wouldn't be bumped and lose some of their precious food.

"Stop!" shouted Victor. "There's no need for this."

Those who hadn't been fed grabbed bowls and dipped them into the cauldron, drinking quickly and dipping their bowls again. Those who were too far away to partake pushed and shoved their way to the front. Fists smacked against flesh. The room erupted into confusion.

"The guards will come," shouted Victor.

The men behaved as though they hadn't heard him. Men thrashed and hit each other as they rolled over the straw beds strewn on the floor. At a monstrous crash, the room fell silent. All eyes turned to the stove and the pot on its side on the floor with the soup pouring out. The room watched in horror as the warm food disappeared through cracks in the floor.

Men rushed to the pot, falling to their knees and scooping bits of potato into their mouths. Others put their lips to the dirty wood to suck in what they could. When the soup was gone, the man from Riga picked up the pot and put it on the side of the stove. The others moved to their beds like ghosts, and fell into them as usual. In the middle of the night, Victor awoke to a shuffling sound, but turned his back to the noise. In the morning, the man from Riga who had caused the soup to spill was found dead in his bed. The poor fellow appeared to have perished in his sleep.

~~

Anton didn't know the village where Ludmelia and Dana had taken him, and wondered why they were stopping in a place that looked uninhabitable. The trio went to a cottage that had been badly burned. The roof was gone. Only the front door and parts of the walls remained standing. A man with an eye patch stepped out from behind the crumbling chimney.

"Come with me," said Ludmelia as she ran to the man. Anton followed. Dana stayed behind.

Simas led them through the remains of a kitchen. A burnt beam lay across the floor near three partial walls. The floor was covered in debris. It was certain the items had once been the possessions of a family: a photo with black edges, a shoebox, shards of paper that might have been letters or newspaper clippings, a child's blanket covered in ashes. Now it was just trash and dead dreams.

Simas drew aside a curtain black from soot, and opened a door. Ludmelia and Anton followed him down into a cellar lighted by a single kerosene lamp. The air was damp, cold, and smelled of mold.

"Sit," said Ludmelia as she placed the two semiautomatics she had been carrying on a shelf. She sank to the floor, her back against the dirt wall.

Anton sat down directly across from Ludmelia, not daring to say a word.

Julius came out from behind the stairs. He held a rifle. Anton made a move to stand. Ludmelia pushed him back with a boot to his chest.

Julius chuckled. "She wants you to rest."

"How do you expect me to rest? Why are we here? Are you holding me prisoner?" said Anton.

"Not at all. You're free to leave anytime you wish," said Julius.

Ludmelia took her hunting knife out of its sheath and held it close to her face as she examined the blade.

"Is there anything to eat?" said Anton, watching her nervously.

Ludmelia put the knife away, stood, and went to a shelf that contained several knapsacks. She opened one, pulling out a piece of bread and a bottle.

She handed both items to Anton and sat back down. The bottle contained water. Anton drank half of it in one gulp. He took a big bite of the bread as Dana came down the stairs.

"Where were you before coming to Utena?" asked Ludmelia.

"In the north, going from village to village, working for a meal and a place to stay, spending a lot of time avoiding work crews and the Russians."

"Why did you come here?"

"I was raised not too far away."

"Why did they let you out of prison so quickly?"

"That was almost two weeks ago. How did you know?"

She glared at him.

"Do you think I'm one of them? Look how they beat me!" Anton unbuttoned his shirt to show the bruises that had turned an ugly shade of yellowish green. "They need me in the labor crew. There aren't that many of us still strong enough to wield a pickaxe and cut trees down all day long. Everyone's old or half lame from a war injury. Every day, all I do is work. I sleep for a few hours, and then work some more. The damn Soviets beat me for offering those soldiers a drink. But I was glad the girl got away. Her father even came to thank me."

"We heard about it," said Julius.

"I just want the Russians out. I don't care what it takes." Anton's heart raced. He took another sip of water.

"Why haven't you already done something?" said Ludmelia.

"I want to stay alive, and it takes a lot to put food in my belly," said Anton, hunching his shoulders.

"We're grateful that you helped Tilda Partenkas," said Julius.

"It was the least I could do," said Anton.

"We could use you right now," said Julius.

"To do what?"

"Damage. But you'll need to take an oath."

"Anything."

"There's no going back once you give your word. Break your oath, ever, and you'll be shot. Understand?" said Ludmelia. She took the knife out again, and ran her fingers up and down the length of the blade in a gentle caress. Anton felt his skin prickle.

"Hold up your right hand." Julius spoke of disobedience that was punishable by death. Divulging anything to the Russians was punishable by death. He spoke of family and love of country. The words meant nothing to Anton. Still, he nodded as Julius spoke.

When Julius finished, Anton said, "Yes, I swear." He took another bite of bread and another drink of water. He fidgeted with the bottle. That they had made him take an oath was ridiculous. He had no intention of upholding it. Words were cheap.

"Come with me. We're on watch. We leave at midnight," said Julius, handing Anton one of the semiautomatics.

CHAPTER 13

In the recesses of the cellar with dirt walls as black as the remains of the house above, Ludmelia lay on two crates forming a crude bed. She was alone with Dana, as Julius and Anton had left for lookout duty. They had taken Simas with them, for he had been pacing in the cellar like a nervous cat. Vadi was already outside. Dana sat on an empty potato sack on the floor next to Ludmelia. He leaned against the crate, looking pensive in the soft light shed by the lamp.

"What do you think about Anton?" Dana stared at Ludmelia as though trying to find meaning in her expression.

"All I know is that we're desperate for men."

"Marius checked him out. Besides, he was willing to kill for us."

"That means nothing."

"He saved Tilda from the Russians. How much does it take to win you over? Maybe he'll bring us luck."

"I don't believe in luck. Besides, this is Julius's decision. Not mine."

"You think it's foolish to take him in so quickly? Maybe you're right, but at some point, we must learn to trust our instincts. What I'm trying to say is that it doesn't make sense to wait any longer."

"What are you talking about?"

Dana took Ludmelia by the hand and pulled her close. "For this," he said, kissing her.

His lips felt soft. She pulled away. "I can't do this now."

"Love is like war. It doesn't come at a convenient time. Besides, there's someone else, isn't there? With you, there's always someone else."

"I can't think about love. We risk our lives day after day, and it doesn't seem to make a difference. People are leaving camp. That's what I think about, and feeding the people we have left, and keeping them as safe as possible."

"I know." Dana put his elbows on his knees and looked at his hands. "A few want to try and leave the country, but it's very dangerous. Simas told me it took a long time for him to coordinate all the units we need for Operation Bolt, and still it's risky traveling to the border let alone getting out. Some people with relatives in the United States are trying to leave through diplomatic channels. Others, like Raminta and Jurgis, just want to stop fighting and settle down to have a family so they can feel some joy before their lives are over."

"There's no joy with the Russians here. The ones leaving think they're going to pop up in another village or town, move into an abandoned house, and live happily. How can they believe they won't be noticed? Someone will say something, and they'll be arrested. We can't protect them anymore, because we don't have the men."

"They're willing to risk it. After all, it's their choice."

"Well, it's a bad choice."

Dana leaned his back against the side of the crate and stretched out his legs. "If Gerta had lived, do you think she'd be proud of me?

"All mothers are proud of their children."

"When I was young, I did whatever I wanted and didn't care what people thought. Now, I'd shovel dirt for the rest of my life just to have another minute with my mother."

Ludmelia pictured the kindly woman who had helped her and Mama after they had fled Kaunas, and her heart grew heavy.

Dana reached into his pocket and pulled out his mother's amber brooch. Ludmelia had found it in Zabrev's office when breaking Dana out of prison in Vilkija in 1944. She'd rescued the stolen brooch and returned it to Dana to give him something tangible to remind him of his mother. The golden stone framed in silver filigree had at its center a perfect little bug and a tiny leaf.

"Sometimes I feel like we're all frozen in time, just like this bug." Dana ran his finger over the stone. "The bug is the only imperfection, but I always thought it made the stone more beautiful. My mother asked me to pin it to her dress once. She stood perfectly still as I pinched the cloth together, trying not to stick her. I was so clumsy. When I finished, it was crooked. 'I have a farmer's hands. They're not meant to handle delicate things. Why did you ask me to do this?' I asked. She said it was because I was her son, and she loved it when I did things for her."

Now, as Ludmelia lay in a dark cellar next to her friend, the memory of their turmoil faded into the past, and she ached from missing Dana's mother as much as she missed her own. She bit her lip. *Partisans don't cry.*

"I want you to have it," said Dana, pressing it into her hand.

"You're going away, aren't you?"

"When Julius is safely out of the country, I'm not going to fight any more."

"But what about the other mission? What about killing those three NKVD officers from Moscow? I need you to help me."

"Anton can take my place. He has time to prepare. He'll do fine. Besides, Vadi will be there."

"Where will you go?"

"I don't know. But I want you to come with me. There will always be another mission. If we don't get help, we can't win, and we shouldn't sacrifice our lives for nothing. I love you, and I think you love me, too. Become my wife. I could make you happy. I would dedicate my life to it. Marry me, Ludie."

Now that she was faced with a decision she had thought almost impossible to make, her heart went to Julius as naturally as a moth to a flame. She felt a moment of cheerful abandon at having made her choice. She would dearly miss Dana, but she would pine for Julius when he left. If she didn't tell Julius how she felt, she'd spend the rest of her life wondering what might have been. She wanted to tell him he would be in her heart no matter how far away he went, no matter how many oceans separated them. She wanted to talk about being together one day, somehow. She wanted to hear from Julius the words Dana had just spoken to her. She hoped she had the courage to talk to Julius of such things without being caught tongue-tied. If words didn't come to mind, her heart would have to speak up, and it would have to be soon.

Then Ludmelia turned back to the face she knew so well, the soft eyes gazing into hers, patiently waiting for an answer. Already, she and Dana had outlived most partisans. If she told him no, he would become sullen and might make a mistake. Keeping him sharp and alert was how she could save him, not by breaking his heart—at least not yet.

She stood and he clasped her hand. "Think about it, Ludie. We'll talk again when Julius is out of the country."

Ludmelia walked away, already dwelling on the cruel reality that the mission to kill those NKVD officers—something that could change the course of their struggle—might fail without Dana.

She glanced back. Dana had already stretched out on top of the crate. His rhythmic breathing told her he was asleep. Ludmelia picked up her gun and quietly climbed the stairs into the dark of the ruined house. Darkness had always comforted her, but tonight, the mere thought of going on missions without Dana rattled her. A figure moved near the front. She spoke the password, and Simas gave the counter.

"Go inside. I'll take over," she said.

"Dana talked to you, didn't he? Not everyone is willing to die for a cause. A tree that can't bend with the wind will eventually break and die."

"You knew?"

"All I know is that he loves you, and was going to ask you something important."

Ludmelia showed him the amber brooch.

"Gerta's pin. Congratulations."

"I didn't say yes."

"You need to make time for love."

"What would you know about that?"

"You're right, Ludmelia. I know nothing of love. Eda proved that. But a few years of living in the woods helps a man get to know himself."

"You weren't alone. You were with Vera. Did you make love to her, too?"

"She was my friend and the best woman I ever knew. She was your friend, too. If you must know, we did, although it's none of your business."

"You've accomplished more than me in that regard."

"You've given your life to the cause. How is that not love?"

Ludmelia frowned. "You know what I mean."

"Your time will come."

"You've become so wise you can see into the future?"

"I've learned to see what others want, even when they can't see it themselves."

"And what do I want?"

"Power, control, and revenge. The same things I used to want."

"I'm nothing like you, Simas."

"The difference is that I've learned patience. And I've learned the toll that power can take."

"I don't want power."

"Maybe you didn't at first, but you do now. Julius and those above him decide the missions to tackle. But you're responsible for carrying them out. You like planning them, running them, and you like having people follow your orders. You like the responsibility of making decisions. When Julius leaves, you'll have even more authority."

"I don't do it because I like it. I do it because I'm good at it, and the people need me. Years ago, you told me it was my duty."

"You wouldn't have done it if you hadn't wanted to. You can lie to yourself Ludmelia, but you can't lie to me."

"You're an old fool, Simas." She gazed out into the darkness. "How far are you going with us?"

"I'm not. I'm going back to Utena to help out in Pagelis's bakeshop for a while." Simas put a finger under Ludmelia's chin, tilting her face upward. "Stay strong. When the men see it in you, they see it in themselves, and we need all the strength we can find."

Ludmelia smiled weakly.

"Goodbye, Amber Wolf." He kissed Ludmelia softly on her cheek and limped back into the house.

~~

Julius was exhausted. He had been outside for only a few hours, but the weight of what he was doing rested solidly on his back. The responsibility of convincing foreign countries to provide aid was immense. But at least he would be out of here and away from this living hell. He'd be able to rest without waking up in the panic that almost blinded him some mornings. He wouldn't see the look of hopelessness in the men's faces. He'd be away from Ludmelia and her intensity that drained what little energy he had left.

He motioned to Vadi that he was going inside. He had tried to convince the large man to get some rest, but Vadi had refused, saying he hadn't been able to sleep since his brother and his new wife, Raminta, had left camp, so he may as well stand watch. As he approached the burned-out house and the position Simas was holding, Julius whispered the password. Ludmelia answered. His heart sank. He didn't know if he had the strength to talk with her, but he would if she wanted to, for his safety depended on her and her gun.

"You should be resting," said Julius.

"Dana's leaving." Ludmelia felt her face get hot. The necessary words had come out, but not the words she had wanted to say. Already she was speechless like an embarrassed schoolgirl.

"I know. He told me earlier today."

"You knew?" Ludmelia crossed her arms, feeling a burn from having been denied the news for even a short time. Thoughts of love vanished.

"He's going to help get me out of the country, and then go his own way. With my blessing."

"Why didn't you tell me right away?"

"He wanted to tell you himself."

"Why are you letting him leave? How are we going to replace him? With both of you gone . . ."

"I'll never deny a good man the right to find his own future. It's the very thing we're fighting for. Besides, soon we'll be getting money and political support. My leaving will help, not hurt."

Ludmelia ran her fingers along the smooth barrel of her rifle. "And what if those powerful men you hope to meet don't listen to you?"

"They must. I will make them listen. I won't stop until they do." Julius stepped closer and gently moved a lock of hair from her forehead.

"After we get you to Poland, I may never see you again," said Ludmelia.

"We can't predict the future, but all you have to do is make sure I get out alive."

"And who's going to replace Dana?"

"We already have a recruit." Julius nodded toward Anton's position near the road. "I hear he's clever and quick. Besides, he knows the area west of Vilnius. He lived there. We could use an extra guide in case something happens. And after what he did today, I'm sure you agree that Anton's a good choice."

"I don't know him."

Julius put a hand on her shoulder. "Sometimes you need to trust another person's judgment. My judgment. I trust him, and you should, too."

"I don't want to trust someone out of desperation." Ludmelia had dreamed up Anton's test to prove his loyalty, and he had passed it. Still, not knowing him made her skeptical. She didn't want to trust anyone just because Julius had said to.

After he left, Ludmelia looked up at a sky that held far too many stars to count, and took a deep breath. She preferred being out in the open and unconfined by walls so she could feel the air on her face. It helped her relax. But tonight, a chill settled into her core. Julius hadn't said that he'd miss *her*. He had only talked about the mission, just as she would have done if she were talking to anyone except Julius. But he had important things on his mind and she knew he loved her. She just *knew* it. There would be time to talk later.

Stirring branches returned an old memory of running through the woods to avoid a Russian patrol. She remembered the explosion that had torn apart a soldier, and feeling glad that there was one less Soviet to worry about. She remembered the feeling of accomplishment when her bullet had killed the NKVD agent in Mr. Zenonas' village. She remembered that horrible sinking feeling when she had heard that Mr. and Mrs. Zenonas had been slaughtered by the Russians.

Danger was always just a heartbeat away. She had given up everything for this rag-tag group of partisans, and yet it wasn't enough. If she were captured, it would affect their lives. If she were shot, it would affect their lives. If she made a bad decision, it might mean their deaths.

Ludmelia couldn't afford any lapse in judgment, any possibility left unconsidered, or any self-pity. Getting Julius out safely was her mission now, and that had to be her only focus. *Will this ever end, Papa?* She waited for the sound of Papa's voice to lull her into the abyss between awareness and dreams when it felt like she was little again, and he was sitting next to her, telling her that everything would be all right. Tonight, she didn't hear him, and her thoughts stabbed like hot pokers as she wondered who Anton Dubus really was, and if trusting him was a mistake.

~~

Downstairs in the cellar, Dana tossed and turned as he dreamed about the soldiers sweeping through Auksia. They came upon the deserted camp, but keep searching, venturing further and further into Auksia, and then the next forest, and the next, with unrelenting purpose and an unending stream of men, killing the partisans one by one until they were all dead. He awoke with a start.

Dana shivered and rubbed his arms, trying to shake off the dream, and remembering that Ludmelia hadn't agreed to marry him, at least not yet. A feeling of inferiority swept over him again. It was a curse he lived with, ever since his first battle, when he had rushed at the Russians like a madman and the Latvian Edvard Urba had given his life to save him. In an instant, Dana's arrogance had vanished, along with his sense of self-worth.

After Edvard's death, Dana had felt tremendous guilt. Sometimes, he could barely stand it. He wanted to leave camp, but there was nowhere to go. Dana stayed and took the worst jobs and most dangerous missions to atone for his stupidity and weakness. It was never enough. He never felt right and whole like a man should feel.

Even when partisans had thanked him after a successful mission, Dana couldn't look them in the eye, for he was sure they were thinking about Edvard. It was far worse with Ludmelia for she had feelings for Edvard. After his death, her conversation came grudgingly. But as time passed, she helped Dana learn to shoot and track. She helped him adapt to the forest and accept it as his new home. For all this, he had fallen in love with her.

Now, he wanted a wife and a son. He wanted to provide for them, even if it meant cleaning Russian latrines for the rest of his life. He didn't care anymore about Soviets or communism. He didn't care about patriotism. He just wanted to live a quiet life and somehow prove to himself and to Ludmelia, that he was a good man after all.

~~

Anton leaned against a tree near the road and his patrol spot, shivering from the cold and feeling very tired. He remembered NKVD training camp, when Svechin had visited him, and had told him of a young partisan the peasants called Amber Wolf. Svechin knew only two things about him. He had light hair and was a crack shot. The peasants revered him, although no one knew anything about him, or at least that's what they said.

Anton had no idea whether Amber Wolf was among this group of partisans. He considered whether Julius could be Amber Wolf, and decided he wasn't. Julius had dark hair and eyes; besides, he was leaving the country. It couldn't be Simas, for he was a cripple. Vadi didn't seem like a leader, although he was big and certainly would be valuable in a fight. Dana's hair was mostly white, and in the sun, it probably had a golden tint. He had played a convincing Russian soldier just hours ago in the woods. Anton had no doubt he was a crack shot. Dana might be Amber Wolf. It was unlikely though, that he had stumbled upon his greatest prize so easily. Still, he would watch Dana just to be sure.

At least Anton's real mission had finally begun. He had gotten through the hardest part of his job, which was finding a partisan cell and gaining their trust, although the woman, Ludmelia, might still be a problem. She was aloof and clearly didn't trust him, but in time she'd come to depend on him. He'd make sure of it. He could charm any woman, and make her do exactly what he wanted. All he had to do was to play his part and wait for opportunity to present itself, just like Marius Partenkas had advised.

~~

Hours later, back down in the cellar, Ludmelia checked the knapsacks. They contained anti-tank grenades, bullets, the few medicinal drugs they had available, bandages, and too little food. She added a few things to Anton's knapsack, but nothing she couldn't live without. She left a pair of binoculars for Julius.

"Where are we going?" Anton whispered as they stopped to get him by his roadside post.

"You'll know when we get there. Now shut up and stay alert," said Ludmelia, shoving his knapsack into his chest. She wanted more proof of Anton's loyalty. So far, he had done well, but it wasn't enough to satisfy her.

CHAPTER 14

At the new labor camp, a guard named Oleg Minsk seemed different from the rest. He was in his midtwenties, and already had a receding hairline. His thin shoulders were permanently curled in a slump. Victor often wondered who the guards were and how they could tolerate this place and this life. Maybe some didn't want to be here, but had no choice. Maybe some were sadistic bastards, here by design. He watched the guards constantly out of fear and boredom, but only when he was sure he wouldn't be noticed, for it would surely have triggered a beating. Oleg Minsk never smiled. Victor wouldn't expect him to, but he never hit anyone either, and only shoved them along when the other guards were watching.

One evening, Victor stood outside the shack to escape its stifling confinement for a few minutes. Across the way, Oleg Minsk was outside, smoking on the steps of the building where the guards lived. It was a palace compared to the housing the male prisoners lived in. Female prisoners lived in similar conditions as the men, behind another locked gate. Victor rarely saw women, except for the few allowed back and forth into the guard's quarters to cook, clean, and entertain them in bed.

Victor watched Oleg smoke, trying to imagine the taste of the tobacco. The guard jerked his head to the side. Was it a gesture? Victor didn't know. Oleg moved his head again in the same way. This time, Victor was sure the movement was deliberate. But what could he want? Was this a test? Was Oleg looking for someone to do extra work, or was it a trap?

There it was again. Victor could run inside and pretend he had seen nothing. But he had, and leaving now might cause a beating. A key to survival was to avoid unnecessary suffering. Victor squared his shoulders, looked to each side to see if anyone was watching, and crossed the dirt yard to Oleg, who had moved into the shadows at the corner of the building. Oleg reached into his pocket and pulled out a piece of bread and a small sausage. He thrust them into Victor's hands.

"Tell no one," said Oleg, walking away.

Victor stuffed the gifts into his pockets and crept back to the shack's steps. What did the gift mean? Why had this Russian given him food? Victor put his hand in his pocket, broke off a bit of sausage, and put it in his mouth quickly. He let it melt there, chewing as little as possible so no one would notice.

When he went back inside, most of the men were already asleep. Victor lay on his bed in the dark, and ate a morsel of the bread and took another bite of the sausage. The act of chewing was a joy. The sausage was packed with flavor.

If he was careful and saved some, the extra food could help him stave off agonizing hunger for a few days. Victor turned his face to the wall and caressed the food. There was so little. He might not survive another day, and the food would be wasted. Victor managed to put aside a few bites for Hektoras before stuffing the rest of the sausage and bread into his mouth.

In the morning, Hektoras was next to him for the long walk to the work area. "Something's different about you. What is it?" he asked.

"Mathematics teachers are just too observant." Victor reached into his pocket for the last bit of bread and sausage, and put it in Hektoras's hand. Hektoras pretended to cough as he put the food into his mouth. His jaw moved slowly, imperceptibly. He swallowed, smiled, and then made a sad face.

"We should have saved it for our escape."

The next night, Victor made it a point to go outside for a breath of air. Each second passed in agony while he waited for Oleg to appear with another gift. The minutes passed. Still no Oleg. If he stayed out any longer, people would notice and ask what he was doing out there for so long. They would suspect something. Victor brushed the tears from his eyes, and went inside to bed.

Nothing happened the next night, or the next. Victor watched and waited. When Oleg didn't come, he convinced himself that Oleg's was a random act of decency, and he should be glad for what he got and expect nothing more.

On the fourth night, as Victor turned to go back into the shack, the door to the barracks opened and Oleg emerged. He jerked his head to the side as before. Victor peered into the yard to see if anyone was watching, then crept to the spot where Oleg waited. This time, it was a cigarette and a piece of pork. Victor took a bite right away. The taste of the cold meat brought the feeling of rapture.

"Why?" mumbled Victor as he chewed.

Oleg shrugged. "I'd want someone to help *me*."

~~

Svechin never liked his meetings with Karmachov, but recently had come to dread them. He climbed the steps in the headquarters building slowly, delaying the inevitable accusations. He seemed to get abused no matter what he did. This time, he had been summoned, and expected the worst. He knocked on the colonel's door, hoping there would be no answer.

"Come!"

The desk dominated the space, and the colonel dominated the desk. He leaned over a stack of papers as if he were going to devour them.

"It's about time you got here," Karmachov growled. "After the Zenonas situation, Colonel Vronsky is coming to Utena to make sure we're doing everything we can to stop those partisans. I don't need my superior hanging around asking questions." He didn't mention that Vronsky, while the same rank, had been recently given more responsibility and broader authority. Vronsky had won the appointment that Karmachov had wanted for himself.

"We'll get the bandits, Colonel."

"Damned right you will. What's your friend Dubus up to?"

"He didn't show up for the work crew this morning. That could mean he's made contact."

"Have you checked where he's staying?"

"Not yet, sir. That might make the locals suspicious."

"Fool! Make sure everyone knows that we're trying to hunt him down. Give him the same treatment as you would give anyone who avoids the work crew. Now what about that man on the road near the

Zenonas farm the day of the assassination? The one that might be Amber Wolf."

"Partisan activity has dropped off recently." No doubt Karmachov was getting angry enough to blind him with a sharp stick, for there were no new leads, and the people in Utena had nothing to say, as usual.

Karmachov leaned across the desk. "Devils lay under still waters. Find him and the rest of those goddamn partisans! I don't care what you do, so long as you find him. I don't care if you have to search every village and forest in this hellhole. Don't come back without him. If that bastard doesn't pay for the deaths of my soldiers, *you* will. Heighten the patrols everywhere. Clamp down so that no one offers those bandits even a morsel of food. Starve them out into the open if you must. Now get out of here!"

After Svechin left Karmachov's office, he leaned against the wall to calm his nerves. It felt like he had just taken a beating. He took a deep breath and continued down the stairs. He had bandits to hunt and no time to waste.

~~

Later that night, Karmachov hit Katya's naked buttocks with a riding crop. She fell against the wall, then slowly got to her feet.

"Those bandits are *your* people." He swiped it across her breasts. "Now they're sending Vronsky here all the way from Moscow to keep an eye on things."

Katya grimaced. Red welts grew on her skin. Her only consolation was that Karmachov was in dire straits over Vronsky's visit. Her tears came naturally, but the sobbing was pure acting. He flung her on the bed and pulled his pants down. His explosion came quickly. Afterward, he lay back and relaxed, looking ridiculous with his flaccid penis and pants down around his ankles. Katya wondered if a whipping was going to be part of his foreplay from now on.

Later, alone in her cell, she let the tears flow again. She had never told Anton their grandmother had beaten her, too, or at least she didn't think he knew, for he would have killed the old hag. Then they'd have been driven out, and Anton put in prison, so Katya had kept the torment to herself. Whenever Katya didn't do enough, or work hard enough, the old woman had smacked her with her cane on the backside, or the back of her thighs; places where the bruising wouldn't show. This was the childhood she knew.

At fifteen, a man selling junk from the back of his bullock cart took Katya into the barn and freed her of her virginity. As a reward, she got a large iron pot that she sold to a neighbor for less than it was worth, but having a few coins empowered Katya, and she resolved to run away before her next birthday. Anton had agreed to go with her.

After months of planning, it came the day to leave. It was in the spring before the backbreaking work of plowing the fields and planting the gardens even started. It was still dark outside, and Grandmother was asleep. Katya was about to take the coins from the old woman's jar in the kitchen, but Anton stopped her. Indeed, Grandmother had counted her coins every night in a ritual to make sure the children hadn't taken any. If the entire jar was gone, she'd have them arrested.

Katya took the jar outside and when she came back, it was full of shit from the pig sty, the coins still visible on the bottom. Anton bit into the back of his hand to keep from laughing as Katya carefully put the container back in its place on the counter. And so they started their new lives together with smiles on their faces.

They had walked for hours that first day. When a farmer gave them a ride in his wagon, they were overjoyed. That evening, they went to a hut in a village and asked a different farmer for some food and to sleep in his barn. The farmer fed the two a hot meal. Anton offered to do chores in exchange for the accommodations, but the man looked at Katya and shook his head. He brought Anton to the barn and showed him where he could sleep. He even gave him a blanket. Katya stayed in the house.

The next morning, when Katya went to the barn to wake Anton, tears ran down the side of his cheeks. "I thought he was being nice to you because you're a girl."

"Don't be naïve, Anton. He was being a man."

"I'll kill him." Anton ran to the door, but Katya stopped him.

"You won't and you can't. Not until we have enough money to pay our own way."

The next night, at a different farm, they posed as husband and wife to save Katya from eager hands. It had worked. The pair did some work, had a meal, and slept on straw in the barn.

Eventually, they made their way west past Vilnius and into the countryside. They scratched together a living doing some work here and there. They spent the first winter with a widow who had a cow.

Katya cooked and Anton took care of the animal. In the spring, Katya planted a garden. In the summer, Anton brought in hay for the winter. They were glad to have a place to stay and food to eat, but the conditions were cramped and the widow treated them badly when she drank. It happened more frequently in the winter than the summer, but the abuse reminded them of their grandmother, so they decided to leave when the weather grew warm again.

The next spring, they heard that a Polish landowner not too far away was looking for a couple to cook, clean house, and tend the horses. They looked and felt tattered as they went down the path to a large house and horse barn. An old man called out to them from one of the sheds.

"We heard there might be work," said Anton. He took off his cap and ran his fingers through his curls. "I spent my life with animals."

The old man squinted at them. His skin looked like leather. "You know horses?"

Anton looked down at his feet. "Pigs, mostly."

The man frowned. "And what can she do?" He pointed at Katya with his chin.

"I know my way around a kitchen," said Katya.

"I bet you know your way around other rooms, too," said the man.

She stepped up to him. "Anton will take care of your horses and learn, while I am in the kitchen. We will do good work for you."

"Well, that may be, but I'm not the one you'd be working for."

Anton took Katya's hand. "Let's go. He's playing with us."

"Wait, children. Wait," said the man, chuckling. "It's my son who is hiring a groomsman and a housekeeper who can cook. Let me go and talk to him."

When the old man returned, Katya and Anton had work, a place to stay, and food. They could barely believe their good luck.

CHAPTER 15

After leaving the cellar, the partisans continued westward from Utena. As they trudged through the cold and dark woods, Anton's elation at having finally infiltrated a partisan cell faded into the hard job of keeping up. He kept his eyes on Dana who was leading. Anton was next in line. Who else but Amber Wolf could deftly wind his way through a forest in the dark?

Snow from leaves and bushes poured into Anton's collar. The melted water trickled down his back, making him even more miserable. He occasionally tripped. Once, he jumped at a movement, only to realize it was an animal. He was keenly aware that he was with the enemy, and could be discovered at any moment from a simple mistake. Any insignificant comment would mean death. He couldn't say anything about Svechin or Karmachov for, as an ordinary laborer, he would have no reason to know them. He resolved to speak as little as possible, like the others, while staying alert to Russian patrols.

Ludmelia walked directly behind him. He could feel her gaze on his back of his head, and it made him nervous. They rested twice, but not long enough to stave off the exhaustion that Anton was feeling. Their midnight trek didn't seem to bother the others at all.

Toward daybreak, they left the forest for a village. A rooster crowed from inside a barn as Ludmelia, alone, took off her cap and hurried across a field to a tidy-looking house, her hair swaying against her shoulders. She went inside, and in a few minutes waved them in from the door. Julius introduced them to Mrs. Rydas, their hostess for the day. They sat down in a neat kitchen to a short prayer, followed by a breakfast of eggs, milk, and bread.

"The Russians are tearing houses apart, looking for places where you might be hiding," said Mrs. Rydas. "They're looking for Amber Wolf." She glanced nervously at the window where Ludmelia and Dana stood together eating bread and sipping hot tea flavored with raspberry juice. Anton raised an eyebrow, and coughed to cover it up.

Mrs. Rydas continued. "They haven't come here yet, but they will. My bones ache whenever Russians are near. They're opening walls. They search barns. When they don't burn the hay, they stab it with pitchforks. They're digging under buildings to find passageways and supplies. Yesterday, four soldiers went into my friend's house on the other side of the woods, and found two mimeograph machines in the cellar with some of those pamphlets you make. They arrested everyone inside and burned the house down. People are terrified."

"We won't be here for long," said Julius.

Mrs. Rydas wiped her eyes. "With my husband gone, what will I do if they destroy my house? I have nowhere else to go. I have no family, and no one to care for me. In a village just south of here, they ripped apart an entire house and barn, but found nothing. Then they burned everything as a warning that said, *don't even think about helping them.*"

Mrs. Rydas went to the stove and picked up the kettle. Her hands shook so badly, she spilled water on the table as she refilled the cups.

Julius glanced at the rest of the team. "Mrs. Rydas, thank you for helping us. We won't stay with you as planned. We'll find another place to spend the day. We'll try not to bother you again."

After they finished eating, Mrs. Rydas looked greatly relieved as her guests thanked her and went outside. The partisans found shelter in a group of hayricks in a field on the other side of the village. The ricks were lined up on an expanse of ground that was bare from the stiff wind, although the west-facing sides of the structures were still covered in snow. The place looked barren and deserted.

Ludmelia picked a hayrick with the largest exposure to the field. She hollowed it out and scattered the hay over the ground. A gust of wind blew it away. Julius gestured at Anton to crawl inside.

Ludmelia scowled.

"Show him how to stay alive," said Julius.

She crawled in with Anton and covered the entrance to the hayrick with more straw. She poked holes so she could see into the field.

"Watch for the Russians from there," she said, pointing to one of the holes as she settled back into the hay.

Anton crawled to his post, leaning on his elbow as he looked out. The air was dusty and smelled like warm bread. He suppressed a yawn. "I'm tired. Hiking all night is new to me."

Ludmelia crossed her hands over her stomach.

"You're a brave woman. You sacrifice so much; friends, family."

Ludmelia yawned. She didn't bother to cover her mouth.

"We're very much alike, you know."

She closed her eyes.

"We've both had a hard life. I had to take care of myself and my sister from a very young age."

"Marius mentioned you had a sister."

The mention of Katya brought to mind Minsk, Svechin, and the Red Army. Anton had to be careful, but maybe he could use his sister to gain Ludmelia's sympathy. He reached into his pocket and handed Ludmelia the photograph of him with Katya.

Ludmelia examined it. She looked at him and smiled before ripping it into tiny bits.

"What have you done?"

Holding the pieces in her fist, she shoved her arm through the hay and gave the shreds to the wind. "We don't carry pictures of loved ones, because the Russians will go after them if we're captured."

He glared at Ludmelia, but her eyes were already closed. He wanted to make the bitch find every shred of that photograph and paste it together for him. He should have expected as much; she was one of *them*. Just a barbarian.

Anton only hoped that destroying the picture wasn't an omen of his fate. His talk of family had caught her interest, though. The next time they were alone together, he'd kiss her, and she would be his. Controlling her should be as easy as finding potatoes in Poland.

The next thing Anton knew, he was running through a fog. Katya was in front of him and he was trying to catch her, but she was going too fast. He started awake to Ludmelia kicking his shin.

"If you need something to keep you awake, you can go outside to watch for Russians. That wind will keep your eyes open, if you don't freeze to death," she said.

Anton took a deep breath and sneezed. When he glanced at Ludmelia, she was lying with her arms crossed, her automatic resting next to her hips. She appeared to be asleep already, but he didn't dare test his theory.

Twenty minutes later, she sat up. "I'll take over. Get some rest."

~~

At dark, Ludmelia, Anton, and the others left the ricks and headed along a deserted road to a brick mill, where two partisans from a group in Ankia joined them. They successfully exchanged the passphrases. This time, one person had to ask how Lena was feeling, and the other had to say Lena was well if everything was quiet, or Lena was sick if something was wrong. The two men took them behind the press shed and offered food. It was just bread and cold Lithuanian bacon, but enough to fill their bellies, partway at least.

The men from Ankia stood watch while the group ate. They were probably in their early thirties, which was a ripe old age for a partisan. The two men moved together as a single unit. When one picked up a gun, so did the other. When one spoke, the other finished his sentence. The men told them that things in the county were bad, like everywhere. The Russians were clamping down with more frequent patrols. Many people were too frightened to help the partisans anymore, although others were enraged by the fresh wave of Russian violence and wanted to help, but often had no food to spare. Partisans all over the country were desperate for reinforcements and supplies.

Anton's eyes glistened at hearing information that reinforced the story Mrs. Rydas had told. He knew this would be good news to Svechin. Unfortunately, there was no way to tell him, even though any bit of information might help the Russians and Katya. Anton had long suspected he was treated so well because Svechin had feelings for his sister and might even love her. Still, Svechin had brought her to Utena. It was possible he had no choice, and it had been Karmachov's idea to imprison her. If Anton found out Katya had been harmed in any way, he'd put a bullet in Svechin's heart, even if it cost him his last breath.

After a brief rest, the men from Ankia guided the partisans further west. A battered delivery truck took them a distance, leaving them on a road alongside a meadow. There were no village lights, and the howl of a wolf was the only sound. They kept walking.

By morning, they arrived at a lightly wooded valley with thick areas of underbrush rimming the open fields nearby. The Ankia partisans said it should be a safe place to rest until dark, as patrols hadn't been seen this deep into the countryside.

The group scattered pine branches along the road to hide their path into the scrub brush. Dana and Vadi went to reconnoiter the area while the rest settled in for some cold breakfast and sleep. A few hours later, Vadi and Dana ran to the makeshift camp. Anton started awake. Ludmelia was up, standing watch. He already heard the faint growl of an engine.

"Russian truck headed this way. Could be a patrol." Dana was panting.

Ludmelia swore. She pointed at a thicket a short distance away. "You and Vadi cover us from there. I'll alert the others."

Awakened, the Ankia partisans moved to the sides, while Ludmelia took a position up front. Anton crawled over next to her. They had a view of the road while remaining hidden. Anton hoped the patrol would pass by, but any movement or sound could alert them. There was nothing to protect them from bullets, just flimsy twigs. He glanced over his shoulder. Julius was so far back in the thicket, Anton could barely see him.

Anton would have to defend himself against his brethren. If the soldiers started firing, they wouldn't know he was their ally. They would be just as eager to kill him as any of the other partisans. The soldiers had no reason to spare him, for as far as they knew, he was a bandit, too. But this was his chance to fight at Ludmelia's side and erase any doubt of his loyalty. He had to show her how brutal he could be. She would expect it. For now, he had to forget about any punishment Svechin might inflict on him, and kill some Russians. Anton was living with wolves, and had to learn how to howl. He glanced at Ludmelia calmly waiting. Something about the position of her head and the slight smile on her face made him think of Katya. He fought his fear and remembered what he had to do.

~~

Ludmelia nodded at Anton, a few feet away from her in the thicket. She was glad he had gone to her side without being told. She couldn't afford to lose anyone, but this relative stranger could protect Julius with his bullets and his body if needed. They both had to do everything possible to keep Julius safe. If Anton did well today, she might learn to trust him.

The sound of the vehicle got louder. Ludmelia watched as best she could through the tangle of shrubs. She listened, barely breathing, her hands steady, her mind focused. Anton was as still as a tree.

A truck stopped and Russian voices came closer, the sound casual, almost as if they were out for a morning stroll. She could see one of them.

The lead soldier was talking about his girlfriend, and how good it was going to be to see her again. Another asked, "With or without clothes on?" The soldiers laughed.

They came closer. She could see two of them. One of the Russians pointed to some branches lying next to the road. He casually used his gun barrel to poke them aside, and then bent down and picked one up. He looked at the ground before going over to one of his companions and whispering in his ear. Ludmelia held her breath. She could see four of them.

Her next action was purely the instinct of a cornered animal. The soldiers looked in her direction. She didn't know if they saw her or not. They simply posed a threat. The only way she could stay alive was to get them first. She dropped one with the first shot. In the time it takes a bird to flutter his wing, she dropped another. Gunfire came from the area where Dana and Vadi lay hidden, and more from Anton, firing next to her. The sound of machine gun blasts filled the little valley. Another soldier fell to the ground as the others scrambled for cover. A bullet whizzed past Ludmelia's ear. She fired again. Broken twigs and bits of leaves flew into her eyes and nose. She could barely breathe. She had to squint to see clearly. She had no place to go; nothing to do but protect Julius and the others. She took a short breath and fired again, and again, and again. Then it was over.

Ludmelia was the first to crawl out from the bushes to the seven Russian bodies lying on the ground. One moaned. Ludmelia took out her pistol and shot him in the head.

She listened for any sounds indicating that Soviet reinforcements were on the way, but heard nothing.

"Julius?"

"I'm all right."

Anton and the men crawled out from the bushes.

"Vadi. Dana. Let's go," called Ludmelia, reloading her weapon. She glanced in their direction. The bush nearest them looked like an insane gardener had hacked away at the branches. Bits of leaves and pieces of twigs covered the snow. Vadi had pulled Dana out and was cradling his head in his arms, rocking back and forth like a mother with her child. Dana's chest was covered in blood. She ran toward them. *Oh God, no!*

She fell to her knees, pressing her hands against Dana's wound to stop the bleeding, desperately trying to save him, just as she had done for Mama so many years ago. Her arms shook. She willed her strength into him, and pleaded with God to spare his life.

Dana opened his eyes. "Ludie. What's your answer?"

"Yes," she choked. It was impossible to say anything else.

The lines softened on Dana's face. The years faded and he looked young again, smiling with that annoying air of arrogance that she had grown to tolerate and even love, simply because he was her friend. His battered body ceased to move, and death took him.

Ludmelia lifted her bloody hands from his chest and leaned back, staring down at the body. They had both run from death so many times, she couldn't believe he was gone. She couldn't move and couldn't think. Her heart was numb. She wanted to stay there and wait for him to open his eyes, but death doesn't allow a second chance.

Vadi cradled Dana's head, mumbling, "Wake up, Dana. We have to go."

Her eyes misted at the big man's tears. She crawled to Vadi, embracing him, and feeling an acute sadness as he sobbed into her shoulder. Ludmelia gave her friend a minute to recover. "Go get their guns." She gestured at the dead Russians.

Vadi slowly got to his feet, picking up Dana's weapon before joining the others as they stripped the guns and ammunition from the dead Russians, putting anything of value into their knapsacks.

"Do we leave him like that?" said Julius.

"He has no one left," said Ludmelia. "His family is dead. All he has is us. It will do no harm if we leave him whole and in peace."

In the early hours of that spectacular morning, there was no time to bury Dana. Ludmelia didn't know if other patrols were in the area, and had to assume there were. But even if they had time and a shovel, the ground was too hard to dig deep enough. All they could do was cover him with a blanket.

As the Ankia partisans stood guard near the road, the others formed a circle around Dana, holding their caps over their hearts, risking their lives to share another moment with their dead friend.

"You were one of the best men I ever knew, Dana," said Julius. "Your country will miss you. I will miss you. Thank you for your service and for being our friend."

Vadi wiped his nose on his sleeve, and pulled Dana back into the thicket. As Ludmelia watched her friend disappear into the brush, she touched the brooch she had pinned inside the hem of her coat. Every day, Dana had become a little more skilled, a little braver, and a little more diligent. He learned from his mistakes. He never gave up. She ached from imagining what he might have done if he had lived, and if she had managed to convince him to stay. Her heartache told her she was mourning much more than the loss of a friend.

Then in a rare sighting, a lone eagle far above them gliding on a draft swooped down to the ground and rose again, this time with a field mouse hanging from its beak.

Life continued. Dana would have told Ludmelia that his death wasn't anyone's fault. He would have said he wasn't lucky, but Ludmelia didn't believe in luck. She believed in the churn in her belly telling her that his death could have been avoided, that he had died for no good reason. In the minute it took for her to reach the Ankia partisans, the churn in her belly had become anger.

She slapped one of them in the face, leaving a swath of Dana's blood on his cheek. "Why did you bring us here, if it wasn't safe?"

"Russians don't patrol this area. At least they haven't for a long time. How could we know?" He rubbed the sore spot.

She slapped him again, anger leeching from her skin. He bent his head.

"Face me like a man!" she yelled.

Julius grabbed her from the back. "They didn't do this. It wasn't their fault."

"Whose fault was it?" She twisted away and glowered at him. She headed across the meadow, the others following in line behind her.

~~

Walking just in front of Vadi, Anton's eyes swam with relief, the scent of Dana's blood diminishing with each step. He was elated at having survived. Anton didn't know for certain whether Dana was Amber Wolf, and would have to wait until the others confirmed it, if they ever did. But if he claimed to have killed Amber Wolf, Svechin might promote him. It might even get him out of this mission. It didn't matter though. For now, he was stuck.

The blood's cold and sharp smell reminded him of the stinking village where he and Katya had spent their youth. He remembered the morning that Grandmother had sent him to the neighbor's house to watch him butcher a pig. He had only been a boy, and Grandmother had wanted him to learn so he could do it himself and she wouldn't have to pay someone else. A gunshot had killed the animal. The neighbor had quickly hung it up by its hind legs. One sure swipe with a knife at the throat was all it had taken to drain the blood. The scent had stayed with him for a long time.

CHAPTER 16

Katya sank into the tub's warm water, relishing every second of the unexpected comfort. The soap smelled so good she wanted to eat it. The watery oatmeal and bread from the morning hadn't put a damper on her appetite, but was better than she usually got. Perhaps her sexual charms were finally softening Karmachov. She hoped so, because she couldn't stand much more, especially the beatings. Katya worked lather into her wet hair, and sank back under the water to rinse it, already feeling a thousand times better.

A knock at the door. "Hurry up," said a gruff voice.

Reluctantly, Katya got out of the tub, reached for a towel, and stretched her thin neck as she patted her breasts dry. They were still round and firm, but each rib showed through the skin below them. Her wide hips held a feminine shape despite her lean physique, and this was both her power and her livelihood. This was why men came to her and why they kept coming back. It had nothing to do with her brains or her ability to carry on bright conversation. With this body, she could be a deaf mute, for men came to her for what was below her neck, and most paid well for the privilege. After all this fighting was over and Anton was safe, she wondered if she'd give up her trade and grow fat. She smiled and thought it might be nice.

Katya glanced at the makeup on the sink and applied some powder and lipstick. She felt old and tired, but her reflection showed a woman who was young and fresh. She looked beautiful. She took her time putting on the silk stockings, enjoying the cool softness against her skin. She put on the slip and combed her hair, drawing it back into a bun, but letting a few curls escape to frame her face. She put on the white blouse with buttons and little collar. The skirt came next, brown wool and well-made. She stepped into black leather shoes with heels and bent down to tie them.

These items were better than the clothes she had brought. Her satchel had been taken away while she was with Karmachov that first night here. She hadn't seen it since, but she still had the photograph of her and Anton. At least that was a blessing.

Her worry was that Karmachov didn't have a generous nature. He would want something in return for the clothes and bath. She steeled herself to the possibilities, and took one last look around the room. It held nothing that could be used as a weapon, so she'd have to keep searching for one. Something small that she could easily hide would be ideal. The next time a guard came into her cell, she would lure him into her bed, wait until he was at his most vulnerable, kill him, steal his gun, and escape to find Anton. All she needed was a weapon and some courage.

Svechin was behind all of this hardship. He had betrayed her. Even if Anton lived, she didn't think she could ever forgive Svechin. It no longer mattered that over the years, as Svechin had risen in rank, he had taken Anton with him. Although Svechin had come from modest beginnings, he had had an uncanny talent for recognizing opportunity. The invasion of Finland had been a disaster for the Soviets, but Svechin had come out a hero for saving the life of a colonel who had become trapped in a snowy ravine. When the war started, Svechin soared through the ranks, finally being promoted to lieutenant. Anton stayed in the infantry, but his old friend got him assignments in areas where the worst of the fighting was over. Anton still fought, but the skirmishes involved fewer men and were over quickly. Then sometime after the war had ended, Svechin recommended Anton for NKVD training.

Katya took one last look at her reflection, breathed in, and opened the bathroom door. The guard brought her to Karmachov's apartment, through his office, and into the dining room.

Karmachov and another colonel sat at the table, finishing their mid-day meal. They might have offered her something to eat, but maybe there wasn't enough food for a hungry woman and two Russians.

She nodded as Karmachov introduced her. The man, Colonel Vronsky, murmured, "What a beauty."

"She's from Minsk," said Karmachov, neglecting to say that she was born here, and implying that true beauties were Russian. He laughed, even though he had said nothing funny. "Go into the other room and get ready."

Seconds passed before she realized what Karmachov wanted. She straightened her back and stiffly crossed the floor to the bedroom, closing the door behind her. She took off the clothes slowly, already missing their feel. When she was done, she got into bed and waited for the first man to come in.

~~

Tilda and Mama stayed in the kitchen with Papa, all of them sitting around the table, a lone candle providing light. Mama and Papa held hands. No one spoke. Well after midnight, after the patrols usually went in, Papa nodded that it was time. Tilda picked up her satchel and tried not to cry. One last kiss from Papa, and Tilda and Mama were out the door.

Tilda didn't think she'd ever see the old house again, nor Mr. Pagelis's bakeshop, the school, nor any of her friends. Once outside the city, they headed north toward Memel on the Baltic Sea, where Mama had family. They planned to use the amber jewelry sewn into the hem of Mama's coat to bribe enough guards to get them passage to Sweden. Hopefully, Papa would join them and they'd all leave the country together. Papa had said he'd try. Tilda had to believe he would. But like them, he would have to walk the entire distance or beg rides from strangers. Train travel was impossible, for they didn't want anyone to know who they were, where they were going, or what they were doing.

Light from the moon provided little help as Tilda jumped over ice-covered puddles. Her feet were frozen. Her back ached. Her arms were stiff. She was miserable. At dawn, they heard an engine. They had barely stepped behind a tree when a truck from the distillery in Obeliai came down the road. Mama ran out and waved to the driver. He stopped, they spoke, and the man nodded. Mama opened the passenger door and motioned Tilda to get inside. After both women clambered in, they were on their way. Tilda thought she was going to be sick from the smell of the liquor, and yet she was glad to be off her feet. While Mama talked to the driver, Tilda fell asleep.

They stopped at a house in a village Tilda didn't know. The driver helped Mama down and offered Tilda a hand as she jumped to the ground. He told them to follow him inside. They entered a small rough-hewn room with a large stove. A green cabinet with flowers painted around the handles stood in a corner behind a table and chairs. The isolation of the village and the simple structure of the cottage made Tilda feel like they were a great distance from home.

A woman sat in a rocking chair next to the stove, sewing. The man spoke to her in whispers, and then left. At the sound of an engine, Tilda ran to the window, only to see the man drive off. The woman got to her feet and told Tilda and her mother to sit. She tended to a pot on the stove and laid bowls on the table. She filled the bowls with porridge, and they ate their breakfast.

The woman asked Mama to tell her the news. Mama didn't say much, for there wasn't much to tell. The Russians were there to stay. What more could a person say? When Mama finished, the woman thanked her, and said she and Tilda could sleep in front of the fire while she went out to tend the chickens. The woman put on her boots and went outside. Mama wrapped herself in a quilt and sat in the rocking chair. Tilda curled up on the floor in front of the stove with a borrowed blanket over her.

Tilda woke to scratching sounds from the rafters. She got up and shook Mama's shoulder.

"Is someone upstairs?" said Tilda.

"It's just mice. Go to sleep."

In the evening, after a meal of tea and bread, Mama and Tilda thanked the woman, and walked away from the little farm, using the scant protection provided by the trees along the road to stay out of sight. After a long night and many miles, they went into another village. Tilda waited while Mama approached a house. She was limping. Tilda hadn't noticed it before. Mama knocked on the door. An old woman opened it. They spoke. The woman pointed to a rickety shed behind the house, and slammed the door shut.

Mama made her way back to Tilda. "There's no room inside the house, but we can stay in the shed all day. It'll be fine. You'll see."

Mama made a nest for them in some dusty straw. Tilda was so cold she took a second pair of trousers from her satchel and put them on. They ate bread they had brought from home. Mama took her boots off. Her feet were swollen and bloody with blisters. "I'll be fine," she said. That day it snowed, and Tilda huddled in her coat next to her mother, wishing she were home.

At dusk, Mama squeezed her feet into her boots, grimacing at the pain.

"Maybe we should go home," said Tilda. Both hands were behind her back, the fingers crossed.

"Papa may already be on the way to Memel."

"Really, Mama?" Tilda's eyes glistened as she imagined how wonderful it would be to see Papa again.

"I pray he is." But Mama's sad expression betrayed her. Papa was going to stay home and pretend everything was fine for as long as possible, giving them the best chance to get to Memel without the Russians even knowing they were gone. Tilda's heart felt heavy as she helped her mother find a stick to use as a walking cane. They made their way back to the road and went even deeper into the countryside.

Near dawn, a skinny dog ran to them, wagging his tail and jumping on them as if he hadn't been near people in a long time. Tilda hadn't seen a dog in years. She greeted him with a hug. Mama shooed him away, but when the dog cut across a field, they noticed a roof through the trees. Eventually, they came to a farmstead with a house and barn at the edge of a yard that looked abandoned: no chickens, no pigs, and no people. Only the windows of the house looked alive as they reflected the golden sunrise.

Mama knocked on the door. No answer. She told Tilda to stay outside, and went in. At Mama's nervous scream, Tilda ran up the steps and into the house. The dog followed. Her mother stood in the sitting room, crying. A woman lay crumpled on the floor in a pool of blood. A man wearing a white shirt, suspenders, and trousers sat across from her, his head leaning over the side of the chair. A dark spatter covered the wall next to him. A line of blood had run down from his head and had pooled on the floor. The dog went to the man and whimpered. Mama pushed Tilda out of the room. The dog followed.

"Where did you get that?" asked Tilda, pointing to the pistol in her hand.

"It was under one of the chairs."

"What happened to them?" said Tilda, shivering from the gruesome sight.

"I think they chose to end their lives."

"Why would anyone do that?"

"Perhaps the future was too frightening for them to bear." Mama found two kerchiefs by the door and used them to cover the dead faces.

They went into the kitchen. Mama searched through the drawers, mumbling about finding bullets. She put the pistol in the pocket of her coat. Tilda found some moldy bread inside a cabinet. She cut off the worst part, putting it on a plate. She lit a fire in the stove and warmed some water. She gave Mama a cup of the hot liquid and a piece of the bread. She even gave some to the dog. Mama took her boots off. Her feet were red and swollen. She said they'd stay here and rest.

Tilda helped Mama upstairs to a bedroom and covered her with a quilt. The dog curled up on a little carpet beside the bed. Tilda got in beside her mother and tried to sleep, but every time she closed her eyes, she saw the bodies downstairs.

When they woke up in the afternoon, Mama's feet were so swollen, she couldn't put her boots on. They had no choice but to stay.

"We should bury the bodies," said Tilda, shivering at the prospect of another day without rest because of the dead people in the sitting room.

"This house is their tomb. We can leave them where they are."

"But we have to."

"The ground is still hard."

"Please, Mama. A shallow grave."

Before Mama could answer, Tilda went outside and found a spade leaning against a wall in the deserted barn. The ground in front of the house was shaded by trees and too hard to dig. But in the back, in what looked to be a garden, the ground was free of snow and softer from the sun. After digging for an hour under the watch of the skinny dog, Tilda hadn't made much progress. She went to the barn and looked inside again before going back into the house.

Completely focused on the job of removing the bodies, Tilda ran upstairs and returned with two sheets. She found an old pair of men's slippers for Mama to wear, and took her by the hand into the sitting room. Tilda decided not to be scared or squeamish as she spread out one of the sheets on the floor. Mama rolled the woman onto it and covered her. Together, they dragged the body into the hallway and through the kitchen to the back door. Tilda winced as the body thumped down the steps to the ground.

"Where's the grave?" asked Mama.

"The ground is too hard to dig a proper one."

"Why didn't you tell me? Now we have to drag the body back into the house."

"Let's take them into the barn."

Mama shrugged and joined Tilda in pulling the woman across the yard. They opened the barn door and dragged the woman inside, leaving her next to a pile of straw.

The second body was heavier, so Tilda got down on her hands and knees on the braided carpet to help Mama roll the body onto the sheet. Death had never been so close. They dragged it from the house to the barn, and lay it next to the other body. Tilda and Mama used pitchforks to cover the bodies in straw. As they worked, streaks of light from the cracks in the wallboards showed dust in the air. When they were done, the makeshift graves looked like two piles of hay.

Tilda didn't even know who these people were, but they had saved her and Mama by giving them a little food and a place to stay. She brushed a tear from her cheek, as her mother leaned her pitchfork against a wall.

"Let's go inside," said Mama.

"Aren't you going to say anything?"

"I have no words for something like this."

The two women crossed themselves and bent their heads. The dog sat next to Tilda, his head lowered as if he was praying, too. When they finished, Tilda scratched him behind the ears.

Back inside the house, Tilda and the skinny dog scoured the kitchen for food. She found some moldy cheese to go with the moldy bread, but nothing more. Tilda cut away the bad part as the dog sat on her foot. She fed him a piece. The dog swallowed it whole.

On the far side of the kitchen stood a door with a wooden latch. Bare wood showed through the worn whitewash. The area around the latch was dark from dirty fingers. Tilda opened it to stairs leading down into a cellar. She lit a candle and crept down the steps, praying she wouldn't find any more bodies. The dirt walls looked frightening in the dim light and made Tilda think of the inside of a coffin. Boxes and pails were stacked in a corner. She turned to go back upstairs when she noticed some shelves along the far wall. One was lined with cans of food: pears, apples, and beets, eleven in all. A nearby bin held a few potatoes and onions.

"Mama!" she cried. "It's going to be all right."

For the next two days, Tilda, Mama, and the skinny dog rested and ate. They had fried onions and potatoes for breakfast. They melted cheese over cooked apples for lunch. They had beets and onions for dinner, and pears for desert. Even the dog ate the vegetables, for there was nothing else.

Finally, after several days of rest, Mama's feet were better and they got ready to leave, packing as much of the remaining food as they could into their satchels.

"Can the dog come with us, Mama?" Tilda had named him Sargas, for he had shown them this place, like a guardian angel. She hadn't told Mama the dog's name, for she had refused to even pet the animal.

"Definitely not."

"But he'll die if we don't take care of him. Besides, he'll protect us."

Sargas looked up at them, his tongue hanging down from the side of his mouth.

"We have this to protect us." Mama reached into her pocket and pulled out the gun.

"Did you find any bullets?"

Mama put the gun away. "We can barely feed ourselves. How are we going to take care of a dog, too?"

"Please?"

"No."

Tilda and Mama went down the front steps, carrying their satchels. Sargas sat on the porch. When Tilda glanced back, the dog ran to her.

"Stay!" said Mama, shaking her finger at Sargas. He wagged his tail.

He sat in the road watching them until Tilda glanced back. He ran to her again. Mama shook her finger again and told him to stay. They repeated the ritual three times before Mama gave up. "He can follow us all he wants, but I'm not going to feed him."

"Thank you, Mama," said Tilda as she hugged Sargas. The dog licked her face.

The next few days brought sore feet, growling stomachs, leg cramps, and aching backs from so much walking. Occasionally, a family would honor them with their generosity and offer food and a place to sleep. Sometimes, shelter in the barn and some milk to drink were all people with hungry stomachs could spare. They spent a few days alone in the woods. With Sargas between them, they huddled together and managed to survive the bitter cold. One day, a truck carrying dry tree branches took them thirty kilometers along their way, and Tilda felt like they had won a prize.

CHAPTER 17

Colonel Vronsky came into the bedroom where Katya waited naked under the sheets. He held a drink in each hand, and the bottle under his arm. He put them on the nightstand, sat on the bed, and took off his boots. "We have a lot in common, my dear. Some people hate us just because of what we do. It seems that much of my job is making my officers miserable."

Already, Katya knew his type: a military man who missed the fighting. His pants came off next. He was surprisingly well endowed. He handed her one of the glasses. His arms were around her before she took the second sip.

Afterward, they drank some more and Vronsky talked about the old days. Katya let him drone on, only half listening, missing the privacy of her cell. He had her again after the second drink.

Karmachov gently knocked on the door. "Colonel Vronsky, we have appointments this afternoon."

Vronsky let his head fall to Katya's shoulder. "Officers in the Red Army have such poor timing." He finished, got dressed, and squeezed her hand before leaving.

Finally alone, Katya stayed in bed as the sounds of voices and laughter filtered in from the next room. Karmachov seemed to be doing all he could to ensure his companion a good time. Eventually, a door slammed and it was quiet. A guard came into the bedroom and flung her old clothes on the bed. He watched her dress from the open door. She didn't even bother to turn her back. None of them would touch her so far, for she was solely for Karmachov and his circle of friends. She wanted the guard to take her, for she would control him after that. Her silence could buy food, clothing, an extra blanket; many comforts. He might even turn his head while she escaped, and she wouldn't need a weapon. She faced the guard as she put on her blouse, letting him see her breasts. She even ran her hand over one before fastening the buttons. The man's face turned red, but he didn't move.

She entered the empty dining room and gazed at the scraps of food on the table. She looked defiantly at the guard as she put a piece of bread and slice of pork on a napkin. One word to Karmachov that he had touched her would end his career, and possibly his life, no matter if it was a lie. She took another slice of pork and lay it on the bread. As she wrapped the cloth around the food, she hid a sharp little paring knife in the folds. It had probably been used to cut the fruit whose remains lay on the dishes. The guard wasn't even looking at her anymore, as if allowing himself the excuse that he hadn't seen her take anything. She put the treasures into her pocket, and descended the steps into the room that was her prison.

When she was alone, she reached up and hid the knife in the window sill where it couldn't be seen. Then Katya put the napkin on the bed. She picked up the slice of bread, and positioned a piece of pork on it with care as if that made a difference. Katya took her first bite and chewed slowly. The food was hardly enough, but a year of feasts wouldn't fill the void in her belly. She sat on the bed, leaning against the stained wall. She gently touched the bruise on her breast that Karmachov had put there. She unbuttoned her blouse and looked at it. The line of purple and red was surrounded by yellow skin.

As she ate, she remembered those sweet years with Anton in Poland. They had settled into a routine working on the modest estate owned by Leon Belzik, who was a Pole. Under the tutelage of Leon's father, Erni, Anton became adept at caring for the horses. After tending the animals in the stables in the morning, Anton often drove Leon to business meetings in the afternoon. At night, Anton would drive Leon to dinners at the homes of families with daughters of marrying age, and sometimes to play cards with friends. Leon inevitably got drunk, and left angry at having lost too much money. Anton would get Leon home and up the stairs into bed. Katya always heard the commotion from the rooms behind the kitchen where she and Anton slept, for once inside his own house, Leon sang old Polish folk songs at the top of his lungs. She would pour a glass of sauerkraut juice from the crock in the kitchen, and bring it upstairs. Katya would hold Leon's head against her breasts as she coaxed him to take a few sips. While Anton took off Leon's shoes and pants, she would run her fingers through his crop of bushy black hair and hum as she would to a baby. Without fail, Leon would come down to breakfast the next morning as spry as a young stallion.

Usually, Katya spent her time alone in the kitchen creating Polish delicacies that a woman from town had taught her to make. She catered to Leon's tastes. His favorite was *bigos*, a hunter's stew made with sauerkraut, fresh cabbage, meats, and spices. Its heady aroma could be enjoyed all the way out in the chicken coop when she went to collect the eggs.

She had duties to perform, meals to cook, and cleaning to do, but she did it willingly and that made all the difference. She and Anton had a place to sleep, food, and a few coins every month to spend as they wished. Despite all the work, for the first time in her life, Katya felt free. More importantly, she felt hope for the future in the possibility of becoming Leon Belzik's wife.

Months melted into years, and with enough food to eat and few worries, Katya's thin frame bloomed into luscious curves. In the morning when she combed her hair, the woman who looked back at her in the mirror wasn't a child anymore, but a fair-skinned beauty. She wondered if Leon had noticed the transformation.

On summer evenings when Anton was home, they'd sit together outside nursing cups of tea while they watched for shooting stars. Whenever she saw one, Katya wished she could stay here forever.

One afternoon, Anton and Leon were out, as usual. Katya put the bread into the oven to bake, and was mopping the kitchen floor when Erni came in and sat down at the table.

"What can I get for you?" she asked.

"I like to watch women while they work," he said.

Katya shrugged, poured him a glass of cool sweet tea, and went back to mopping the floor. He stared at her bare feet as she swept the mop back and forth over the wood, staying as still as a hot pig in a trough of cool mud. The mop bumped into his foot. He didn't move. She swirled the mop under his chair. He still didn't move. When she hit the chair leg with the mop, Erni smiled and Katya decided the floor was clean enough.

She put the cleaning things away, and went out to the garden. She came back carrying cucumbers and dill in her apron. The kitchen smelled like warm butter. Erni was at the table, gruffly giving orders to two men. She recognized them as the field hands who helped during the summer. She put the vegetables down on the table, and felt the men's gazes on her as she bent over to take the bread out of the oven.

Erni followed the men outside. His trouser legs flapped against legs bowed from spending too much time on a horse. He leaned to the side with each step, as if he needed to use his entire body to make forward progress. It amazed her that the handsome Leon had come from the loins of this scrawny man. All she knew about the mother was that she was dead, but she must have been beautiful and elegant, for Katya saw these traits in Leon, and they couldn't have come from his father. Katya touched her breast and thought of Leon's head resting against her.

As she peeled the cucumbers, she imagined what life would be like as Leon's wife. Probably not much different than it was now, other than sleeping next to him in his bed, and possibly hiring someone to help in the house. For the first time in her life, she would give her love freely, never again in payment for a meal or a pot. Anton would live with them, and he would never again have to sleep in a barn. He would have a job forever, and a home. Maybe he'd find a wife one day, and they'd all live happily together in the big house.

Katya sliced the cucumbers, added a dollop of sour cream from the crock on the shelf, and some chopped dill. Yes, one day she would be mistress of this household. She *knew* it.

She was in the dining room putting out the cucumbers, fresh bread, and a small roast when Anton and Leon returned. Leon and Erni sat down in the dining room to their modest repast. Katya and Anton went into the kitchen for theirs.

About halfway through the meal, Leon came into the kitchen. "My father would like to see you in the dining room," he said.

The pair exchanged a glance and followed him. Erni sat at the head of the table with his hands stretched out on the cloth. Leon sat down. Katya and Anton waited.

"My father and I want you to know how happy we are that you came to work here," said Leon. "You've become dear to us over these past few years. You've both found your way into our hearts."

Katya held her breath as she smiled and clasped her hands together.

Erni, who had been staring down at his food, spoke up. "Get to the point, dammit!"

"Katya, my father would like to ask for your hand in marriage."

Katya's smile faded. She had been foolish to dream of love. She had been foolish to imagine for even a moment that her desires would ever be met in this life. Love didn't matter. There was nothing to think about. This was her chance to secure Anton's future. She would be foolish to say no to Erni's proposal for it meant food, comfort, and a place to call home. "Yes."

Surprised, Anton whispered, "Are you sure?"

"Of course, she's sure," snapped Erni as he waved them away.

Back in the kitchen, the brother and sister stared at their food. Katya was the first to pick up her fork.

"You don't have to do it," said Anton.

"I'll do it for the both of us."

"But Erni?"

"He's not so bad. We won't have to worry about anything ever again."

"We could find another place to live and different jobs."

"Anton, I said yes."

On Sunday, Katya stood in a little church wearing a brown suit that had belonged to Leon's mother. Erni was in a baggy jacket and wool pants. Anton and Leon stood beside the couple, bearing witness to their vows given in front of the town's priest and in the sight of God. After the blessing, Erni clutched Katya's arms and drew her close. At the last second, she turned her head to the side and his lips pressed into her cheek.

They went home, and Erni got drunk in the spacious dining room while the others ate delicacies made by a local woman hired for the occasion. Sitting in his usual spot at the head of the table, Erni claimed in a slurred voice that his mother had descended from the great line of Casimir. Leon sat to his right, rolling his eyes, and Katya to his left, looking down at the napkin covering her lap. Anton excused himself for a made-up emergency in the stable. Erni told them about his pony and his French tutor. Leon yawned, made his excuses, and left the room. With Katya captive to his company, Erni continued his soliloquy and went on to speak of the band of ruffians he had encountered one night in Lublin. He had dispatched them all with one hand while the other held a glass of beer. He hadn't spilled a drop.

When Katya was about to scream from boredom, he stood and swayed as he extended his hand to her. She took it. Later, lying next to him in the bed, Katya noticed the scent of tobacco and boiled cabbage. She breathed through her mouth and thanked God that his lovemaking had been brief.

During that first month of endless dinners and making love every night, Katya couldn't believe the old man had such energy. Eventually, to Katya's surprise, Erni hired a cook. At first, Katya thought that the matronly woman from town would be a problem. Perhaps Erni had already grown bored and wanted a new woman. Katya went into the kitchen often to see if Erni was there, but he never was. It seemed that the cook was content to make their meals and go home to her own family at the end of the day. And Erni seemed content to bring Katya to his bed every night.

Sometimes at dinner, Erni lingered alone with Katya, telling her sweet stories of his father and his childhood. Without liquor, he didn't exaggerate his experiences. His father had been a merchant who had fallen on bad times. Erni and his mother came home one day to find him gone and the store in debt. She sold everything to cover expenses. The man who bought it, Count Belzik, had taken pity on her and her child. They married a year later and moved into the grand house. Erni spent much of his youth riding his pony, and trying to understand why his father had hated him so much as to leave without even a single word of goodbye.

Years passed, and Count Belzik died. Erni's mother passed on a few months later, and the estate went to him. He married the cook, a graceful woman who loved music. They had a son and named him Leon. "You see, Katya, how I'm partial to women who know how to cook." He held his sides when he laughed and to her surprise, she laughed, too.

~~

The Auksia forest surrounded the jeep as it sped down the road. Inside were Svechin and three heavily armed soldiers, including a driver. They turned onto a dirt road broken by mounds and ruts, leading farther into the trees. Bushes rising out of the snow between the tracks were cut down mercilessly as the jeep rolled over them. The scent of pine was powerful.

The jeep came to an abrupt halt at the old sawmill that served as Anton Dubus's home. Svechin got out first and listened for any signs of the living. He sent two men into the woods. The third man went inside and emerged at the door a moment later, shaking his head. Anton wasn't there. Svechin hadn't expected him to be, but he had to be sure. By missing the labor crew that morning, it meant that he had been in an accident, had run away, or had contacted the partisans. They had found no bodies along the road, and no deaths had been reported. Anton would never put Katya in danger by running away. If Anton was with the partisans, he had already accomplished something. Chances were slim that he might also be with the one they called Amber Wolf, but it was possible.

It was also possible Svechin had seen Amber Wolf along the roadside with that woman. He had thought the man was old from his clothing and hair. But now he wasn't so sure. Back then, he didn't think the pair could possibly be dangerous. If they had deceived him, they wouldn't do it again.

A dusting of snow had obliterated any footprints along the path leading to the shack. Svechin went inside. Nothing there indicated a struggle. He examined the wall board lying on the bed and the empty hiding place. Again, nothing. He went outside and ordered the men back to the jeep. As they drove, he decided to revert to the only source of information he had, namely the villages. Eventually, someone would talk. He would make them. Someone would offer information he could use, even if he had to interrogate every damn person in every damn village in the entire stinking country.

CHAPTER 18

Along the way westward toward Marijampole County, several farmers who held a vile hatred for the Soviets provided the small band of partisans with food and shelter. But more often, they slept on mattresses of pine needles piled over the snow, and under low branches hiding them from sight. Unfortunately, the branches also prevented the sun's warmth from reaching them. Every evening, as they got ready to continue their journey, the cold seized Anton's back with stiffness that turned to agony by morning. He was amazed that the others bore the discomforts without comment. He began to think that the partisans were a race of super-beings impervious to hunger, fatigue, and cold. But he knew better. They were just like his grandmother had been; tough and quiet. Ludmelia never missed a shot, and Vadi had the uncommon ability to spring from sleep to alertness in a mere second. He never seemed to get tired. He often volunteered to stand watch so the others could rest. "You need it more than me," he would boast.

In the morning, the Ankia partisans brought them to an abandoned blacksmith's shop to rest during the day. Being inside felt like luxury to Anton. He found a spot on the dirt floor, and using his knapsack as a lumpy pillow, settled back. He closed his eyes, but not all the way. He was in the habit of opening them just a crack to observe the others. While it was unusual, Vadi was inside, too, leaning against the cold forge. The others were outside standing guard and reviewing plans.

Vadi waited for a few minutes before untying his left boot and taking it off. Anton noticed a scent that reminded him of stale fish. Vadi took off his sock to reveal a bandage covering his toes. He winced as he unwrapped it. The big toe was swollen and red, its nail missing. The middle one was completely blue, either from a bruise or frostbite. Anton tried not to cringe as Vadi examined the foot, rewrapped it, and pulled his boot back on, grimacing all the while. When he was done, Vadi crossed his arms and closed his eyes.

Anton's first reaction was disgust. These people didn't have the sense or means to take care of themselves. He wondered how Vadi could stand to even walk. The man must be determined, and able to stand a good deal of pain.

Anton shuddered the thoughts away, and turned to his accomplishments. He had already done much of what Svechin wanted; he had infiltrated a partisan camp, and while he hadn't killed Dana himself, the man was dead. He could even claim to have killed the great Amber Wolf, even though he had no idea if it was Dana, for no one could dispute it. He knew that the partisans were planning to escape from the country, although he didn't know precisely where they would cross the border. But now that Anton knew how skilled and resolute they were, he couldn't possibly break away and get word to Svechin. His task of doing additional damage seemed harder than ever.

~~

Svechin gazed into a valley that held a few scrawny trees and a good deal of underbrush. Seven soldiers had been ambushed in the area. Damned partisans. Due to delayed communications from the local NKVD office to Karmachov and then to him, it had taken his team too much time to finally get to the site. He had ordered the bodies be left where they were, but the dead soldiers had been taken away. Only one body remained, and it wasn't a Russian.

The jeep had stopped upwind of the site, and he could already see red that looked like raspberry syrup against the snow. Svechin followed footprints to an area where twigs and stripped leaves covered the ground. The paw prints of wolves were everywhere. The adjoining bushes, while providing cover, were not in a good defensive location. This encounter couldn't have been planned. The bandits should have been surprised by the patrol, but seven dead Russians compared to the one dead partisan indicated the bandits had been ready. It could have been an ambush, but if it had been, the partisans would have taken away their dead. These people were on foot, and had neither the means nor time to take care of a body.

The corpse had been dragged out from the brush. Svechin squatted down and pulled away the blanket covering it. The man's skin was gray. The eyes had been eaten, and the body had been gnawed on by sharp teeth. Svechin stared at the gruesome face, noting the unusually light color of the hair. It took him a moment to recognize this as the man he had met along the road to the Zenonas farm.

Oddly enough, the bandits hadn't obliterated this man's face, although wolves had done a decent job for them. Svechin carefully examined the area, looking for more signs. He walked in ever-widening circles away from the bloody snow, looking for boot prints. He wanted to know the direction in which the partisans were headed, and how many there were. Unfortunately, he couldn't tell partisan boot prints from the Russian ones, due to the cursed incompetence of the men who had ignored his orders to stay out of the area. If he had time to deal with them later, he would. After searching for over an hour, he finally found several prints in some wet dirt. They were smaller than the rest, and most significantly, the imprint wasn't as deep. They belonged to a small man, or a woman. Svechin thought of the woman he had met on the road to the Zenonas farm, and wondered if she was with them.

Svechin lit a cigarette and considered likely places they might be headed. Kaunas, Marijampole, and Trakai were among the many possibilities. Russian targets were everywhere, but why would a band travel through dangerous and open territory? Perhaps this group had special skills needed for a special purpose.

It was certain he was on the trail of a group of partisans, whether or not the dead man was Amber Wolf. He remembered the man's companion. She had amber colored hair, but the partisan hero couldn't be a woman. Partisan women were sharpshooters, but for a woman to be revered as a warrior was too bizarre to even consider.

Svechin and his men left the scene. At dark, they pulled into Ukmerge, a nearby city with a barracks. Narrow cobblestone streets wound past the buildings in the oldest area. Houses lined the broad avenues. It was a quaint and lovely place, but he barely noticed, for he was still preoccupied with discovering the partisan objective. After a beer at a bar with his men, and a meal of *galumpkis*, rolls of ground meat covered in cabbage, they drove back to the military facility and quartered for the night.

Svechin lay down on a cot in a small, stark room with a metal locker, worrying about Katya's safety and damming fate for putting him in this impossible situation. He thought about all the little reports that had recently come to him from interrogations in the villages: a farmer had seen a group of people led by a small man or possibly a woman crossing a field at evening near some hay ricks; a boy had noticed strangers following a woman into a neighbor's house. None of it added up to more than bits of unrelated information. However, if he assumed the events were related, they indicated a possible trek westward. He thought about it until fatigue overcame him and he fell asleep.

Hours later, Svechin started awake. *The partisans were headed for Poland. They were leaving the country.* He pulled on his boots. He had to put the border guards on alert. If his hunch was right, he might get those bandits yet.

~~

The Ankia partisans hurried the group to the next rendezvous point, a lone hillock just off the road. They waited while Vadi scaled the rise, coming back with two more men. Both leaned forward as they walked, as if constantly battling the wind. The grins on their faces made them look like they were out for a good time.

"Have you seen Lena?" asked one. Stiff brown hair stuck out from the edge of his cap.

"Yes. She's well," said Julius. He embraced both men and introduced them as Polish scouts, Tymon and Tolek. They shook hands all around before saying farewell to the Ankia partisans, except for Ludmelia, who stood by with a scowl on her face, her arms crossed.

~~

Several uneventful days later, Ludmelia and her companions were outside the little town of Sintautai near the former Lithuanian-German border. Poland lay on the other side of the frontier that was known as Lithuania Minor, formerly East Prussia. It was sparsely populated by Lithuanian families trying to scratch out a living off the battle-scarred land. While it would be difficult to cross terrain badly gnarled from the war, the area was guarded less closely than the minefields protecting the concrete pillboxes marking the border gates in Punsk to the south. In the frontier, there were few people to help them, but there were also fewer Russian patrols.

The partisans spent the day resting in a cemetery down the road from a church with two spires. The upright gravestones gave shelter from the wind, and the ones that had been toppled provided a dry place to sit or even lie down once the snow had been brushed away. Young fir trees grew everywhere, including on top of graves, and offered a hiding place for the partisans. After they settled in, the Polish scouts handed out camouflage coverings made from white tablecloths. While little more than crude hooded ponchos, the casual observer could easily mistake a partisan who was wearing one for a dirty pile of snow.

"Did you make these yourselves?" said Ludmelia, putting on the garment.

"What, you think I couldn't?" said Tymon, laying aside his Blyskawica submachine gun.

"I was wondering if you have a wife at home."

"I did, once." It was the first time since they had met that Tymon stopped smiling. "She was in Warsaw in 1939, taking care of her mother who had fallen from a ladder and broken her leg. She was using it to climb an apple tree, because she wanted to make pies. You'd think a sixty-five-year-old woman would know better. I didn't want my wife to go, but you know how women are with their mothers. When Hitler bombed the city, they were both killed."

Ludmelia touched his hand. It seemed that everyone she knew had a sad story to tell.

After eating a cold breakfast, Vadi and Ludmelia left the cemetery to stand guard. During the day, they spelled each other for the occasional twenty-minute nap. Ludmelia preferred it to hours of sleep. After what had happened to Dana, she was long past trusting the group's safety to anyone but herself. She was tired, but the catnap quelled exhaustion. Besides, she hadn't slept well in years, and Dana's death had only aggravated an already bad situation.

The few houses in the area were spread apart and none were in the immediate vicinity of the church. There were trees and bushes in and around the cemetery, but the area beyond it was open enough to provide a view of anyone approaching either on foot or in a vehicle along the road. The day passed by peacefully.

At night, using two borrowed rowboats, the partisans got on the Sesupe River and went into the frontier. They disembarked near a field where the weeds were as tall as men. They passed a farm that had been burned to the ground. The black rafters leaning against each other groaned in the piercing wind. Road signs were smashed at the crossroads. At one point, a wild pig crashed through the trees, coming to an abrupt stop in front of the partisans. It gazed at the group for a second, then squealed and ran away.

Ludmelia glanced at her companions, all hardened fighters in dirty clothes with guns strapped to their backs. She smiled. "I guess we're the scariest thing that pig has seen in quite a while."

Occasionally, they noticed the smoke from a chimney, or a dog barking. The families who had stayed were too poor to move, so they lived in extremely stark conditions. The partisans didn't want to burden people who had nothing to share, so they made do with the supplies on their backs.

Once, a truck with three men inside passed by as they hid behind a grouping of fir trees. Ludmelia thought they were either patrolling the area or looking for loot in the wreckage. The partisans gingerly crossed a frozen swamp and came upon an abandoned railway line with buildings that had been wrecked by bombs. The nearby sleigh tracks looked old, so they entered a ruin of two walls meeting in a corner among piles of bricks and stones. Vadi found a small collection of dented food tins that had been hidden under crushed mortar from some fallen bricks. They even risked a small fire to warm themselves, as the area was large and completely abandoned.

They continued their trek toward the border with Poland. The remnants of the fighting between the Nazis and communists became even more apparent in the wire entanglements, masses of timber, and wide anti-tank ditches. Crossing the trenches became a problem, as most were full of water and the ice wasn't always solid enough to hold their weight. They crawled across a few on their bellies. Where necessary, they used the timber to form makeshift bridges.

When fresh tracks from trucks and skis gave notice of border patrols, Ludmelia knew they were close. From that point on, she and Anton used a branch from a fir tree to wipe away their footprints when the wind didn't do the job for them.

At sunup, they made camp in a thicket. Vadi and Anton stood watch while Tymon and Tolek chattered like two old hens, seeming even more relaxed now that they were so close to their native land.

"I'm glad the Russians don't charge us every time we go through the border," said Tolek, "or we'd be paupers. But then again, we *are* paupers. But we're lucky to be alive. The Russians came close to catching us a few times."

"What part of Poland are you from?" asked Ludmelia.

"We were born in Suwalki."

"Are you farmers?"

"We're partisans." Tolek grinned. "Our parents were professors at the University of Vilno before the war, but they left in 1936 for a place in the country. They thought that if the Nazis ever invaded Poland, it would be better to be a farmer than an educated Polish citizen."

"Vilno is the same as Vilnius. You lived in Lithuania."

"Before the war, Vilno was part of Poland."

"It's the heart of our country. The only thing Stalin ever did for us was to return Vilnius to its rightful owners."

"You have it now. But be careful, my beauty. I was trained by Polish paratroopers and know how to take things back so you wouldn't even know they were gone."

Ludmelia smiled and leaned forward. "Tell me about your friends."

"Our government went into exile in London at the start of the war, and many of our soldiers escaped to Great Britain. Thousands volunteered for special training by Polish and British special operations operatives, eventually parachuting into Poland for special missions."

"You were trained by spies?"

"It was a secret organization with secret missions. During the war, they smuggled money in for the Home Army that was trying to gain strength for an uprising against the Nazis. In Poland, some served as radio operators and airdrop coordinators. Some even forged documents. They ran secret military schools. That's where I learned anti-tank warfare."

"What were they called?"

"You already know too much. I can tell you though, that many were dropped into the Warsaw area to join the resistance and free the city in 1944. But the Soviets who were supposed to help us, didn't. Churchill pleaded with Stalin to send in men, but he didn't. By the time the allies delivered support, it was too late. Most of our men had been already killed by the Nazis." Tymon spat on the ground.

"If the British know what's going on here, maybe there's hope for us yet."

"We've been able to communicate using transmitters, but there aren't many."

"We've built a few ourselves, but they don't work well."

"And you know the situation in Poland is different from what's going on in Lithuania."

"Why aren't the British helping you?"

"After the war, the West didn't stand up to Stalin on our behalf, either. We're a Soviet-occupied country, just like Lithuania. The difference is that the Soviet yoke is lighter in Poland. We're communists and have our own communist leader. Our churches are open while yours are closed. We've had few deportations, while the Soviets seem hell-bent to send all of you Lithuanians to labor camps. Your farmers are being forced into collectivization, while ours aren't, at least not yet. But don't get me wrong: it's bad in Poland, just not as bad as in your country. You react in anger to the Soviets, so they use violence against you. More than that, they use violence to try and control you, and you don't like being controlled." Tolek took out a flask.

"It's dangerous to drink," said Ludmelia. "We have to stay alert."

He shrugged. "It's turpentine. I was going to put some on the soles of your shoes so the dogs can't follow our scent."

"Why do you think dogs are coming after us? No one knows we're here."

"It's a precaution, my beauty."

Ludmelia held out her hand. Tolek grinned and passed her the flask.

Later that morning, the Polish scouts left for a position where they had a view of the border, to spend the day watching the patrol patterns of the guards, to note numbers, schedules, and anything passing along the road.

Ludmelia proceeded in the opposite direction, to a spot where she could keep an eye on Tymon and Tolek, as well as any Russians who might come into the area. The expanse of dead earth in front of her extended to a highway. The area had been cleared of debris. On the other side lay a fence about two meters high, forming the barrier that made Lithuania an island unwillingly separated from the rest of the free world by lengths of barbed wire.

When a breeze picked up, she heard the faint sound of Russian voices. A ski patrol of two men came into view, but they were following the road, and soon were out of sight. Under the cloudy sky, Ludmelia gazed to the land beyond the fence and wondered what it would be like to be free.

CHAPTER 19

In the outskirts of Memel, Mama and Tilda hid their satchels under a hedge as Sargas ran around the area, sniffing trees before choosing one to piss on. The air smelled salty, and Tilda could hear the faint rumble of the sea. Mama held her hand, and they walked into the city as if they belonged there. But as they approached city center, Tilda realized that no one belonged there. A spire leaned against a pile of rubble that must have once been a church. The streets were virtually empty. Occasionally, a Russian mother with her child could be seen hurrying along. An eerie silence made the place seem like it was populated by ghosts. They walked along, just like a mother and daughter coming home from errands, instead of fugitives planning to break out of the country.

They went to visit Tilda's aunt, passing her house once, and then again, just to be sure someone was home. It was hard to tell. They went up to the door anyway. It seemed a lifetime had passed before someone answered their knock.

The door opened a crack to an unsmiling female face with very pale skin. "What do you want?"

"It's me, Ana," said Mama.

The face disappeared and the door began to close, but before it did, Sargas managed to squeeze inside.

Tilda was crestfallen. To be turned away by Mama's family was horrible. How could they do this? Where would they go now, without help? And what about Sargas? Would they return her dog or keep it for themselves?

Angry, Tilda raised her fist to pound on the door, but her mother stopped her. They waited.

The door opened again. This time, the light was off. A hand grasped Tilda's arm, pulling her inside and down a narrow hallway where another door creaked open. Light from an oil lamp brightened a kitchen whose windows were covered in black cloth. Sargas ran to Tilda and licked her hand. Ana hugged Mama.

"It's been so long, I wouldn't have recognized you as my niece if you weren't with my sister," said Ana before kissing Tilda.

They sat at a table next to a man in a black jacket who was chewing a cold pipe. "Welcome to our home." Ana introduced him as Petr, her husband. Mama hugged him, even though it was the first time they had met. Tilda hugged him, too.

As they spoke in hushed voices, Ana put a kettle on the stove and food on the table. There wasn't a lot to eat, but enough to put the gnawing hunger at bay. No one spoke until all the food was gone, for the food got all the attention there was to give. Even Sargas got a bone to chew.

When the meal was finished, the adults talked. Mama told them why they had come. She cried when she explained that Papa had stayed in Utena to give them a better chance to escape. She told of the soldiers who had tried to harm Tilda. Sargas sat next to Tilda as she scratched behind his ears. He went to the stove, curled up in front of it, and went to sleep. Tilda yawned. The voices became a dull murmur, then quieted completely.

When she awoke, Ana took her into the bathroom. A few inches of water lay in the tub. As Tilda undressed, Ana returned with the tea kettle and poured in all its steaming water. It was still cool, but Tilda took her bath. Later, she put on a clean borrowed nightgown, and lay down in a real bed all by herself. She hadn't felt so good in a long time.

The next day, Tilda and Mama huddled in a bedroom upstairs, the shades drawn and curtains closed to the sun. Ana brought them tea and bread for breakfast. Later she brought up some soup for lunch. After dark, when Petr came home, they all went down to the darkened kitchen. He had their satchels with him.

"I'm sorry you had to hide upstairs all day," said Petr. He looked nervous. "No one must know you're here. Almost everyone fled for their lives when the Russians came, near the end of the war. Ana and I stayed. Where would we go? This is our home and we had just gotten married. The Soviets didn't harm us, but they destroyed everything; the churches, the town square. They left our city in ruins.

Recently, Russian families have come here to live. We pretend we're happy to see them, but every time they move into an abandoned house, I pray for the people who left. The Russians are finally rebuilding the city center. That's where I work. But it barely seems like home any more. When the Germans were here, I pretended I was German, because my mother was German. When the Russians came, I pretended I was Russian. Half the time, I don't know who I am anymore."

Sargas sat on the floor next to Petr and licked his hand. "You shouldn't go out of the house while you're here. But if you must, you'll have to speak Russian."

"I speak it," said Mama. "German, too. And Polish, and a little bit of English." She opened her satchel and pulled out the gun. She handed it to Petr. "You can have this."

Petr looked like he had won a prize. He hurriedly put on his coat and rushed outside with the weapon. When he returned, Ana was dishing out bowls of soup.

"Thank you," said Petr. "It's hidden well. I hope I never have to use it, but I feel better knowing I have one."

"There are no bullets," said Mama.

"That's all right." Petr smiled, sat, and said a prayer to the Holy Father, thanking Him for the food, their visitors, and the gun.

"It's almost impossible to get out of the country now," said Petr, wiping his mouth. "After the war, they let the Germans out, because the Russians considered them refugees. You'll have to say you're German citizens, too. It's a risk, because it's been years since the war ended. With the right bribes though, we might be able to get you out. We'll have to get identity papers for you and Tilda. Do you have any money?"

"I have my jewelry," said Mama. She went upstairs and came back down with her coat. She unpinned a small velvet bag hidden in the lining. She took out an amber pendant trimmed in gold, an amber necklace, two amber rings, one set in silver and the other in gold, and an amber locket.

"It's dangerous, Petr," said Ana. "If the Russians find out . . ."

"Come with us," said Mama.

"It's very expensive," said Petr. "I know from my friend who tried to get his mother out. There should be enough for one set of papers. I don't know about the second set."

"If Tilda gets out, that's all that matters," said Mama.

"I don't want to go alone," said Tilda.

"You will do what I tell you to. It's your life we are trying save. The rest of us have lived. We've had our day. It's your time now."

"No, Mama."

"You will, my dear, if you have to—if there's no other choice." Mama clutched Tilda's hands. "Know that it's what I want. It's my dream for you to get out and have a good life. It's Papa's dream too. It's all we ever wanted."

A few days later, Petr announced that there was enough money for two sets of papers, and Mama cried.

"What about Papa? What if he comes? What will we do?" said Tilda.

"I wish we had that problem."

"But we have no money for his papers. And what if he gets here after we're already gone? He can't stay here. It would put Ana and Petr in danger. But if he's not at home, the Russians will go looking for him."

"He's not coming, Tilda."

"Of course he is. You said he was. He wouldn't leave me forever. He must come. Please, Mama. He has to." Tears streamed down her cheeks.

"He wants us to get out. We may never have another chance."

That night, Ana let Sargas into Tilda's room. The girl fell asleep while crying into the fur around the animal's neck.

Two days later, Tilda and her mother stood in a line waiting to board a trawler headed for Sweden. Everyone around them spoke German or Russian, and already it didn't even seem like they were in Lithuania anymore. Even so, Tilda's heart was back in Utena, with Papa.

The Russian soldier spoke to Mama in German, and she answered in German. Sargas sat patiently at Tilda's side, wagging his tail. Mama had taught her some phrases, but they were talking too fast and Tilda couldn't understand what they were saying. She tried not to look confused.

The soldier looked down at Sargas. He scratched the dog's ears and asked Tilda a question. Mama nodded and smiled. Tilda smiled, too, and nodded because her mother had nodded. The soldier took hold of Sargas's collar, and waved Mama and Tilda on.

"*Bitte*," said Mama. She took hold of Tilda's arm and started walking. "Keep smiling and don't look back," she whispered.

"Why isn't Sargas coming with us?"
"They won't let him on the boat."
"No!" Tears trickled down her cheeks. *Not Sargas, too.*
"Keep walking."
"What will happen to him?"
"He'll be all right."
"No, he won't."
Mama's fingers dug into her arm.
"You're hurting me," said Tilda.
"Just do as I say!" Mam's voice cracked.

CHAPTER 20

Victor looked around nervously before taking two cigarettes from Oleg, and putting them directly in his pocket.

"I'm leaving," said Oleg. "They're moving me to another camp."

Dumbfounded, Victor thought of the food and cigarettes, and how much he would miss them. He remembered how good the sausage had tasted and the soft inside of the bread. He remembered treating the bits of nourishment as treasures akin to gold. Oleg shrugged and walked away. Only then did Victor realize he hadn't expressed his gratitude for the kindness, and it was too late. Running after Oleg would draw attention and that wouldn't be good for either of them. Victor returned to the shack and touched Hektoras's shoulder. He was already on his mattress. "I'm trying to sleep. What do you want?"

He told Hektoras about Oleg. While Oleg had never approached him, Hektoras enjoyed the treats that Victor had shared.

"No one will ever help us like that again," said Hektoras. "The years will pass even more slowly, and in the end, we'll die. My son will become a man without ever knowing his father." He pulled out a worn photograph from his breast pocket and kissed it.

"We've survived this long. We'll survive longer."

Hektoras turned with his face to the wall and didn't say anything else.

The next morning when Victor awoke, Hektoras was still in bed. Victor flamed the fire to life and heated the tea. Hektoras got up as usual, but there was no friendly banter today. Hektoras was glum, and looked more depressed than usual. Victor worried that his friend had just given up.

The men ate their breakfast and lined up for the long walk deeper into the forest. As Victor waited at the end of the line, Hektoras spoke to one of the guards. They escorted him away. Victor couldn't imagine where they were going. Hektoras hadn't said he was sick.

A few minutes later, a guard approached Victor. "Come," he said.

"What is it?" asked Victor.

The guard poked him with his automatic.

Victor felt what little energy he had fade away to worry. His first thought was that someone had seen Oleg give him the cigarettes last night, or had found them hidden under his bed. Punishment would absorb what little resolve he had left. He could almost feel death breathing against his neck.

Maybe bad news wasn't coming. Maybe he'd be set free and be in Kaunas before the week was out. Maybe he'd see his family in a matter of days: beautiful Ludmelia, Matas, and the love of his life, Aldona. It was possible. A man could hope.

He was escorted into the guard's quarters, and down a long and dim hallway. It felt like his fate waited behind the door at the end. Victor brushed the dirt off the front of his coat, put his cap in his pocket, ran his fingers through his hair, and walked purposefully into the room. It had a long table with chairs in the middle. Another row of chairs stood along the far wall. Hektoras was sitting in one of them. Victor felt a rush of relief that his friend was there. Maybe they both would be released, and Hektoras would finally see his son.

An officer in military uniform sat behind the table. Victor had never seen him before. He was thin and looked weary, like the rest of the guards. Several folders sat on the table. The officer shuffled through them, and opened one.

The guard pushed Victor forward.

"Victor Kudirka," said the officer as he read from a paper. "You are charged with treason against the motherland, for forming a unit of the Brothers of the Forest in the Vilkija area in Lithuania, and organizing attacks against the Soviet military."

Victor gasped. The meaning was clear, and defense irrelevant. He wouldn't see his family again. The accusations were painfully accurate. His body began to shake. It was as if all air had left the room. "Again, please," said Victor.

The officer shrugged and repeated the words.

This time, the accusations merged into the sound of betrayal, for no one knew anything about him except Hektoras, his friend and confidant. Victor turned to the row of chairs where Hektoras sat looking down at the floor.

"Can anyone validate these accusations?" asked the officer.

Hektoras slowly got to his feet.

"Don't," said Victor, but he knew that he didn't have a chance in the battle that poised his life against Hektoras's son.

"I can validate the accusations," said Hektoras. He held his hands in front of his crotch and looked at the officer. "Victor Kudirka confessed all of those activities to me."

Victor watched Hektoras's blank expression, and resolved to fight.

"Yes, I said those things," said Victor. "But I was making up a story to pass the time. They were just fabrications of my imagination. I taught history. The stories I created mixed the past and the present into fantasies. I know nothing of partisans or warfare. I teach for a living. What do I know of fighting? I was entertaining my friend."

The officer let Victor continue. Victor spoke of Lenin and extolled the noble social experiment that had led to the greatest nation on earth. He spoke of Father Stalin's cunning and fortitude during the war. He spoke of the bravery of Russian soldiers in their fight against the Nazis. In the end, Victor leaned against the table exhausted, but full of hope that his words had saved him and that a miracle was about to happen.

"Hold him for interrogation," said the officer. A guard took Victor by the arm, and guided him to a seat next to Hektoras.

The officer opened the next folder in the stack on the desk. He ordered Hektoras to come forward.

"What's your occupation?" asked the officer.

"I'm a mathematics teacher in gymnasium," Hektoras stammered.

"Where do you live?"

"In Trakai, with my family."

"Why haven't you come forward about Victor Kudirka until now?" asked the officer.

"I don't know. I wasn't sure. I needed to know more. He told me about his past not so long ago." Hektoras scrambled for his words. "Well, I . . . when am I going to see my son?"

"You've been collaborating with a traitor. You'll be spending the next twenty years at hard labor."

"You said I'd see my son!" Hektoras choked back a sob.

"You will, but not for twenty years."

Hektoras lunged for the officer. "You bastard! This was all for nothing. You promised me!" A guard blocked Hektoras's way, and another hit him in the head with the butt of his gun. He crumpled to the floor.

Victor didn't want to feel satisfaction at Hektoras's sentencing, but he did. The Soviets had avenged this betrayal. Victor laughed out loud. Many men had refused to talk for fear of saying something that could be used against them. Victor had faith that men of intelligence could be trusted. He had been wrong. But the man who had betrayed him had been punished with a twenty-year sentence. Tears rolled down Victor's cheeks. He pointed a finger at the officer and kept on laughing, but stopped when the guard raised his gun.

Victor spent the night staring at the walls of a cell. It would have been better if he had been shot right away, as he knew it was coming. Execution would have been a relief instead of being kept for additional questioning. Finally, he fell asleep and entered a dream where his family hovered around him like woeful spirits.

A guard opened the cell door and dragged him into another room. From the windows, it looked to be the middle of the night. As with all rooms in this accursed place, the lighting was dim. The furnishings were only a desk, a lamp, and a chair. The officer from yesterday sat at the desk. The light reflected off the planes of his face, giving him an unworldly glow.

The guard shoved Victor into the chair. It scraped backward on the dirty floorboards.

"Victor Kudirka," said the officer.

"Yes," said Victor.

"It's good that you're talking already. It will save us both time and energy."

"I have nothing to hide."

"Tell me about the Brothers of the Forest."

"It's a resistance group in Lithuania."

"How many of these groups are there?"

"I have no idea."

"Where are they?"

"You said they were in the Vilkija area." Victor paused. It had been years since the meeting at the homestead with Simas and old Mr. Ravas. They were both probably dead by now. He didn't expect that any partisans had a long life. The truth he knew was dated and useless. He couldn't understand why the Soviets were still interested in that tiny cell from years ago.

A guard hit Victor's leg with a club. The crack of bone sounded and then Victor's scream.

"Tell me," said the officer.

"Go to hell."

The guard hit the broken bone again. Victor screamed a second time. It didn't matter what he said anymore. It just didn't matter.

"What other cells did you help organize?"

Victor's mind cleared. *They want the leaders of the cells in other forests.* Could the Soviets possibly have found his list? He remembered their kitchen in Kaunas, and the two sheets of paper containing names and instructions for Aldona hidden behind the bread in the corner cabinet, along with his letter to the Lithuanian Army. He exhaled, recalling his instructions to Aldona to destroy the documents if anything happened to him.

"I organized nothing."

"I don't believe you," said the officer. "Tell me and live. Otherwise, I'll have you shot for being a traitor." The officer gestured to the guard who stepped forward and hit Victor's broken leg a third time. He passed out.

When he awoke, he was in the same place, his leg throbbing with fresh pain. Victor didn't know how much time had passed. The officer continued as if it had been mere seconds. "And your propaganda pamphlets? Where did you distribute them? Who took them?"

"Students at the university. That's all. So they wouldn't forget who they are."

"They're Soviet citizens!"

The interrogation continued for what seemed to be hours. The officer asked questions, Victor answered them, conveying no information. He didn't know if his family and friends were safe, but his silence could protect them. He felt satisfaction knowing his last act on earth would be saving the people he loved by saying nothing. An eternity later, it was over.

"He's not going to say anything more we can use. Get rid of him," said the officer.

Victor didn't remember anything else.

When he opened his eyes, Victor was on the floor of his cell. He had to blink several times to focus. At first, he didn't know if it was morning or evening. He tried to move, but his body felt like it had been hit by a train. He couldn't move his leg, and it hurt when he touched it. He looked down. It had swollen to twice its normal size.

He tried to use the pain to clear his mind. If the Soviets were asking about the Brothers of the Forest, it meant they were still active and still a threat. Victor managed a chuckle. Perhaps the sapling he had planted years ago had grown into a tree. It would be a joy to be in the forest with his brethren, fighting with other patriots. He longed to see Simas, his crusty friend, eye patch and all. He thought of Gerta and Bronai Ravas and their kind natures. He thought about his children, whom he had raised to survive all circumstances. Or at least he had tried.

Two guards came in and dragged him from the cell. All he wanted was for the nightmare to end. They went outside. It was very cold. Dawn was breaking.

"I need a coat," said Victor. "I'll freeze out here."

The guards laughed as they threw Victor into the back of a truck. He could barely stand the pain. Victor reeled at the bodies stacked on the floor, already stripped of shoes and useable clothing. Their skin was uniformly gray, the limbs hard like sticks.

Victor retched, but nothing came out. These were the dead collected from the shacks. They were the bodies of the poor souls who had not survived the night. Two prisoners sat near the front, where some heat from the cab drizzled through. Victor recognized them. They looked like shells of men. They avoided his gaze.

This is it, thought Victor. *They're taking me to die.* Had he wasted his life writing those pamphlets and making those plans? All of it may have come to nothing, but they had interrogated him for specific information. His work had mattered. His life had mattered. The people he had left behind had used his ideas to accomplish something. They had built an organization. If Ludmelia or Matas were alive, and knew what he had done, they would be proud. There was always a chance they knew, even though he had kept secrets to keep them safe. Even if no one knew it was he, Victor Kudirka, who had planted the seeds for the Brothers of the Forest, it was all right. He wouldn't have wanted anyone to be hurt for knowing.

The truck screeched to a halt. Victor fell against a stiff body with eyes frozen in an expression of awe. *Hektoras!* Victor yelped, and pushed away from the body. He didn't want Hektoras to die, not really. He regretted ever thinking of vengeance. They had been friends, but friendship meant little here. Victor knew that now, and it had been a brutal lesson to learn. Perhaps the poor bastard dreamed he was with his son and his wife at the very end. Maybe Hektoras had escaped in those last moments for a place of peace, and Victor envied him. Victor tried to close Hektoras's eyelids, but they wouldn't move, so he sat next to his dead friend and stared up at stars he would never see again.

The guards opened the tailgate and pulled Victor from the truck. They dragged him to a tree near a gaping hole in the earth where thousands of bodies already lay in everlasting rest.

"At least give me one last cigarette," said Victor.

The guard, a man Victor had never seen before, pulled one out of the packet in his pocket, lit it, and gave it to Victor. He stayed with Victor as he smoked. When the cigarette was gone, the guard helped Victor lean against a tree before stepping away to join the other guards.

As Victor slid down the bark, distinct images stepped out from the collage of his life. Victor pictured his wife, Aldona, her soft arms embracing him. He pictured Matas, standing straight and tall, eager to be like his father. He pictured Ludmelia, her amber hair, her smile, her laugh, and he could feel her strength seep into him. He thought back to the camping trips with his children, teaching them the mysteries of the forest. He thought of the nights they had spent sleeping near a campfire under the stars, and the banter. He pictured the stunning green trees, and breathing air so crisp he could feel it in his toes. He thought of his love for his precious country. He pictured Simas and Dana, and old Mr. and Mrs. Ravas who had opened their hearts to him and his family. He pictured the university classrooms and the fresh faces of the students that had greeted him every year in their quest for a bright future. He closed his eyes and filled his lungs again. He pictured his friends drinking tea in the dining hall as they talked about politics, world events, and their country's future. He was a lucky man to have such memories.

The guards raised their automatics. As gunfire cut the air, Victor proclaimed his heritage one last time. "As Lietuvis!"

CHAPTER 21

Ludmelia spent the day gazing at the land beyond the iron fence. The wide swath of open area down to the road and beyond it into Poland looked smooth and clean under the snow. A long stretch of road extended in both directions. The trees standing in the distance looked welcoming. Ludmelia wondered what it would be like to taste freedom. She wondered if the dirt had a different flavor, or the air a different scent. She wondered if at night, the stars shone brighter.

People in Poland lived in relative peace from the Soviet occupiers, Tymon had claimed. The infrequent patrols, the factory work, and supplies from Moscow made it feel free. She wouldn't need a gun or a knife to defend herself. She could spend the night sleeping, instead of worrying about a Soviet raid. She could speak openly with strangers and not fear repercussions. Going to school, finding a husband, and having a child seemed possible beyond the fence. At home, those things were just a dream.

She ached for Papa's guidance, telling her it was all right to leave the fight and move to a better place. She wanted him to tell her she could walk away from the suffering and live in Poland, or even escape to the West with Julius. Given the chance, most people would. But she knew warriors didn't run. They stayed to fight the battles no one else could, and when they couldn't fight any longer, they helped their cause in other ways.

Her mission to see Julius safely out of the country was almost over. It would be done tonight. In Poland, they would rendezvous with a Lithuanian family whose son would take him to an airstrip and a plane that would fly him to France. All the risks and sacrifice to get Julius out were for a promise that by some miracle, he could bring down that barbed wire fence and allow them to join the rest of the free world. Unfortunately, she thought Julius was as likely to succeed as she was to reach the age of thirty.

Ludmelia wanted true freedom on her own soil, not the borrowed freedom from visiting another place. She wanted to raise any children she might have in her native land. Fighting was her destiny, not leaving to support Julius's dream. In a few hours, he wouldn't need her protection anymore. It was time for her to continue the struggle that so many people were abandoning. After tonight, her mission wasn't to help Julius anymore. It wasn't to patiently wait for his declaration of love. It wasn't to leave her country. It was to kill three NKVD officers from Moscow. If she didn't have help, she wouldn't survive. But she'd rather die fighting than leave her beloved land.

The others were eating from the dented food tins as Ludmelia came into camp. She smelled the scent of sweet syrup. "After we get you out tonight, I'm going back to take care of those three NKVD officers from Moscow. I'm not going into Poland."

"Aren't you going to escort me to the rendezvous?" said Julius.

"You're safer in Poland than at home. You can do the rest yourself, with the men. You don't need me."

"I need your protection."

"And I need to stay and fight. No one else is willing to do it."

Ludmelia expected Julius to argue with her. But instead, his face became red and he looked away. "Take Vadi with you, dammit. It'll be extremely dangerous with only the two of you, but you could pull it off. It'll be suicide if you try it alone."

"Vadi can stay with you. I don't know—maybe he wants to get out of the country, too."

Vadi opened his mouth to speak, but only managed the groan of a tired, lonely man as he shook his head. His eyes misted over. Ludmelia touched his hand.

"I'll keep Anton with me. I don't need the rest of you," said Julius. "I'm risking my life getting to the West, and if that's not enough for you, I don't know what is."

"You're leaving because you can't fight anymore. Or is it because you don't *want* to fight?" Ludmelia's anger surprised even her, but she knew her words were true.

"I've done as much as anyone for our cause. More than most."

"Have our lives become too hard for you to bear? Are you trading our freedom for a soft bed and plenty of food? Why are you really leaving us, Julius?"

"I'm sick of your constant badgering. Not everyone is as strong as the great Amber Wolf. When I get to the West, I'm not going to sleep outside just so I can be like you. But tell me, what have you done? A few killings? Blown up a few bridges? How has that mattered?"

"I've planned and carried out every mission assigned to me, even when others couldn't because they were too scared. You forget the fury of the Soviets in 1945. I helped hundreds of people escape deportation. Each person I saved meant that a family remained whole. Do you know what it's like, not knowing where your father is or if he's ever coming back? My men attacked the polling stations in 1946, making a public sham of the rigged Soviet elections. I got rid of collaborators and officials. Your leaving will amount to nothing. We all deserve a better life, but you're the only one who is going to get it."

"I'm sorry you feel that way, but I'm leaving anyway. And I'm going to work until I get us the assistance we need, or die trying." Julius sat down on a fallen tree trunk. It wobbled and he almost fell. "When you finish your next mission, go to Utena and find Simas. He'll be working at Pagelis's bakery. He'll tell you how to get in touch with a partner cell once things cool down."

"Simas is an old man. He's not good for much."

"We need him."

"We need you, too." Ludmelia scowled. "The most important work we can do is over there." She pointed toward the east and home. "You've risked our lives, and the lives of two Poles, to get out. Dana died for you. You must want to leave very badly to abandon us."

"Enough! You wear me out. I'm tired. Of this struggle, of the Russians, of living like an animal. I'm tired of *you*!"

Ludmelia spat in his face. She stood defiantly before him, daring him to react, but he didn't. His words were a blow, but they rang true, and truth brought clarity. Any hint of love had been a ruse to give her the strength to carry out missions too dangerous for anyone else. She felt like a fool for thinking he had feelings for her. She no longer trusted that Julius's motives were pure and for the good of them all, because by leaving, he was helping himself more than anyone. She remembered years ago when she had stopped trusting Dana, too. But he had worked to regain her support and love. Over time, he had become a warrior. Julius wasn't a warrior, at least not anymore.

"You've become a savage, Ludmelia, just like the worst of the Soviets," said Julius, wiping her saliva from his cheek.

~~

Anton had to pull his cap down over his eyes to hide his shock. *Ludmelia is Amber Wolf.* It all made sense, now. Her brazen attitude, fearlessness, cunning, and unwavering dedication to her cause meant that she was the partisan hero. How could he have missed it before? It wasn't Dana or Julius. *It's the woman! She's his prize.*

Anton got to his feet. "I want to stay with Ludmelia. I want to stay and fight."

"Go ahead, dammit," Julius hissed. "I don't need any of you."

As he settled back down, Anton wondered how she was going to assassinate those NKVD officers, for her gunshots were sure to be heard all the way to Moscow. If he killed her before she killed them, it might get him and Katya out of this mess. He just didn't know how he was going to do it.

~~

Although the sky was dark and wisps of clouds floated under the stars, the snow radiated the little bit of moonlight left, giving an unearthly glow to the area around the border. The war debris on the rise directly bordering the road was gone, but the snow recorded every boot print. Using her best instincts to determine a path, Ludmelia guided the others down to the road. While Vadi stood watch, she had the others wait as she and Anton crossed, going immediately to the fence, where they frantically cut strands of barbed wire. When the hole was barely big enough for a man to pass through, Ludmelia waved Julius across. He paused for a second and looked at her before crawling through. Tolek followed next.

"Goodbye, my beauty," said Tymon, kissing Ludmelia on the mouth.

She handed him the tin of turpentine. "Keep him safe."

Then Tymon, too, went through. Ludmelia moved the cut wire back so that the breach was less noticeable at a quick glance, although anyone looking more closely would be sure to see the damage. Vadi and Anton erased their footprints with a fir branch and they went back up the rise.

They were about halfway up when the lights of a truck shone off in the distance. A spotlight on the vehicle washed over the fence.

There was plenty of time for Ludmelia and the others to get away, but if they did, the patrol might find the cut wires and assume someone had escaped. Julius and the Poles would be in jeopardy. The three separated and waited with their bellies in the snow as the vehicle came closer.

At first, Ludmelia thought the spotlight had missed the breach. When the truck backed up, she got to her knees and opened fire. Vadi and Anton joined her. The return fire was spotty and pointless against the partisan bullets, and soon stopped altogether. When Ludmelia signaled the others to stop firing, the truck moaned, as if it had been pummeled by a giant.

Ludmelia was sure that Julius and the Polish scouts had heard the noise and would take all precautions possible. If she were with them, they might survive. Without her, she didn't know if they would, but it was too late to help them. The headlights from more trucks appeared in the distance, headed her way. She and the others had to leave. If she acted quickly, she could divert at least some of the soldiers away from Julius.

~~

Tilda cradled her mother's head as they lay on the floor of a deck crowded with people. The trawler rocked back and forth over the waves. Occasionally, spray splashed over the sides and onto the deck. People moaned at the shock of cold, but no one moved. Tilda gazed out at the dark sea, missing Sargas. Around her, mothers tried to comfort their children between dribs and drabs of sleep. Husbands sat with their arms around their wives trying to share warmth. Here and there, a man or woman looked back to the country they were leaving.

Mama's lips fluttered as she breathed. She was finally asleep. Tilda's eyes filled with tears. Already she missed Utena. She missed the places she knew in town: Mr. Pagelis's bakery, the park where she had gone on picnics with her parents, the secluded lake where Papa had taught her how to swim, school and her math teacher who had told her how talented she was and who gave her the hardest problems to solve. She missed the pride she had felt when she finished them, knowing she could solve even harder ones. She missed her friend, Ona, and their silly conversations that sometimes involved more giggling than actual words. She missed breakfasts with Mama in the warm kitchen, and her bed. How she missed her bed.

Above all, she missed Papa. She didn't think her life could go on without him, and yet here she was with Mama on a trawler out on the Baltic Sea. She prayed to God he was still alive, and that she might see him again. One day, when she was grown and rich, she would come back and force the Soviets to let him out of the country. She would bring Papa to her elegant home somewhere near the sea. They would join Mama and laugh, remembering all the good times.

Tilda wiped her eyes. Their future wouldn't be an easy one. No one in Sweden would be there to greet them. They had no friends, and no money, as all of Mama's jewelry was used to procure their travel papers. They would have to scrounge for their meals. They would be glad to work, but there might be no jobs. Even if they found a way to make money, they couldn't stay for very long. They would have to move, for the Russians might force the government to send them back. They might have to make their way to another country, and then another, always searching for a permanent home. Their future wasn't guaranteed, but once away from their homeland, they had the possibility of success. At least Tilda hoped so. As the ship rocked over the waves, she felt herself moving farther and farther away from Papa and the country of her birth, on into the black unknown.

~~

Svechin walked along the terrain bordering the mine field at Punsk. From a distance, the rolling field looked peaceful and open, except for occasional clusters of trees and low shrubs. The swath of land directly along the border had been plowed before the mines had been placed. Frozen clumps of dirt were visible through the melting snow. A lone road extended into Poland beyond the check point's pillboxes that were painted red on the Lithuanian side and black-and-white stripes on the Polish side. He was convinced that anyone trying to escape through the mine field had to be insane, but that was the nature of the people he was seeking.

He realized Anton Dubus was rarely on his mind, but this partisan called Amber Wolf consumed his thoughts. His assumption that the bandits were headed for Poland was only a guess. They could be anywhere. Success felt like an impossibility. Perhaps he should leave the army, find a job somewhere in the countryside, and marry a woman who would bear him fat babies. When he was younger, Svechin would have snickered at the image of himself as a father. Now, the thought of babies made him believe something was missing in his life. It wasn't wise to consider marrying a woman who made her living from men. But if he could take Katya away from that life, he could make her happy, provided he could get her out of Karmachov's prison alive.

Svechin had taken the precaution of alerting all border patrols to a partisan band trying to escape the country. The border supervisor at Punsk, a short man with a big moustache, had refused to believe Svechin, claiming no one would even try to get through his mine fields, let alone his guards. Svechin had to point out that escapees were partisans, likely to do as much damage in Poland as they had in Lithuania, not that it mattered to the supervisor. At one point, Svechin just wanted to shoot the man, but managed to convince him the partisan threat was genuine by offering to put an end to the supervisor's lowly career.

Svechin considered going through the border himself to see if he could pick up the partisan trail. The process of getting out was slow and tedious, though, and the supervisor wasn't inclined to expedite anything involving Svechin and his men. Once across, Svechin would have to mobilize the Polish frontier guards and begin a search. After all, they knew the area and he didn't. Besides, he had no authority in Poland. All he could do was to find the partisans and hand them over to local authorities, or kill them and be done with it. Svechin needed a stroke of genius or a miracle to find the people he was tracking. As he lit a cigarette, he hoped for both, but in the end, he decided not to bother crossing into Poland. If the partisans had escaped, they were no longer his problem, and he could safely claim he had driven them out of the country.

He and his men went to spend the night in the barracks where the border guards lived. Svechin's room was tiny, but at least he was alone and could spend some time thinking. In the middle of the night, he was woken from a restless sleep with word that there had been a breach in the wire bordering Poland in the frontier to the north.

CHAPTER 22

Katya kept Colonel Vronsky company for several nights in a row. The reprieve from Karmachov was a blessing. Vronsky didn't bother her as much, for he simply liked a lot of sex. She could live with that. Karmachov, on the other hand, got a little more nervous and a little angrier each day his superior was in Utena. She could tell from the guards, who seemed more jittery than usual. She occasionally heard Karmachov ranting at them.

The next time Katya was brought to Karmachov, it was in the afternoon. He was sitting on a chair in the bedroom, sipping a drink. Katya wasn't sure where Vronsky was or what Karmachov wanted her to do, so she sat on the side of the bed and waited.

"You're not doing a good job with Vronsky," he said.

"What?"

"I want him to be so happy he forgets why he's here. I want him to stop asking questions, reviewing my reports, checking on the condition of the soldiers. I want him to stop poking around. Make him ecstatic!"

"If he wants a drink, I get it for him. If he wants to go to bed, I go with him. What more can I do?" She had the feeling this conversation wasn't going to end well for her.

"You impudent bitch! You're alive because of *me*. You'll do as I say if you want to stay alive." He reached for the riding crop. "You're going to be here a long time, so you'd better get used to taking orders."

"But you said I'm here only until Anton finishes his work for you."

"Forget about Anton. Anton's dead," Karmachov lied. He laughed as Katya's expression turned to wide-eyed sorrow.

"Anton's dead? Is it true? Please tell me. I must know. I'll do anything."

"Of course, you will." Karmachov tossed the riding crop across the room, flung her on the bed, and quickly pulled his pants down. His explosion came quickly. As he lay back, Katya saw the look of satisfaction on his face.

Katya always thought she would have felt something when it happened. She and Anton were so close; certainly they would share that last moment of consciousness that came before death. After all, she had always known what he was thinking. She had always known when he was happy or sad. Now, she would never see him again. She'd never hear his voice.

Karmachov had her three times that afternoon. She held back her tears so he wouldn't know how deeply his words had cut. It was the hardest thing she had ever done.

Later, her cell, Katya cried as she prayed to God to take her, too. She didn't want to believe Anton was gone, but it had to be true. No one would be so cruel as to lie about something like that.

The way Karmachov was using her made her angry, but Anton's death made her want to use the knife she had stolen on herself. She knew now she'd never leave this cell. She wasn't here to make Anton do a job. She was here because that's what Karmachov wanted. Svechin had brought her here and had done nothing to help her. He hadn't protected Anton enough to keep him alive. Svechin had broken his *promise*.

For the first time in her life, she didn't even want to breathe. She had come close to this once before, but Anton had been there to help her through. It was during her last days with Erni. Unfortunately, as Erni got even older, his rants came more often and sometimes even without the help of liquor, just like Karmachov. Erni's lies became more extravagant. Often, he didn't know the day of the week. He forgot the name of his horses. One day, he told Katya he attacked a man he had found in the stables. It had been Anton, but Erni hadn't recognized him.

Despite her husband's senility, Katya became pregnant. Erni was the father, although she could hardly believe it. A man of Erni's age couldn't possibly sire a child. Furthermore, after her previous entanglements, she was sure she couldn't have children. But in three months, there was no doubt. Erni was going to be a father again. Katya found herself humming, glad to cement her place in the family, secure Anton's future, and have a little one to love, as her mother had loved her. The difference would be that Katya would never leave her child, no matter what happened.

When Katya told Erni the news of his impending fatherhood, the expression of pride on his face told Katya he was pleased.

"You make me feel young again. Like a stallion," said Erni.

Katya looked out the bedroom window as she buttoned her skirt.

"The men in town envy me for having such a young wife. Now, they'll envy me even more for being a father again at my age." Erni grinned. He was missing two teeth on the left side of his mouth. They had fallen out last year, when he was chewing on a ham bone.

Katya held no illusions about love. Erni wanted her because she made him feel like he could live forever. In return, Katya enjoyed the many comforts that Count Belzik's money could buy, and in mere months, she would have a baby to love.

Katya had told Anton the news when they were sitting on the step enjoying the last cup of tea for the day, and watching the stars.

"Now there are three of us to feed," said Anton.

"Erni will take care of us. There's nothing to worry about."

"And what do we do when that changes?"

"It's not going to change." Tears stung Katya's eyes. "I did all this for you, so you wouldn't have to worry anymore. Stop being angry all the time. Things will be fine. Just wait and see."

A few weeks later, Katya awoke with terrible stomach pains. At first, she thought it was something she had eaten, but no one else in the family was ill. Her urine turned red and she knew it was over. When she had told Erni that the child was gone, he slapped her face. "What did you do to my son?"

"Nothing. It just happened. There was nothing I could do to stop it."

"My friends will laugh at me and say I was lying about becoming a father." He slapped her again. She smelled liquor on his breath. "You killed my son!"

"It just happened, Erni. I didn't do anything. Why would I want to hurt my own child?" she cried.

"I can't stand to look at you."

"Please!" Katya fell to her knees and wrapped her arms around his legs.

"I can't stand to look at you."

"Don't send us away! Where will we go? What will we do?" Katya sobbed into his trousers.

Erni left the room. Katya heard him yelling at Leon, instructing him to make sure she was out of the house as quickly as possible. Later that day, she and Anton packed their things. Leon stole into their rooms and handed Anton an envelope full of money.

"I'm sorry. You know how he gets. Good luck to you both." Leon left quickly, leaving the door ajar.

Anton and Katya left for Minsk later that day, hoping a better future would find them there.

~~

Just over the border to Poland, Julius and the Polish scouts broke into a run at the sound of machine-gun fire. They weren't being fired upon, but it was too close to ignore. Desperate to find a place to hide, they entered a village, where their steps mingled with a hundred others. They passed right through. Instead of stopping in a place the Russians were sure to search, they opted for the cover of the woods. They ran through land that had fewer scars from the fighting, and no trenches to cross. They paused briefly in the forest to catch their breath before moving on. Traversing the forest at night was slow, but the telltale green of Soviet-made tracers lit up the sky, and the men went faster. Before dawn, they were at another village that looked strangely familiar, almost like the villages at home. Here, the terrain seemed natural and held no signs of the war. Vegetation was plentiful in the healthy trees and shrubs. Groupings of carved crosses marked the road intersection, as was common in Lithuania before they had been destroyed. The houses were neat. Some doors were even decorated with homemade wreaths of pine needles and berries. One barn door held the carving of a steed.

Tymon had to go to three different farmhouses before anyone answered his knock. Finally, a man in a nightshirt opened the door. Tymon asked to rent a sleigh and horse. They argued for several minutes, finally settling on a high price. The man insisted that his son, a lad of twelve, go with them to ensure the horse and sleigh returned to its owner.

The boy wasn't happy to be rousted from his warm bed. Julius and Tymon hid in the back of the sleigh, while Tolek sat with the driver. He had the boy whip the horse into a gallop.

With many kilometers behind them, they slowed. In over an hour, they were close enough to their destination to make the rest of the journey on foot. As the men climbed down from the back, Tolek instructed the boy to continue to the next village before turning the horse homeward.

Tymon led them to a house, where they were welcomed. Even though they were in Poland, the family, Mr. and Mrs. Stelmokas and their son Leonas, spoke Lithuanian as did many of the families in the area. Mrs. Stelmokas brought Julius, Tymon, and Tyvek bowls of soup and thick slices of bread. As the men ate, she had Julius remove his shirt, and stitched up a rip in it.

"How can it be that it's more peaceful here than at home?" asked Julius.

"The Nazis ruined Poland. They destroyed my beloved Warsaw." Mr. Stelmokas blew his nose and wiped his eyes. "After the war ended, we had two years of civil war. No, we don't like the Soviets, and we don't like communism, but we have to rebuild. Moscow is helping us. Already we have factories and jobs. People are putting their lives back together. While we have our own leader, it helps that he's nothing but a diluted version of Stalin. All of this makes the Soviet burden lighter to bear."

"It seems that the Soviets continue to take their fury out on Lithuania, though."

"You are like bees stinging the bear's ass. How can you expect it not to become angry? You refuse to lie down and die, which is what they want. During the war, the Soviets won battles through sheer numbers of men. Stalin's army is the biggest the world has ever seen. How can tiny countries like Lithuania and Poland hope to do damage against such an army?"

"That's why we need help from the West."

"People are leaving your cause, aren't they?" Mr. Stelmokas stared into Julius's eyes. "Can you blame them?"

"If we joined together, we would both be stronger. It would make a difference."

"A lofty goal, but we can't. We're too weak from the fighting. The Nazis left us with nothing. We have to gain our strength again and that may take years, even decades."

"But we'd be much stronger together. The Russians would fear us. It's the only way we can win."

"Others have tried to bond our two countries together in agreements, but there is violent history between us. Besides, what can you and I do? We're just men." Mr. Stelmokas put a hand on Julius's shoulder. "My son, you're going to have to get used to people telling you they're not going to help, for one reason or another."

Julius put on his mended clothing. "It's time for us to go. Leonas, I'm in your hands." He said goodbye to Mr. and Mrs. Stelmokas, embraced Tymon and Tolek in farewell, and followed Leonas out the door.

~~

Svechin and his men sped north toward the frontier. All he knew was that there was a breach in the fence, and a patrol had been ambushed from the Lithuanian side. Four men dead. Guards were pursuing bandits on both sides of the border. Svechin bet that he would find Anton on the Lithuanian side, with at least one guide, for Anton would never abandon his sister. Anton would sacrifice his personal freedom for his family. When Svechin was younger, he would never have sacrificed anything for a woman. Now he wasn't so sure. Before he met Katya, he had never imagined that a woman who made her living from men could ever interest him.

Svechin assumed the partisans had escorted someone to the border and had gotten them out before heading back to their forests, or someone had escaped from Poland to join the partisans. What other explanation could there be for a breach in the fence and partisans headed eastward? If Anton was among the group who had killed the soldiers in the patrol, it meant he was playing the deadly game of helping the partisans, instead of focusing on his mission to destroy them. Other officers thought their men were expendable, but Svechin didn't. After all this trouble, if he found out that Anton was aiding the bandits in any way, Svechin would introduce his friend to God, with the help of a Russian bullet.

~~

Vadi ran for the sanctuary of the trees while Anton and Ludmelia fled in the opposite direction, toward bushes and a network of trenches. She ran from a hail of bullets as she pulled Anton alongside her, jumping down into a trench. They crashed through ice into freezing water, but she didn't have time to care. She fired on the Russians as tracers lit up the sky. As she switched guns, Ludmelia heard more firing directed toward the Soviets from a location in the trees to the left. It must be Vadi providing cover. She said a quick prayer, climbed out of the trench and raced for the relative safety of the trees. Anton scrambled after her.

Ludmelia motioned Vadi to follow them as he fired another long burst into the Russians. She passed through a cluster of elms into an area where the trees had been all but destroyed. Jagged trunks looked like broken soldiers. Snow-covered branches covered the ground. She ran along a twisted path through the dead foliage. She glanced back. Anton was still there, but Vadi was nowhere in sight. The sound of explosions gradually became more distant as they ran in the direction of a village holding an old barracks for Russian soldiers that she had visited years before, while seeing her friend, Danute, who lived in the area.

After crossing a vile expanse of thorns growing up among rusting wire that tore their trousers and scratched their legs, they came upon a stream. Ludmelia and Anton splashed in. A shock of cold ran through her body. Her feet were numb within seconds. Anton took her hand as they stumbled across. They ran to a meadow, where they stopped for a short rest. Sitting next to her, Anton couldn't seem to stop shivering.

"Are you all right?" asked Ludmelia.

Anton shrugged but managed a smile. Without her, he would surely be dead by now. Ludmelia was saving his life. "Thank—"

More machine-gun fire, closer this time. "Let's go," said Ludmelia.

Her gun and knapsack bounced against her back as she went as quickly as possible. Shortly, her tired legs were guided more by will than energy. Anton lagged behind.

"Hurry up," said Ludmelia.

In a little while, Ludmelia let Anton rest while she lay a false trail to the village and barracks. She did the best she could in the dark, although she was sure a good tracker could still follow them. Ludmelia hoped the Russians weren't so careful or observant. She would have liked her trail to be longer and more elaborate, but it was better than nothing. It might at least delay their pursuers for a while.

Anton looked better when she returned. Acting more on instinct than good sense, he drew her close and kissed her. "I didn't want to die without kissing you at least once."

Maybe she was so tired and angry that she didn't know what she was doing, but Ludmelia kissed him back. The touch of his lips made her heart race. His breath gave her strength. She allowed herself to feel joy. She wanted to stay in the moment, but knew they had to leave. She broke their embrace, and headed away from the barracks.

As the sun came up, they came to a village of burnt houses. Cottage after cottage had been either ruined or damaged. Most barns were gone; occasionally, one stood undisturbed. A silence of isolation permeated the area.

Ludmelia led them to a dwelling next to a barn that was mostly intact. Her old friend Danute stood in the doorway of a house that looked like it had been damaged, but it was still standing. There was a roof. The door was a ragged yellow. Danute wore a skirt, a man's shirt, and a stained apron. Her brown hair was piled up on top of her head. A scar ran from her left ear to her throat. She smiled as she came out to greet them. "Have you seen Lena?" she asked.

"Yes, just the other day. She's concerned about her health," said Ludmelia.

Danute rushed them inside. Ludmelia had met the woman years ago, when the partisan work was just beginning. Danute had helped with missions in Vilkija before marrying. A pregnancy had prevented her from working alongside the partisans in their camps, so she and her husband had moved to this area near the border, where they had a farm. During the war, Danute and her husband had survived by escaping to the woods whenever they had the slightest inkling that the Soviets might be close. Once, he wasn't quick enough, and the Soviets shot him as he ran to the trees. After the war, she had stayed, and the location of the farm proved to be a valuable asset to anyone trying to get out of the country.

Danute brought them into a barren kitchen. Every surface had been scrubbed clean. The sole plate and cup on the table showed a solitude that saddened Ludmelia, for every day she was with people she trusted and who trusted her. Danute still helped the cause, even though she lived with memories and ghosts. Ludmelia wondered what nights were like in this village of ruin.

Ludmelia and Anton rubbed themselves down with rough cloths to help the circulation and warmth return to their legs and feet. After putting on dry clothing, Ludmelia immediately began cleaning and oiling her weapons. Anton sat beside her, doing the same. As he pulled apart the gun, he faltered, and the barrel fell to the table. His face was gray with exhaustion.

"Careful," said Ludmelia, smiling.

Anton wiped his forehead with a hand, and continued.

Danute heated milk and cooked some eggs.

"Russians are chasing us. They're sure to be here before too long," said Ludmelia.

"I'll be fine. They never hurt me. Whenever they come here, I give them something to eat, and they go on their way."

"You're not going to be safe here forever," said Ludmelia

Danute slouched and creased her cheek in a twitch. "The Russians think I'm a deaf half-wit, especially with this old scar. I got it years before the war, when my brother and I were playing. He was chasing me and I fell against a spade," she explained to Anton, touching the rough skin. "Besides, the Russians don't come here that often. And no one is safe anymore; here or anywhere else."

After the quick meal, Ludmelia went to the window and looked out over the broken landscape. "Come with us, Danute. At least you'll be with people."

"I won't leave my family."

"Your family is gone."

"You need someone here to keep watch and help when the need arises. A position this close to the border is valuable. The Russians know me. They don't suspect me of anything. I'm all right here."

"Danute . . ."

"My parents, my brother, and my husband are all out there under the oak tree behind the barn. My baby's there, too. This is where I belong."

"No one belongs here. Come into the forest with us, and we'll look after you. You won't be alone anymore." She touched her friend's face, and had the odd premonition she was looking into her own future.

"Go. There's no time to argue."

The women hugged. Ludmelia and Anton were outside when they heard the far-off rumble of engines. They broke into a run. As they turned toward the forest, Ludmelia glanced at Anton, grateful she wasn't alone, and glad that he knew how to shoot. But he looked exhausted. She wasn't sure they'd both get away.

CHAPTER 23

Svechin and his men joined up with the guards who were pursuing partisans on the Lithuanian side of the border. The entourage included a tracking dog, a Laika crossbreed named Rimsky that had been trained at the Red Star Kennel in Moscow. The trail they followed was complex, but the group was expert in tracking, and the signs they found led them to a little cottage in a burned-out village.

Svechin came through the door as Danute was stacking the clean plates in the cupboard. His men followed. Two spoons remained on the table as evidence of her recent guests. Her face twitched. She lay a rag over the spoons, not sure if her new visitors had noticed them.

Svechin walked through the room to the bed. A few items of clothing hung on hangers dangling from a rope stretched wall to wall. Svechin moved them aside. Two pairs of trousers were wet. He stamped on the floor and listened for the hollow sound that indicated a hiding place. He even looked under the bed.

"Are they still here?" Svechin said.

Danute raised her hands as if confused.

He grabbed her wrists and shouted. "Do you think I'm stupid? Where are they?"

She looked at him fearfully.

"How many?"

Svechin let go of her and went to the door. "Try and make her talk. If she doesn't want to, shut her up for good."

Two soldiers crossed the floor as Danute let out a blood-curdling scream. It was the last sound she made.

Outside, Svechin stopped and listened. Nothing. Two sets of footprints led through the rubble into a barn with a sagging roof, open doors, and a partially missing side wall.

He had his man check inside. The soldier thrust a pitchfork into a stack of hay. Svechin stopped him. "Don't bother. They're not here."

"Shall I burn it, sir?"

"No. They know we're chasing them, but they don't necessarily know how close we are. Let's keep it that way."

Svechin and the trackers turned toward the woods. On a whim, he knelt beside Rimsky and let the animal sniff the handkerchief Anton had left in Karmachov's office after the interrogation just a few weeks ago. Svechin had kept the cloth, thinking that it might be useful one day. He had been right. After sniffing Anton's blood and sweat, Rimsky barked and strained against his leash.

~~

Ludmelia could hear barking as she reached into her knapsack for the tin of turpentine, then remembered she had given it to Tymon. She did the only thing she could do—go back to the stream. They ran as fast as they could, dodging mounds covered in snow. Barbed wire pulled at Ludmelia's trousers, ripping the cloth and cutting her skin. She didn't even break her stride. There wasn't time.

At the stream, she and Anton splashed in with their boots on. The first step into the freezing water was a shock, just like before. The second step was painful, and the third numbing. She struggled along, finally going deep enough to let the current move her. Anton was alongside her. With all the hardware strapped to her back, Ludmelia had to pull hard with her arms to keep her head above water. She was so cold even her mind was dazed.

She pulled against the water with arms she couldn't feel. The current moved her along quickly. She was so cold she could barely breathe. She couldn't see Anton anymore, and if he needed her, she didn't know if she could save him, let alone herself.

At a curve, the current pulled her under. Death by drowning had never even occurred to her, as she was sure a bullet would end her life. She flailed. Her arms felt heavy and cold, like spent mortar shells. She tried not to panic. There was no air. Her lungs burned. She squinted into to the swirl. It was beautiful, and the bubbles were playful. She felt an instant of peace, and was glad to be conscious during her last moment. She thought of Dana, Vadi, and all her friends. She remembered Mama, and Matas. She felt that Papa was close. She kicked and clawed her way up toward the sky, toward Papa.

Her head broke free and she gulped air. She kicked, saw Anton, and caught him as he went under. Grabbing onto his collar with fingers that could barely move, she half-swam, half-dragged him to shallow water.

~~

Rimsky led the Russians toward the stream. They tripped and fell in the dark, swearing. The dog skidded over an ice-covered trench. Svechin and the men inched across as they listened to the ice crack. The last one to cross, Svechin's driver, panicked and ran. He fell through. The men managed to get to him, dragging him to safety. Already he was blue and shaking.

Svechin was angry, cold, hungry, and disgusted as they made camp in the wild. They built a fire, but it did little to calm Svechin's nerves. If his enemy was out there, he couldn't see them through the trees. He wouldn't put it past these people to hunt him as he was hunting them. After eating, he ordered the men to stand guard in shifts, and he sat with his back against a log, watching the fire with Rimsky, as his driver hugged a blanket and waited for his clothes to dry.

Svechin was glad that it was Anton's scent the dog had identified. At least he was alive, and with someone who probably knew their way through the woods. Svechin felt it in his bones that he was getting close.

~~

All Katya did was to pace in her cell, crying because Anton was dead. Occasionally, she stopped to curse Svechin and Karmachov before going back to her tears. The sour smell from her waste bucket permeated the room, but she barely noticed. She hadn't seen Karmachov in a few days, and it was for the best. She couldn't stand that fat pig anymore. His vile nature made her sick. It felt like she had no hope and no control, just like during those years after Erni had told her to get out of the house. She and Anton had been alone again, without a home or family to go to, and it had been terrible. They decided to leave the country and its bad memories, so they moved to Minsk. There, she convinced Anton to enter the army. It was the only solution she could think of that allowed him a chance to work for his future, and be away from her so she could support herself.

After Anton left, Katya took whatever comfort she could from the money she made on her back. When she wasn't thinking about Erni and his strangeness, or the baby she had lost, she thought of Anton. At least he wasn't alone, and the chances of his finding people who would help him were good. That was when Svechin had come into their lives.

During the war, she rarely saw Anton, yet she wrote him faithfully in her childlike script; Grandmother hadn't believed that women needed much of an education. Hope of a bright future for Anton was what she clung to as men grunted their satisfaction into her neck. She wondered if somewhere in the vastness of Mother Russia, Mama was doing the same thing. Alone in the cell, the memory of all the men who had abused and used her twisted into a tempest named Karmachov.

Katya took the knife from its hiding place at the window and lovingly ran her finger along the blade. It had a film from fruit and cheese that had become moldy and dry. She brought it to the pail that held her waste and dipped it into the filth. She held it up to dry, and watched the brown harden on the blade.

She didn't think about she was going to do. She just went through the motions that seemed right, even instinctual. She tucked the knife into her underclothes, not worried that it might cut into her skin and fester. A little blood would only prove to her that she was still alive. Katya went back to the cot and waited. She would wait forever if she had to.

Late that day, a guard came in. "He wants you."

Katya climbed the stairs with the determination of a woman about to meet her destiny. With each step, she unfastened a button on her blouse. At the top of the stairs, she let it fall from her shoulders. The guard stared at her naked breasts as he opened the door for her.

Karmachov sat at his desk. "I see you missed me." He took out his pistol and locked it in a drawer in another of his foreplay rituals. He seemed unusually relaxed, even happy. "You only have me to worry about, now. Vronsky's gone, thank God. He said he had a wonderful time. Can you believe it?"

She walked past him into the bedroom. She took off the rest of her clothes quickly, letting them drop to the floor. She hid the knife under the edge of the mattress. Karmachov caught her bent over next to the bed and she thought her plan had been foiled, that he had seen the knife. She froze. He was on her in a minute, excited and ready. Men were always excited by her body. This wretched beast was no different from anyone else. And yet, he *was* different. He had controlled Anton's well-being, and now Anton was gone.

This overgrown animal had tried to further his career at the expense of her beloved brother. She'd had to endure much hardship throughout her life, but this was too much. Finally, his rhythm against her stopped. He squeezed out a grunt, exited her, and fell onto the bed.

"Take my boots off," he said.

Katya pulled one off, and then the other. His feet smelled like a dead horse.

"Undress me," he said. "I like to watch your breasts when you move."

He sat up and Katya peeled off his jacket. She unbuckled his pants and pulled them down. She took her time draping them over the chair. She glanced at his face. His eyes drifted shut, enhancing the look of fulfillment on his face.

When Katya came back for his shirt, he clutched her arms and shifted her position so that she was sitting on top of him.

"You're the best whore I've ever known, Katya." He closed his eyes again and sighed as he became hard against her. "Do what you do best."

She leaned forward, and snuggled his neck as she reached under the mattress for the knife. She lifted her hips just enough, and as she came down around him, he moaned. She felt it in her groin.

She thrust the knife into his chest, guessing at the location of his heart. All her anger and grief faded away. She was in control, and it felt good. She bared her teeth as Karmachov's eyes popped open in an expression of shock. Blood flowed onto the sheets. She twisted the knife, making sure all its filth stayed inside him. He grabbed her neck and squeezed. She just smiled, not resisting, not particularly caring what he did next.

"Guard!" he called. His voice was low and weak.

He managed to lift her by the neck until she was off him. She was amazed that his erection was still intact. She couldn't breathe. It didn't matter. She heard commotion at the door. Then came a sharp blow to the back of her head, and she fell into unconsciousness.

CHAPTER 24

Ludmelia and Anton had stayed in the stream beyond what her senses told her they could withstand. When they finally came out, she simply didn't know if they were far enough along that the dogs and men wouldn't find them. She and Anton staggered to the shore. He fell to his knees. She helped him up. Even though they were on dry land, she had to look down at her feet constantly as she walked, because she couldn't feel them. She stumbled. Anton took her arm. At the next step, she fell heavily against a tree, and Anton sank to the ground. She didn't even feel bruises she knew she had, she was so numb. She helped Anton to his feet, and faltered along. She kept going, as it was vital to find a place to dry off and warm up.

Anton kept up with her at first, but fell behind. "Is that you, Katya?" His speech slurred.

"Quiet," whispered Ludmelia.

Anton opened his jacket, stumbling off into the woods like a man possessed by the devil.

"Damn," murmured Ludmelia. She followed him, and found him face down in the snow. He would be impossible to carry, so as she shivered, Ludmelia gathered anything she could to form a nest. She wanted to make a fire, but if the Russians were near, they were sure to smell the smoke.

She rolled Anton onto a bed of pine needles and twigs from a fir tree. She rubbed his chest and struggled to get him out of his wet jacket. She wanted to curl up in the snow and go to sleep next to him, but forced herself to try and save him.

Ludmelia sensed someone was there before she could see or hear anything. She went for her gun, but her hand was so cold, she could barely grasp it. *This is it*, she thought as she clawed to free the pistol from her belt.

"Ludmelia," whispered a voice.

Vadi.

He took off his coat, draping it over her. Then he lifted Anton over his shoulder, and went into the trees. Ludmelia followed in his steps, half numb, barely aware. Soon they came to a dilapidated shack.

Vadi kicked the door open and walked right in.

A woman in a patched skirt and a man's sweater picked up a piece of wood from the bin and held it over her head, poised to strike. "What do you want?"

"We need you to help us. If you don't, we'll help ourselves," said Vadi.

"What if they find you here?"

"Hope that they don't."

Ludmelia went inside, closed the door, and collapsed to the floor. She felt herself being lifted and her clothes taken from her body. She sank into a bed. Someone rubbed her legs and feet. Her hands ached. The last thing she remembered was the smell of shit. Then everything went dark.

The next time Ludmelia opened her eyes, it was dawn. She was in a bed covered with rags, but she was warm. It felt so good, she thought she had died. Anton was in another bed. She watched his chest until it moved, and breathed a sigh of relief.

She was in a shack with a dirt floor. A fence made of tree branches isolated a corner of the room, where a horse stood on straw covering the floor. A coop held a few chickens clucking for their breakfast. She couldn't tell whether people were living in a barn or animals were living in a house.

Vadi sat in a chair next to a fire. His semiautomatic lay across his lap. An old couple, man and woman, hugged each other as they sat on a bench along the far wall. When Vadi noticed Ludmelia sitting up in bed, he smiled.

"Get us some food," said Vadi. The old woman reluctantly stood and went to the chicken coop. The birds clucked as she reached under them for the eggs. Vadi came over and sat on the side of the bed.

"How?" asked Ludmelia.

"I drew the guards off, giving you and Anton a better chance to get away."

Ludmelia clasped his hand. "We went to see Danute. I asked her to come with us, but she refused."

"I went there, too, but she was already dead. They killed her."

Another one gone, thought Ludmelia.

"I couldn't bury her. I didn't even say a few words. To be left like that lying in your own blood is a horrible thing. I'd want someone to take care of me in death, but there was no time. I didn't even cover her. I thought the Russians might double back. I drank her milk and ate her bread, but didn't say the Lord's Prayer for her soul in heaven." Vadi wiped his eyes.

"How did you find us?"

"There were five Russians and a tracking dog, so I followed them. When they went to a stream, I knew you'd used it to get away. I guessed how far downstream you'd be, and managed to find you while the Russians made camp. I guarantee it was farther along than the Russians would think possible, although this group seemed to know what they were doing. It was good you could still walk. I found this place the last time I visited Danute, and got you here as fast as I could."

He lowered his voice so the others couldn't hear. He gestured at the old couple. "They think I'll kill them if they don't cooperate, but I wouldn't. They're just old, poor, and very scared."

"Eggs are ready," said the old woman.

"The Russians will be on our trail today. I'd like to let you and Anton rest, but we need to get out of here. There's a road not too far away. We'll have to be careful, but it'll be easier than going through the forest."

~~

Anton lay in the dirty bed, his eyes open a crack, listening to Vadi and Ludmelia. He felt much better than last night. Most of all, he wasn't cold anymore. He needed days more of rest, but that wasn't possible. With some food and dry clothing, he'd be all right for a little while.

Anton had no doubt Ludmelia and Vadi would kill him if they found him out, but they had saved him. Vadi had helped them get away from the soldiers. Then he had found them wet and freezing in the dark and brought them to this place. Ludmelia had refused to let him drown in the stream. These were brave people risking their lives for their country and their friends. Russian bullets weren't going to change their determination. They were never going to give up. They might be killed, but they would never be truly defeated. He might be able to destroy this group, but if others had the same determination as Vadi and Ludmelia, they weren't going to fail, even if it took the lives of their children and their children's children.

He had thought Ludmelia heartless and barbaric for destroying his picture of Katya, but she had compassion, and was afraid of nothing and of no one. Everything she did was with a cool air of deliberation. For men to live like dogs was one thing, but for a woman, it was remarkable. She had forsaken everything to fight for her ideals. He had never known anyone like her.

Days ago, Anton had thought he'd become Ludmelia's master with a kiss. Instead, in the second she had kissed him back, her world threatened to become his. He saw the two of them making love with an intensity he had never known. But it had to remain a fantasy. He couldn't even dream about living under Ludmelia's spell. Having seen how critical she was to partisan missions, he could deal a blow to their organization by killing her when the opportunity arose. It would be hard, because he no longer wished to hurt her. But he had to for Katya's sake.

He couldn't let himself fall into Ludmelia's eyes, for he might never find his way out.

~~

At first light, Svechin and the others followed the stream's banks to pick up Anton's scent. An hour later, Rimsky finally started barking. They followed him through more of the horrendous terrain and found tracks: two sets of boot prints. Farther along, they found a pile of fir branches formed into a nest that someone might have slept in. More tracks led to the scent of wood burning, the curl of smoke from a chimney, and a pauper's shack.

The Russians went in without bothering to knock. An old woman was lifting dirty straw into a bucket with a pitchfork. She froze at the sight of the soldiers. Rimsky ran to the bed and barked.

"Who was here last night?" said Svechin.

The woman hunched her shoulders and shrank back, but she didn't put down the pitchfork.

"Talk!" said Svechin.

The woman looked confused.

"You don't speak Russian, do you? Well I don't speak Lithuanian, so there we are."

"I speak a little."

Rimsky pawed the side of the bed.

"How many were there?"

The woman held up three fingers.

"Was one of them a woman?"

The peasant looked down, slowly nodding her head.

"What color was her hair?"

"Like amber."

Svechin's instincts told him that his nemesis, Amber Wolf, was the woman. She had been on the road near the Zenonas farm; he recalled the lock of amber hair that stuck out from her kerchief. Her companion had been found dead, and it was probably her shallow boot print he found in the snow nearby. He remembered the reports from the village interrogations of a woman seen traveling with a small group of men. A woman with amber hair had been in this hovel just last night. He had been on the right trail all along, and was so close to capturing her, he could smell victory.

It was unlikely the old woman could tell him anything more. The bandits wouldn't have discussed their plans in front of her. They would have been secretive and sly as they always were.

"Shall we burn it, sir?" asked a soldier.

Svechin looked around the pitiful room. Burning would improve it as it would make the stench more bearable. "Let's go. If they're still in the area, I don't want them to see the smoke."

If he missed capturing Amber Wolf this time, it would mean either a bullet to his head or spending his retirement in Siberia. He had to pick up the trail again, and fast. He had no choice.

Rimsky led Svechin and the men to the only road in the area. The dog's mouth remained closed and his tail was set, indicating he was keen on the scent. Rimsky walked for several kilometers without wavering into the weeds and trees. Svechin's hands began to sweat. He could sense they were getting close. No one spoke. Rimsky didn't bark, just walked at a quick pace, the others following.

An engine sounded in the distance. Svechin couldn't tell how far away. A jeep appeared along the road before too long. *Damn.* The partisans were sure to hear it too, and would take extra precautions to stay out of sight. The jeep stopped, and the soldier inside asked for Lieutenant Svechin, reporting that Karmachov was dead.

"Are you sure?" Svechin chided himself for asking such a stupid question, but he couldn't help his disbelief, thinking the news was too good to be true.

The soldier reported that the commander had been stabbed to death. Svechin turned away so the men wouldn't see his face. With Karmachov gone, he had no one threatening him with long trips to Siberia. Further, Svechin would assume temporary command. He didn't have to continue trekking through fields looking for bodies, or harassing old women for bits of information.

He gazed down the road. Part of him would miss the quest for the bandits, as they had challenged him like no one before. He would have liked to find the partisan woman and know whether she was really Amber Wolf. He imagined even liking her, for she was deadly, cunning, and unique. Even so, he would have had to kill her, eventually. For now, she would remain free, another wild creature in the woods. Svechin scratched behind Rimsky's ears, got into the jeep with the soldier who had delivered the message, and ordered everyone else to continue hunting for the bandits.

During the ride back to Utena, Svechin's relief was palpable. He wanted to celebrate with vodka, a good cigar, and Katya. The first thing he would do is get her out of that damn prison. If he could convince her to stay, they might find a way to be together. It struck him that Amber Wolf was like Katya: both were extraordinary women. While he regretted giving up the hunt, he was also relieved, because he wasn't sure he would have found her. She had eluded them for years. He was hopeful that his men, Rimsky, and the expert tracker would find her, but wasn't sure they would.

~~

Back at headquarters, Svechin got a quick update from one of the soldiers and went right to Katya's room. She already looked half dead. He sat next to her on the bed. "The men know what you did. By now, everyone in Moscow probably knows what you did. Why? I could have let you go. Now I have to make you answer for your actions."

"Get away from me." A tear trickled down her cheek.

"All I can do is make it quick for you. They told me Karmachov had died in pain. He was weak from losing so much blood, and the infection festered. You won't suffer though; I'll see to it."

"I don't care what you do to me. Anton's dead. Get the hell out of here."

"Anton's still alive."

"Karmachov told me he was dead days ago. How do I know you're telling me the truth? You've lied to me before. The two of you are just the same. I hope you burn in hell."

"A tracking dog picked up Anton's scent. You killed Karmachov because you thought Anton was dead? You killed him for nothing."

Katya gazed at him with a look of contempt in her eyes. "Karmachov deserved to die. You lied to get me here. You're lying to me now. You said nothing would happen to Anton, and now he's gone."

"I think he's alive."

"Did you see him? Are you sure?" Katya's expression softened. She looked even hopeful.

"No."

"He's dead. I know it. I can feel it."

There was no point in arguing any more. "I'll stay with you when it happens."

"Don't bother. Two people I'm glad I'll never see again are you and that wretch."

"I'm sorry."

"Get out!"

Svechin stood, looking down at Katya. He wanted her to forgive him for what he had done and what he was about to do. He wanted her to know that the few hours they had spent together had been among the sweetest he had ever known. He wanted her to say that in another life, she might have loved him; but none of that was to be, for sometimes our hearts take us where we shouldn't go.

The next morning, four guards unceremoniously shot Katya behind headquarters. Svechin gave the order himself. As difficult as it was to say the word that ended her life, he couldn't bear delegating it to someone else. He winced at the gunfire, and turned away as she collapsed to the ground. He told himself that at least she was at peace, but that, too, was a lie. All she was, was dead.

CHAPTER 25

It was market day in Birzai. A town in northern Lithuania close to the border with Latvia, Birzai's redeeming qualities were a ruined castle, the oldest artificial lake in the world that peasants had dug with the aid of hand shovels and horses, and good homemade beer. More produce was out on the tables than usual, although far less than during the years before the war. Soviet sympathizers intent on impressing the important guests, three NKVD officers from Moscow, had rarer items out; jams, jellies, and sausages. A man with one leg even had a tray of sweet cakes for sale. People carried in modest amounts of beets, carrots, and other vegetables, placing them on tables or in small bins. A woman wearing a flowered kerchief ladled out cabbage soup from a large pot hanging over a small wood fire, its sharp and savory scent filling the air. A skinny boy with stringy blond hair and wearing trousers patched at the knees stood next to a bowl of eggs. Voiced blurred amid the occasional whinny of a horse. Wagons were parked on the south side of the market, where small groups of men stood together talking for a moment before fanning out.

In the middle of the commotion, a grandmother in a long skirt, an old brown coat, and a wool kerchief over her head sat on a stool at one of the tables. The few jars of honey from last summer's bees were in front of her. She took one and wiped it in her apron, admiring the golden glow. Soldiers walked through the market, along with the three visiting officers, who were examining the selections on various tables.

Two additional soldiers watched from the edge of the square. Both had on the fur hats Russians liked, the ear flaps tied on top. Both men wore greatcoats. One man was very large, the other slight, his hair tucked completely into his hat. They went into the square and wandered through the stalls and tables, looking as though they wouldn't lower themselves to purchase such common wares.

As the old woman watched the NKVD officers approach, she casually took two jars of her precious honey off the table and put them in her coat pocket to save them from potential Russian thievery. She glanced at the sack by her feet and reached down to pick it up.

"I haven't had good honey in a long time," said one of the NKVD officers in perfect Russian.

The grandmother squinted at the man as if she didn't quite understand what he was saying. She leaned over the table as if to hear better while her hands, hidden from view, placed the jars of honey back into the sack.

The officer spoke louder as he examined the honey. "Do you speak Russian?"

The old woman shrugged.

He held the honey up to the sunlight. His companion, another of the three NKVD officers, joined him and grunted approval as he picked up a jar and put it directly into his pocket.

"It's almost as golden as the honey we have in Moscow. You want it to be a little bit cloudy though, just like this."

The grandmother glared at him, wondering if he was going to pay for it, or just put it in his pocket like the other Russian thief.

A young woman in a long skirt and oversized jacket walked past them and put a basket of potatoes down on the other end of the table. She smiled and nodded hello. She was pretty, but looked very tired. The skin on her hands was rough and scaled. She took out a few potatoes and piled them up in a display. She absentmindedly drew her hand over her forehead, dislodging the brown head-covering and revealing her amber-colored hair.

"It's better if you keep them all in the basket," said the old woman. *Stupid girl is going to lose all her potatoes to thieves if they're out on the table like that.*

The young woman winked at the grandmother, glanced over her shoulder, and nodded. Curious, the old woman followed her gaze to the blond Russian in the greatcoat. He was looking directly at her. He looked tired, too, and sad, as if he was about to do something he didn't want to. As he reached for the pistol in his hip holster, the young woman pulled a pistol out of the basket of potatoes and shot the two NKVD officers near the table. In the time it takes for a bee's stinger to pierce through human flesh, the jar burst and a red dot appeared on the forehead of the man examining the honey. Blood and honey spattered over the old woman.

Through the smoke, she saw the blond soldier in the greatcoat aim his pistol at the young woman. His knuckles were white and his brow creased. He looked like he was in agony. He hesitated until the young woman noticed him. When she did, he either couldn't move or chose not to. A look of surprise crossed her face as she shot hit him in the chest and brought him to the ground. The man smiled as he fell. His hat dropped to the side, revealing a crop of curly blond hair so beautiful as to be the envy of any woman.

More shots exploded as the young woman ran through the square. She fired again, dropping the last NKVD officer. In a heartbeat, a Russian soldier, the big man, was on her heels, shouting, "Stop!"

The market erupted in a confusion of machine-gun fire, shouts, and screams. Bits of vegetables flew into the air. Tables and carts overturned, some by bullets and others by people using them as shields. "Ilya!" shouted a voice. The sound of explosions was laced with cries from the frightened and the dying.

The old woman dove under the table. Two of the NKVD officers lay not a meter away. The thief faced her, his eyes wide open. His body was still. She reached out into the madness and pulled the jar of honey from his pocket. She put it in her sack and held it to her breast as she prayed to God not to see heaven today.

~~

Anton's betrayal stung like a bullet as Ludmelia fled from the square and the soldier pursuing her. It had taken all the strength she had to run after watching Anton's body crumble to the ground. She was amazed at how relieved he looked when she shot him. A bullet pinged against the brick wall of the building next to her. She ducked, and kept on running. She darted around a corner and stopped in a doorway. She knocked once. The Russian chasing her turned the corner. She glanced back at him. He was gaining on her. The door opened. Ludmelia rushed inside. She closed it, pressing her back against the wood.

A second later, a single knock sounded. She answered it.

The Russian soldier came inside.

"You all right, Vadi?" she asked.

He nodded.

"Anton was going to kill me," she hissed.

He nodded again.

"Lock it," said the gruff voice of an old man as he stepped out from the shadows.

Ludmelia did as she was told, and then took off her skirt and handed it to the man. She rolled down the legs of the trousers that had been hidden underneath. She felt around her head and mumbled, "Where's my kerchief?" She pulled out a cap from her coat, put it on and quickly tucked in her hair. Vadi took off his greatcoat and hat, revealing laborer's clothing covered with dirt. He tossed his coat into the old man's arms.

They followed the old man through a dim kitchen to a back door leading to a cross street, where a truck from the dairy processing plant waited with its engine running. The truck headed along its usual route, finally dropping Ludmelia and Vadi off at a wood not far from the brewery outside of town. The pair managed to get out of sight just as a delivery truck passed by, no doubt on the way to a local communist bar. A military truck going in the other direction forced it to stop. Ludmelia and Vadi disappeared through the trees as Russian soldiers barked orders at the driver.

The sun was already below the trees and the sky golden as Ludmelia and Vadi arrived at the small bunker in the woods. It was one of many that had been built during the war as safe places for partisans to spend the night when it had been too cold to sleep outside, or when they needed to hide from the Russians. The air in the small room smelled sweet and felt damp from the dirt. As Vadi brushed away their tracks, and replaced the camouflage that hid the entryway, Ludmelia cleared a layer of dust from the table. She pulled out food she had brought, lit an oil lamp, and settled down on the shelf lining the wall.

As Ludmelia chewed bread that was tasteless to her palate, she realized even hunger didn't bother her anymore. Nothing bothered her. Not killing, not the threat of loneliness, not even the prospect of life without love. Her best years were gone, and she had spent them killing Russians.

"Anton fooled us all. Even Julius. You're the only one who didn't trust him," said Vadi coming inside. "How could he betray us like that? How could he betray his country? He was born here. To try and kill any of us meant that he was content with the Reds destroying our culture. For that alone he deserved to die."

"I'm not going back to Utena."

"That's all right. If anyone has earned a rest, it's you. In fact, I'll stay with you, and we can go back together when you're ready. We should stay out of sight, though. After killing those three NKVD officers, the Russians will be out for blood. If we're going to stay here, we'll have to find some food." Vadi sank his teeth into a cold boiled potato.

"No. I'm never going back." Ludmelia felt a weariness like none she had known before. Her judgment had failed her. Love had failed her. She didn't trust anyone anymore; not even herself. There was nothing left of her to give.

"But you have to. Where will you go? What will we do without you?"

Ludmelia moved next to her friend. She embraced him, and he leaned against her. She felt his head rest on her shoulder, and his gentle breathing. She kissed his cheek, which was damp with tears, picked up her gun and knapsack, and left the bunker. She made her way deeper into the forest, sure that Vadi didn't understand why she was going off by herself. Maybe even she didn't know the reasons, only that she wanted to feel something other than the usual cold numbness that had become even sharper with Anton's death. She had wanted Anton to live and to love her, for she was sure at this point that no one else would. By killing him, it felt like she had killed love itself. God meant her to be alone for the rest of her life as surely as she could fire a gun.

When Anton had pointed his pistol at her, she'd had no doubt he was going to use it. He was a traitor, a spy, and a plague on the earth for selling out his country. What was he promised in return? Gold? Praise? In the instant before she shot him, she knew her instincts had been right all along, that she should never have trusted him. She promised herself she would never trust anyone again. But she had needed him for the mission, and to soothe her heart. She had used him just as much as he had used her. In the end, she had killed him without wavering, even though it caused her more pain than she thought possible.

~~

The forest helped her through those first days alone, with a cold snap that forced her to fight to stay warm, even though she didn't want to fight for anything anymore. She already felt like an old woman who had lived her life.

She chose to go to Kaunas. There, she might be able to hide by not hiding at all. She was so thin she looked frail, hardly the image of a partisan. With her hair neatly tucked in under a kerchief, and wearing a dress, she was certain to go undetected.

Ludmelia trudged along roads and cut through forests, some familiar, some unknown. Most nights she slept in barns or sheds, where she curled up in loose straw to stay warm. Once, she was so hungry and cold, she stole into a barn and drank warm milk from a cow's teat.

She didn't have to use her rifle, although a Russian patrol passed within spitting distance of her hiding place one night. Angry and forlorn, she wanted to fire on them, but her instinct to persevere won the day, and she let the Russians pass.

Coming into Kaunas, she found a pile of sticks on the side of an apple orchard and hid the gun. She told herself she'd come back for it in a day or two, but she knew she wouldn't.

Wearing filthy trousers and a tattered coat, she hid in a shed just inside the city limits and waited for dark. She sat on the dirt floor facing the door, next to two rusty hoes and a broken bucket. Her back leaned against a wall. She knew she smelled bad. She hadn't felt water against her skin in weeks. She was grimy, and could feel the dirt caked on her face. She took the hunting knife out of her boot and held it in her hand, ready to slash anyone who disturbed her. The fatigue was so overwhelming she believed she would never rise from the floor. But well after sunset, her instincts drove her up and out, onto the road, and she walked into the city of her youth. As she made her way through the streets to her old house, she acted like a wild animal, jumping at every sound, hiding at every motion. She paused at the house where the Partenkas family had lived years ago and thought of Tilda, wondering if she was all right. An unfamiliar figure moved in the window. Ludmelia hid behind a tree: squatters no doubt. She moved on.

Finally, she made her way to Mrs. Dagys's house, hoping the old woman was still alive.

Ludmelia climbed the steps and knocked. Her heart raced as she waited, not knowing who might see her and what they might do. She glanced at her childhood home next door and considered going inside. But the windows had been smashed. Papers and empty bottles littered the step. A curtain snagged on some broken glass hung outside the window. She turned away to avoid the sadness from seeing the happy memories of her youth in ruins.

She was about to leave when she heard a noise. Ludmelia almost ran away, but the door opened just a crack. The old woman showed her face and scowled. "Who are you and what do you want?"

"It's me, Ludmelia."

"Don't play games with me, young man."

Ludmelia removed her cap and her hair fell to her shoulders.

"*Dieve*," said Mrs. Dagys, making the sign of the cross. "Thank God you're alive." She pulled Ludmelia inside and closed the door. Her hug was the first human contact Ludmelia felt since she had left Vadi. The old woman felt thin and frail through a dress that hung from her shoulders.

They went into the kitchen. Mrs. Dagys set out a crust of bread, a bowl of cabbage soup, and a glass of vodka. Ludmelia ate quickly. When the food was gone, she sat up and scanned the stove, looking for more, but there was none. With a pang in her heart, she realized she must have just eaten Mrs. Dagys's supper, and the poor woman would go without food tonight.

Ludmelia drank another glass of vodka. It helped warm her as Mrs. Dagys chattered, but Ludmelia barely paid any attention. She made her excuses, and went into the bathroom to wash in the unheated water, although after the freezing stream, it didn't feel so bad. It quickly became brown. She changed the water and washed again. She had to cut out knots in her hair with scissors before she could comb it. She put on a spare nightgown Mrs. Dagys had given her. It smelled fresh and felt soft against her skin. Ludmelia crawled into a bed for the first time in ages. She tossed and turned, and finally moved the quilt to the floor. She wrapped herself in it and lay on the hard surface, where she finally fell into a restless sleep, her knife within easy grasp.

In the morning, Ludmelia unpinned Dana's brooch from her coat hem, hiding it inside the hem of the curtains in the bedroom. She put her clothes into the tub, and scrubbed them by hand. Each time she changed the water, it turned brown again. Eventually, she gave up, hanging the badly worn garments up to dry on the string over the tub. She wanted to burn them, but she might need them again, as they were all the clothes she had. She borrowed a dress from Mrs. Dagys. It had a simple flower pattern that had been washed so often it had faded to an indistinct blur of pink, blue, and yellow. It felt odd to have a skirt brushing against her legs. She had to borrow shoes and socks, too. Mrs. Dagys gave Ludmelia the last piece of jewelry she owned, and hugged her again before she left the house wearing Mr. Dagys's coat. It was too big, but it was warm. Ludmelia went to a black-market trader where she exchanged Mrs. Dagys's beautiful amber wedding ring for rubles and food. As she walked back to the house, Ludmelia felt guilty for selling the ring instead of the brooch Dana had given her, but she couldn't bear to part with it.

~~

Svechin felt old as he climbed the steps to Karmachov's office, carrying the picture of Katya and her brother under his arm. He put it down on the desk next to the battered typewriter from the file cabinet. Svechin sat down in Karmachov's oversized chair and considered what he would say in the report he was about to type.

He was relieved that the partisans killed the three NKVD officers from Moscow when they were in Birzai instead of Utena. He was also truly saddened that Anton Dubus was identified among the dead.

He included Anton in his report to Colonel Vronsky, who was now Svechin's superior. According to the men in the barracks, Vronsky had visited Utena while Svechin was gone, and had a wonderful time. Svechin called Dubus a patriot who under Svechin's leadership, had led Soviet troops to a partisan cell and had caused several partisan deaths. Unfortunately, the bandits had discovered Dubus's true identity, and had shot him. Svechin didn't know if this was true, but it was close enough.

Svechin lifted his fingers from the typewriter keys, speculating that Amber Wolf was behind the Birzai assassinations. Who else would be so brazen as to kill three NKVD agents in broad daylight in a crowded market? It had to be Amber Wolf. It could be no one else. The soldiers present had confirmed seeing a woman with golden hair fleeing the scene. One soldier had pursued her, but none of them would admit to it. No doubt it had been one of her associates. Of course, none of the locals had seen anything. A young woman firing a gun had somehow remained invisible. In the end, Svechin mentioned nothing about his speculations. If Amber Wolf had caused the assassinations, it was in Birzai. She was someone else's problem now. Instead, he wrote that Amber Wolf was probably a woman. His proof was scant, but he thought it to be true even though he was sure it would be met with disbelief. He wrote that after tracking her across the country and relentlessly attacking her companions, her resources were so depleted that she was rendered ineffective.

Svechin concluded that the partisan offensive in Utena had been effectively neutralized. Personally, he believed Amber Wolf was still out there. He hoped to God that she would at least stay out of his area for a while. If she did, he felt certain he could do what was expected of him. If she returned, he had plenty of subordinates to send into the wild to track her down. Their likelihood of success would be slim, though, for her ability to elude Soviet troops was astounding, even remarkable. His men, Rimsky, and the expert tracker had come back from the frontier empty-handed, and they were among the best.

When he was done with the report, he looked around the office that still held Karmachov's presence in the rose plates, demitasse cups, and food crumbs. He picked up the picture of Anton and Katya, the closest people he had to family, even though both were gone. They seemed so young and happy. That's what he wanted to remember, but the picture brought him to tears. He gently laid it facedown on the desk.

Over the next month, much to Svechin's delight, partisan activity in Utena did indeed dwindle to almost nothing. For leading the team that drove out the bandits, Svechin was given a new rank, a promotion, Karmachov's permanent job, and a mandate to keep the area secure and free of partisan activity. In Moscow, the officers nicknamed him the Partisan Slayer.

Svechin hired two Lithuanian women to scrub and polish Karmachov's rooms. The Colonel's personal belongings and his portly body had already been shipped to his long-suffering wife, living somewhere in the bowels of Mother Russia.

Svechin added a few choice pieces of his own furniture, and replaced Stalin's portrait with a Monet reproduction. The silver-framed picture of Katya and Anton remained where he had left it.

Maybe one day he'd be able to look at it again.

CHAPTER 26

Ludmelia stayed with Mrs. Dagys, cleaning her house, coaxing her to eat the little food they had, and listening to the stories about Mr. Dagys and their life in Kaunas before the war. The simplicity of how they had lived made Ludmelia envious. Mrs. Dagys had kept house and gone to market every day while her husband worked. When the Soviets had invaded in 1941, he had died fighting them, but maybe that had been a blessing, for he hadn't seen that hollow look develop in his wife's eyes, or watched her body shrink from hunger. He hadn't seen the ferocious Soviet anger hell-bent to ruin his country.

Mrs. Dagys seemed happy that Ludmelia was there, but the old woman grew progressively weaker. One night, Mrs. Dagys didn't want to go to bed. She sat in the sitting room telling Ludmelia how she folded her husband's pants, making a crease with her hands before hanging them up. It was a ridiculous thing to talk about, and it was as if she was stalling for time. After a while, Ludmelia insisted that Mrs. Dagys get some rest. Ludmelia helped her into her nightgown, and tucked the old woman in as usual. She kissed Mrs. Dagys on the forehead. As she was turning to leave the room, Mrs. Dagys stopped her. "Stay in my home forever if you want, but don't run away from life, my child. You've seen the worst. Now, go out there and look for the best. Find peace and joy. You may have to search hard to find it, but it's there."

In the morning, Ludmelia found Mrs. Dagys dead. She sat on the bed holding the old woman's hand as it grew cold and stiff, all the while thinking about Mama and how much she missed her.

She dressed Mrs. Dagys in a black dress, put her in a cart, and brought her to the church. A caretaker happened to be there. It was a voluntary position, as the church was still closed and the priest gone. The caretaker found a man to help him dig a grave next to Mrs. Dagys's husband. The cross Mama had left was gone, but Mrs. Dagys had replaced it with a homemade one. Ludmelia made another from wood she found, and put it on Mrs. Dagys's grave after saying a prayer thanking her for her help.

Afterward, Ludmelia wandered through the cemetery. The grass over some graves had been cut short, but most were untended. The crosses and markers looked as if they had grown up organically among the wildflowers and tall grass. She found the stone marking Matas's grave and touched it, hoping Matas could feel her hand. She said a prayer for her brother, and asked him if he knew where Mama was. He didn't answer. The rosary beads Mama had draped over his stone were gone. Ludmelia got to her knees to pull a few weeds, and found the beads in the dirt. She brushed them off, kissed the cross, and put them back on the stone so everyone would know the person buried here was still loved. Ludmelia wanted to believe that finding the rosary beads had been a sign from God that she belonged here in Kaunas.

At first, Ludmelia told herself she would stay in Mrs. Dagys's house for just a little while. It didn't feel right to claim anything so valuable for her own. The only thing Ludmelia owned was Dana's brooch, and she kept it with her always, pinned to the inside of a pocket.

One evening, Ludmelia went out on the front step and gazed at her old house, thinking she should perhaps move there, or at least go inside for some of Mama's clothes to wear. The broken windows and trash meant the house had been ransacked. She didn't know whether it had been soldiers looking for loot, or a family desperate to find something they could exchange for food. The urge to go inside was overwhelming, and yet, she knew she wouldn't see the tidy closet near the front door where Papa had kept the rifle that Matas had used to fight the Russians. The pleasant sitting room with the hand-embroidered linen was probably a tattered mess, if any of the furniture even remained. Her bedroom upstairs had probably been searched, contents of drawers thrown to the floor, the clothes gone, her childhood toys taken or broken. Ludmelia didn't have the strength to go inside.

It took weeks, but finally Ludmelia admitted to herself that Mrs. Dagys's house was her new home. The few neighbors left on the street were accustomed to seeing her, and assumed that Ludmelia was a relative, a story she never denied.

Whenever she passed the Partenkas house down the street, she prayed that the family was safe and well.

Ludmelia got a job at a bakery, where she worked for food. The work wasn't steady, but it was enough to sustain her. The owners liked her and when the husband died, the wife asked Ludmelia to take over the baking. It wasn't long before she was making bread that would have rivaled Mrs. Pagelis's, back in Utena.

Baking brought a sense of fulfillment that Ludmelia cherished. The bakery was always warm and dry. She enjoyed watching the yeast bloom, like life itself. She liked the feel of the dough as she kneaded it. The smell of bread baking calmed her. The work of providing food made her feel that she was doing something real to help people, and it was satisfying.

One day in the summer, a knock on the back door startled Ludmelia away from her poetry. She had taken up writing for the comfort of the words. She hid the pencil and paper under the carpet before going to see who it was. She opened the door to Vadi's kind face grinning down at her. She pulled him inside. In the dark hallway in the back of the kitchen, Ludmelia and her old friend embraced.

She gave him a plate of food; potatoes and boiled cabbage. As Ludmelia watched Vadi wolf it down, it occurred to her that she had never seen him enjoy a leisurely meal.

"How did you find me?" she asked.

"We knew where you were. I just wanted to give you some time before coming to visit."

"Are you still fighting?"

Vadi looked down at the empty plate and shook his head. "A few men are still in Auksia, but many have moved on."

"And what are you going to do?"

"I'd like to stay here with you." He had a hopeful look in his eyes, and a smile on his face.

Ludmelia refilled the plate, setting it down in front of Vadi. As she watched him eat, she decided that Raminta had been right. It didn't matter what a man did. It was more important that he was courageous and compassionate.

They were married two days later. For Ludmelia, it wasn't love, but she wanted to give love a chance. Fighting had frayed the rope joining her to humanity. Vadi represented the single thread that remained, and she wanted to hold onto him, and let him pull her back to grace.

An elderly neighbor, once a captain in the Lithuanian Army, performed the wedding ceremony in Mrs. Dagys's sitting room. Ludmelia had dusted the furniture for the occasion, and collected wildflowers in the cemetery for a bouquet. She wore a brown suit from Mrs. Dagys's closet. Vadi wore a gray suit that had belonged to Mr. Dagys. It fit his waist, but the sleeves and pants were too short. Ludmelia didn't care. Vadi was a good man who loved her, and he was one of the few people she trusted. He gave her hope that one day she'd become just an ordinary woman living an ordinary life, and it sounded wonderful.

On their wedding night, Ludmelia went upstairs first. She put on a long nightdress and got into bed, feeling nervous. It made no sense, for she had lived with danger for many years. A man she had known for a good part of her life shouldn't make her jittery. The windows were open. A warm breeze freshened the air. Her pistol was on the nightstand as usual.

She waited, but Vadi didn't join her. She hadn't heard him go out. She wondered if he was having second thoughts, already regretting their marriage. She picked up her gun, more from habit than a sense of danger, and went downstairs. She found him on the floor in the sitting room, a cushion under his head, fast asleep. She knew the exhaustion he still must be feeling. He was still wearing Mr. Dagys's trousers and shirt. She pulled off his shoes and belt, and covered him with a blanket from upstairs. She stretched out next to him in the darkness, listening to the sounds: his breathing, a vehicle driving down the street, two distant voices speaking Russian, a cricket. He slipped his arm under her neck, and kissed her. Ludmelia curled into his warmth. She awoke the next morning to the chirping of a few lonely birds, surprised she had slept so well.

The days, months, and years that followed were blissfully the same. Vadi helped her in the bakery during the day. They shared a meal together at night, and slept in each other's arms. Vadi made her feel cherished, and over time, it made her human again. She considered herself a lucky woman to know such love.

~~

Vadi died ten years later, of a bad cold that developed into pneumonia. Ludmelia buried him in the same cemetery where Matas and Mama lay, and Mr. and Mrs. Dagys; her friends and family. Sometimes, visiting her husband late in the day, for she only went out in the sunlight when she had to, she wished Dana were there, too. But she knew it would be hopeless to try and find him. He was gone to the elements, and she was sure he would have preferred it that way.

As time passed, Ludmelia sought company. She became involved in a group discussing a new government. It formed the seedlings of an independence movement that Ludmelia hoped would take hold. Most of them felt that they would never live to see their ideas put in place, nevertheless, they talked about how they would quickly organize elections, and operate as an independent nation. They talked about diplomacy, and whether they could ever forgive the United States and Great Britain for ignoring their desperate plight. Of course, the conversations were illegal, and if the Russians found out about their little society they would have all been sent to a gulag. Still, their words gave them hope for the future, and it brought Ludmelia a sense of unity like the one she had known while living in the forest with the partisans those many years ago.

Over time, Ludmelia came to understand that words could inspire and affect people more powerfully than any gun. Words were the secret to securing the state of a nation, for they could describe the heart and desires of the people, something bullets could never do.

Five years later, a butcher and widower originally from the village of Varniai asked Ludmelia to marry him, but she refused. She told him she was too old to adjust to living with anyone again.

Once a week, she still went to the butcher's shop for a piece of meat. When he died, he left his shop to his granddaughter, and his money to Ludmelia; fifty thousand rubles. He had kept it hidden in a tin box under a loose floorboard beneath the bottom drawer of the table where he cut and wrapped the meat. Months before his death, he had told her where it was. She thought he was joking, for no one had that much money, especially a butcher in a communist country. After the funeral, she went to the shop and let herself in with the key hidden in the dirt at the corner of the building where it always was.

Ludmelia pictured her friend with his ample waist talking and laughing behind the blood-spattered table as he cut small pieces of meat for his customers, and wrapped them in paper. Ludmelia had always gotten a little extra. More on a whim than anything else, she took out the bottom drawer of the table, and under a false bottom, found the tin box. Maybe there would be enough money inside to buy some bread and a sweater, as the winters bothered her now that she was older.

The tin was full of rubles. She had never seen so much money, and had never dreamed she would be so wealthy. She brought the box home and hid it inside the potato bin in the basement. Ludmelia used some to buy herself a good winter coat and some extra food. She doled out the rest, little by little to help sustain orphanages filled with children who had lost their parents to the Soviet aggression.

As the years passed, Ludmelia spent more time at home, thinking about the people and events of her life, wondering why she had survived when others hadn't. She thought about the numbness she had forced upon herself when she was young to help survive the horrors. Vadi's love and time had lifted that feeling, although a bit of it was still there.

More and more often, she reverted to writing poetry. One poem she entitled *Dana*, began:

A spotted eagle lifted my love from the meadow as he lay sleeping

It was one she never finished.

CHAPTER 27

1991 – A New Beginning

The air felt cold as Ludmelia slowly climbed the steps in the stadium, cursing the stiffness in her old legs as she used the cane to bear some of her weight. Her legs had never been the same since those hours she had spent in the frigid stream in the frontier near the border with Poland.

A spry man with black hair rushed to her as Ludmelia struggled to mount the very last step. He offered Ludmelia an arm to steady herself.

Ludmelia took it and sat heavily, thanking him. The man went to a seat a dozen rows away. All the seats around her were empty, although a few people were coming to fill them, even at this early hour. Maintenance staff in navy blue overalls climbed the steps to the right, while a loud blast came from the sound system, followed by "Testing, one, two, three."

A gray-haired woman came up the steps and sat next to Ludmelia.

"Tilda Partenkas," said Ludmelia, clasping the woman's hands. "I never thought I'd see you again. When I got your letter saying you'd be here today, I was overjoyed. I'm glad you thought to contact Mrs. Dagys. I've been living in her house for years, although she's been gone for quite a while."

"I tried contacting all the people I knew, but I think most are gone."

"Everyone who can be here today, will be. It's too important a day to miss. Maybe you'll recognize some faces." Ludmelia touched Tilda's cheek. "You look the same as I remember. What have you been doing all these years?" She pulled down the purse strap from her shoulder, searching inside for a handkerchief. After carrying a gun for so many years, she was still comforted by some weight on her back.

"My mother and I got out through Sweden in 1948, but we didn't settle there, or else they would have shipped us back. We traveled on to Britain." Tilda looked down at her hands. "I haven't seen Papa since we left Utena, and now he's gone."

"By the time I moved in with Mrs. Dagys, squatters were living in your old house. I never saw him." Ludmelia reached over and patted Tilda's arm. She knew what it was like to lose a father.

"I went to school. I'm a nuclear physicist."

"A nuclear physicist?" said Ludmelia. "So smart! You must know all about that damned power plant the Russians built at Ignalina. Bigger than Chernobyl, they say."

"We call the plant at Ignalina the Amber Widow."

Ludmelia raised an eyebrow.

"There was a power surge in 1983. Nothing came of it, as there were precautions to prevent a disaster. But there's a flaw in the design. Many people died at Chernobyl. More may die at Ignalina. That's why we call it the Amber Widow. But still, it may be our means to keeping the Soviets away forever."

"It won't be long until the Soviet Union is history. If Gorbachev had been in power after the war, our lives would be very different now. We need to join NATO, don't you think?" Ludmelia touched the handkerchief to her brow.

Tilda glanced over her shoulder before speaking. "We can never trust the Russians. Amber Widow may be our greatest ally."

"What do you mean?"

"If they ever try to come back, we have to be ready to take the fight to *them*."

"How is that possible?"

"Fear. Just the way they controlled us for all those years."

"Are you talking about a bomb? A bomb is a bomb. Russia's too big to bomb."

"An atomic bomb would bring them to their knees, but that's not what I mean. Nuclear waste presents us with very interesting possibilities. Only God protects us until we figure out something for ourselves." Tilda put her hand on the old woman's shoulder. "Your days for worry are over, Ludmelia. Know that others will take care of our children and their children, and their children. The new generations will become like the old ones. And they will be free. Always and forever. I will do everything in my power to make that happen."

Ludmelia wiped her brow again.

"Are you all right?"

"I'm just tired. It's an important day and I'm thinking about all my friends. You may know some of them. Do you remember Julius?"

"No."

"We used to call him Lightning. We got him out through the Iron Curtain, and he managed to get to the United States."

"God bless him."

"He spent his life trying to convince their Congress to take action against the Soviets for crimes against humanity, and to provide financial and military support so we could defeat the Soviets. He made the news from time to time, but nothing came of it. After a while, we stopped hearing of him entirely."

Ludmelia wiped her nose with the handkerchief. "My friends, Raminta and Jurgis. Do you know them?"

"No."

"They left camp in 1948 and found a place to live not far from here. Raminta had a baby girl and two baby boys. They named the girl after me, and one boy after his uncle, Vadi. They named the other boy Jonas." Ludmelia smiled. "Raminta and Jurgis are gone, but their children are having babies. I never saw Tolek or Tymon again after that mission in 1948. I don't think they made it, but we can hope."

Tilda shrugged. She looked confused, but kept on smiling.

"I married Vadi. He was one of the finest men I ever knew."

People began filling in the seats around them. Even though Ludmelia knew Papa couldn't possibly be alive after all these years, she looked at every face, hoping to see him.

"Did you know Dana Ravas?" said Ludmelia.

"No."

"He was killed in 1948. He gave me this pin when he gave me his heart." Ludmelia put her hand on the brooch with the bug and tiny leaf encased in amber pinned to her coat. Today was the first day she had worn it openly. "Isn't it beautiful?"

Tilda nodded.

"I'll tell you a secret."

Tilda leaned closer.

"They used to call me *Amber Wolf*." A little boy holding his mother's hand squeezed past her. "I wish you luck and success," she said to the child.

Ludmelia wiped her eyes. It was hard remembering everyone, yet she had to. Especially today.

Then she noticed an ancient man standing near the side banister. He looked so thin and slight she thought he might blow away in a gust of wind. His skin was like leather, but the eye patch gave him up. *After all these years, could it be? He has to be over ninety.* She clutched the handkerchief to her heart, and stood. Tilda jumped to her feet and took Ludmelia's arm.

"I'm all right," said Ludmelia, waving her away.

As Ludmelia went to the man, the years faded away. She felt young and strong, and as if she could accomplish anything. When she got to his side, her vision blurred for the tears.

He put his arms around her.

"Simas," she whispered. They held each other for a long time.

Tilda pointed at them, mouthing the words *Amber Wolf* to the people around her. The news rippled through the crowd. Within minutes, a cluster of people had gathered around the pair of partisans, shaking their hands and saying that their father, grandmother, or friends had spoken of them. Some people cried. Others kissed their cheeks. Many told Ludmelia and Simas how grateful and proud they were of what they had done for their country.

Ludmelia thought of Vadi and Dana, hoping they knew they wouldn't be forgotten; that they, too, were heroes. They all were.

Simas took her hand and began singing, just like he had that day almost fifty years ago in the forest outside of Vilkija. The crowd hushed at his shaky voice. A few people joined him. More voices chimed in as the music floated up to the heavens. The hymn they had all learned as children, and that their parents had forbade them from singing in public because of what the Russians would do to them, was finally simply, proudly, and openly theirs.

When the song ended, a tall lanky man in a brown suit, Mr. Vytautas Landsbergis, leader of a free Lithuania, stepped up to the podium. He raised his arms to the joyous cheers of the crowd. Ludmelia was certain their friends in heaven could hear that, too.

We're free at last, she thought, *at long last.*

THE END

ABOUT THE AUTHOR

Ursula grew up working on the family dairy farm started by her grandparents, who fled Lithuania for a better life in the U.S. After losing her father at an early age, Ursula overcame poverty and went on to college.

Armed with a degree in physics and an advanced degree in mathematics, Ursula entered the job market when mini-computers were "the new thing." She provided solutions addressing major business problems in the areas of security and messaging. While all this was going on, Ursula and her husband, Steve, had a beautiful daughter.

After decades working, Ursula left the high tech industry and began writing fiction. She took many courses and attended numerous writers' workshops where she found the friends who continue to help and inspire her.

Ursula writes gripping stories about strong women struggling against impossible odds to achieve their dreams. Her work has appeared in *Everyday Fiction*, *Spinetingler Magazine*, *Mystery Reader's Journal*, and the popular *Insanity Tales* anthologies. She is a board member of the Seven Bridge Writers' Collaborative. Ursula teaches classes on writing and publishing, and is a professional speaker, appearing regularly on TV and radio. Her award-winning debut novel, *Purple Trees*, her WWII thriller, *Amber Wolf*, and the enchanting Peruvian folk tale, *The Baby Who Fell From the Sky*, are available on Amazon and other fine retailers. *Amber War* is Ursula's third novel.

Ursula is available for speaking events and lectures on writing and publishing. For more information, contact her at urslwng@gmail.com or visit her at http://ursulawong.wordpress.com.

Connect Online:
Website: http://ursulawong.wordpress.com
Email: urslwng@gmail.com

Other works by Ursula Wong

Amber Wolf

Purple Trees

The Baby Who Fell From the Sky

With other Authors

Insanity Tales

Insanity Tales II: The Sense of Fear

Insanity Tales III: Seasons of Shadow: A Collection of Dark Fiction

Looking for something great to read? Get Ursula's award-winning mini-tales, guaranteed to shiver, shake, and make you laugh. All you have to do is tell her where to send them. You'll get one to start, and a new one every month. Sign up at http://ursulawong.wordpress.com.

LIST OF CHARACTERS

Algis – Lithuanian partisan.
Ana – Mrs. Partenkas's sister.
Erni Belzik – Polish horseman and land owner. Katya's husband.
Leon Belzik – Polish land owner. Son to Erni.
Father Burkas – Priest and Lithuanian partisan.
Mrs. Dagys – Neighbor to the Kudirka family in Kaunas.
Danute – Lithuanian partisan.
Anton Dubus – Red Army soldier recruited to infiltrate the partisan organization in Utena.
Katya Dubus – Anton's sister.
Eda – Simas's old girlfriend.
Hektoras – Mathematics teacher. Victor's friend in the labor camp.
Julius – Lithuanian partisan leader.
Jurgis –Lithuanian partisan. Brother to Vadi, husband to Raminta.
Kazi – Lithuanian partisan. Stasys's brother.
Colonel Karmachov – Leader of the Red Army division in Utena county.
Aldona Kudirka – Victor's wife. Ludmelia's mother.
Ludmelia Kudirka – Amber Wolf. Sharpshooter, Lithuanian partisan. Daughter to Victor and Aldona.
Matas Kudirka – Ludmelia's brother.
Victor Kudirka – Ludmelia's father. History professor interred in a labor camp in Siberia.
Oleg Minsk – Soviet prison guard in Siberia.
Ona – Tilda's friend.
Operation Bolt – The mission to get Julius out of Lithuania and seek help from the West.
Mr. Pagelis – Lithuanian partisan supporter. Bakery owner.
Mrs. Pagelis – Lithuanian partisan supporter. Bakery owner.
Marius Partenkas – Lithuanian partisan. Laborer. Father to Tilda.
Tilda Partenkas – Daughter to Marius.
Petr – Ana's husband. Mrs. Partenkas's brother-in-law.
Raminta – Lithuanian partisan. Wife to Jurgis.
Dana Ravas – Lithuanian partisan. Loves Ludmelia.
Gerta Ravas – Dana Ravas's mother.
Rimsky – Tracking dog.
Ruta – Julius's friend from university.
Mrs. Rydas – Lithuanian partisan.
Sargas – Tilda's dog.
Simas Vargas – One-eyed Lithuanian partisan.

Stasys – Lithuanian partisan. Kazi's brother.
Mr. and Mrs. Stelmokas – Polish partisans.
Leonas Stelmokas – Polish partisan.
Lieutenant Yuri Svechin – Colonel Karmachov's aide.
Tolek – Polish partisan. Brother to Tymon.
Tymon – Polish partisan. Brother to Tolek.
Edvard Urba – Latvian partisan.
Vadi – Partisan. Brother to Jurgis.
Vera – Doctor. Lithuanian partisan.
Colonel Vronsky - Russian officer. Karmachov's superior.
Lieutenant Roman Zabrev – Russian officer.
Mr. and Mrs. Zenonas – Farmers. Lithuanian partisan supporters.

READING LIST

And Quiet Flows the Don, Mikhail Sholokhov, Forgotten Books, London, UK, 2017.

Bloodlands: Europe Between Hitler and Stalin, Timothy Snyder, Basic Books, NY, NY, 2012.

Fighters for Freedom, Juozas Daumantas, The Lithuanian Canadian Committee for Human Rights, Toronto, Ontario, 1975.

Forest Brothers 1945: The Culmination of the Lithuanian Partisan Movement, Vylius M. Leskys, Baltic Security & Defense Review, Volume 11, 2009.

Iron Curtain, Anne Applebaum, Doubleday, New York, 2012.

Life and Fate, Vasily Grossman, NYRB Classics, New York, 2012.

No Simple Victory: World War II in Europe, 1939-1945, Norman Davies, Macmillan Publishers, London, UK, 2006.

Savage Continent, Keith Lowe, St. Martin's Press, NY, NY, 2012.

Showdown, The Lithuanian Rebellion and the Breakup of the Soviet Empire, Dr. Richard Krickus, Brassey's Inc., 1997.

Stolen Lives, Jan Kusmirek, Derwen, Pembroke, Wales, 2010.

Tarp Dvieju Gyvenimu, Vytautas Alantas, Lithuanian Book Club, Chicago, 1960.

The Rise and Fall of the Third Reich, William L. Shirer, Touchstone, NY, NY, 1959.

Made in the USA
Columbia, SC
06 February 2018